En Garde, My Love

By
Amy Corwin

Copyright

En Garde, My Love
(Fencing for Ladies, previous title)
COPYRIGHT © 2016 by Amy Padgett

Contact information: contact@amycorwin.com
Cover Art by Amy G. Padgett
Publisher: Fireside Romance
Editing Services Provided by: Vince Dickinson

Publishing History
First Edition, 2016

Synopsis

In defiance of Society's strictures, Lady Olivia is fascinated by fencing and determined to share the thrill of facing an opponent with a foil in her hand. Defying convention comes at a cost, however. While her family agrees to allow her to found the Fencing Academy for Ladies, she must agree to a betrothal to the extremely eligible, but insipid, Lord Saunders. It seems like a fair compromise, so she agrees, even though Lord Saunders makes no secret of the fact that he disapproves of her academy.

Unfortunately, tragedy strikes the day before her school opens. Lady Olivia discovers a dead body in her office with a marble cherub in place of his head. And she unwittingly leaves a trail of footprints through his blood, blood so fresh that it is still sticky. There is no sign of anyone else in the building—just Lady Olivia and the still-warm corpse.

Scandal erupts, and Lord Saunders demands that she close the academy and conform to Society's dictates. She stubbornly refuses until a second body is discovered. Desperate, Lady Olivia turns to dashing fencing master, Lord Milbourn, for help. While the handsome master fencer is clearly hiding his own dark secrets, her heart tells her to trust him.

Torn between her growing love for the attractive and enigmatic Lord Milbourn and her promise to Lord Saunders, Lady Olivia is determined to fight for her heart's desire, whatever the cost.

Table of Contents

Contents

Chapter One

Lady Olivia Archer threw the bundle of letters onto her writing desk, nearly tipping over the silver inkwell at the edge. She had thought her Fencing Academy for Ladies was so dashing, so exciting, that it would prove wildly popular with her friends and acquaintances, who insisted they yearned for a chance to do something *outré,* or at least different. Apparently, the prospect of crossing swords with other ladies was less enchantingly *outré* than she'd anticipated.

Why didn't they understand how exciting it could be?

If only they could feel the exhilaration she'd experienced when she'd first crept into her brothers' lessons. Of course, Edward had blocked her way, wanting to throw her out, claiming it was wildly inappropriate for her to join them and that she was only interrupting their lesson. Harnet and Peregrine had snorted, shook their heads, and looked to the instructor to make the final decision.

Their teacher, the former Alexander Bron, now the Baron Milbourn, laughed and said sardonically, "Why not, *mi niña bonita?*" That had been the first time he'd teased her with that annoying phrase, *my pretty little girl.*

Annoyance had flared to life inside her, and she'd frowned at him, watching his maddening grin widen. She'd had enough sense, though, to swallow a sharp retort, and the effort that took was rewarded. He had nodded and allowed her to join them.

She didn't realize what she'd so innocently walked into however. Her brothers didn't approve of her presence and were determined to test her mettle. They'd all teased her — as well as each other —

mercilessly, but they soon discovered that instead of making her run away in tears, she'd adored their challenges and sharp mockery. She whipped them with retorts as sharp as their own, and they gradually accepted her as a worthy opponent.

Finally, in some magical way, she was one of them — at least when she had a foil in her hand. She felt accepted and filled with sizzling energy as she flung insults at their heads and her blade slid against theirs. Her laughter mingled with their snorts and chuckles as they tried to avoid the humiliation of being bested by their own sister.

During those brief hours, she had control of her life and destiny, and she had never felt closer to her brothers. Those lessons had been a precious time, perfect and so full of joy that the mere thought of it lifted her spirts and made her smile. The tingling feeling of her blade rasping against her opponent's foil as she tested his arm never failed to thrill her. Even Peregrine forgot to stammer when he held a foil in his hand and faced her.

"Watch for an opening — now!" A slow, proud smile would break through Mr. Bron's somber expression and his black eyes would glow when she slipped in under Peregrine's guard. "You did it, *mi niña bonita*. Good."

He'd been proud of *her*, then. She could face her brother and, at least on this occasion, win.

She'd felt as if she were dancing three feet above the wooden floor.

"Bit of luck, there." Peregrine had wiped his forearm over his forehead and grinned at her. "Won't happen again. You cannot live on luck, you little devil."

"Skill, not luck, Perry dearest." She'd laughed and saluted him with her foil. "You do realize you have a left side, do you not? You left it woefully unguarded."

"Your sister speaks wisely," Mr. Bron said. "The kitten has claws, Mr. Archer. Do not leave yourself open."

"Wisely — for once — you mean." Peregrine snorted and nudged her shoulder with his fist. "And none too soon, if you want the truth. I doubt it will happen again." Despite his words, the twinkle in his gray eyes showed his pride in her. He'd never been a sore loser — all of her brothers were admirable that way — and when he cuffed her again as they headed for the door, an elated laugh burst out of her.

The world had seemed golden-bright with possibility. She could accomplish anything when she held that foil in her hand. And for once, she wasn't just some porcelain figurine, waiting to be wrapped in brown paper and string and handed over to the first man who bargained for her, destined to be unwrapped and carefully set for display on his mantle for the rest of her dull and placid life.

The brief, glorious memory faded, leaving her feeling even colder as she glanced around the Ivory Drawing Room. The large, airy room was usually her favorite, but today, she shifted restlessly, the thin slippers on her feet doing little to protect them from the cold. She glanced at the huge bow window, framed with sweeping ivory satin curtains edged with gold trim. Normally, the wide expanse let in the light and an exciting view of London life in the street below, but now sleet smeared the window obscuring the view. A gust of icy February wind rattled the panes and one of the curtains billowed out, brushing the delicate white-and-gold damask chair next to her. She rubbed her arms.

The morning had been gray and bleak, the sun unwilling to peek out from behind the thick clouds hanging low in the London sky. Even the passersby hurried along the walkway below with hunched shoulders and the occasional slip when they stepped on a patch of ice. Even the normally glorious painting of dawn over Olympus gracing the high coffered ceiling seemed dull. The rich rose, blue, and gold-gilded clouds had lost their color under a gray pall, and the gods and goddesses themselves seemed tired. They stared so dismally at each other that Olivia could almost see them shudder in despair over their presence in chilly London rather than sunny Greece.

She glanced around, noting the shining, clean surfaces on all the small occasional tables. Except for a few forlorn vases of hothouse flowers and the occasional small Egyptian statue given to them by the Duchess of Peckham after one of her trips to the Nile Valley, the room was perfect. Cold and without the warmth it used to have when her mother used to leave all her bits and pieces all over the sitting room. Half-finished embroidery, magazines, books, and lovely sketches were scattered about when she was alive — always giving her something to talk about with her visitors and set them at their ease. She'd laugh, shake her head, and pick up an item at random to show a guest and suddenly, they were old and comfortable friends.

Right now, the only cluttered surface was her desk. With an exasperated sigh, she leaned her hip against the edge of her slender, swan neck-legged escritoire and aligned the letters on top with one cold fingertip. Disappointment tightened her mouth. She flicked a quick glance at her younger sister, Margaret, sprawled over one of the ivory and gold couches with a book in her lap and one arm draped over the back of the couch. Olivia willed her to leave, but Margaret remained, a secretive smile on her mouth as if perfectly aware of Olivia's desire for privacy.

As Margaret stared at Olivia, her smile grew thoughtful. She always seemed to know when Olivia was at her lowest and rarely missed an opportunity to relish it thoroughly.

"The post brought you quite a number of replies, Livie. You must be terribly pleased," Margaret said with patently false innocence. Her blue eyes glinted with merciless amusement. "How many students have enrolled in your fencing academy now?"

A pitiful three. Today's mail only contained one more acceptance, bringing the total to an even four. Unfortunately, the most recent lady to register her interest was the one Olivia least wanted to accept. Miss Cynthia Denholm was her oldest friend, so she *had* to invite her. However, Cynthia was a strapping, energetic young lady who would most assuredly outshine all of them, including Olivia, through sheer force of will and muscle.

Assuming Cynthia even allowed Olivia to teach and didn't simply take over the class herself.

Suddenly tired, Olivia smiled at her sister, pretending a serenity she was far from feeling as she perched on the edge of a settee. "How many? I have not had time to count them all yet. Why do you ask? Are you interested in learning to fence?" She hummed thoughtfully and gazed down at the letters. So many polite refusals. "I may be able to find a place for you, if you wish."

Her careless words failed to impress Margaret. She tilted her head to the left, her sardonic gaze all but accusing Olivia of lying.

Instead of voicing the disbelief so clearly written on her face, she said, "Oh, I would not dream of taking one of your valuable seats. Not when so many ladies are interested."

Touché.

Olivia bit the inside of her cheek to stop a sharp retort and smoothed her expression again. When Margaret's gaze drifted to the pile of letters, Olivia scooped them up and held them against her waist.

"Did Lord Graybrook fail to meet his appointment?" Olivia assumed a more direct approach to disconcert her sister. Margaret wasn't the only one who could recognize a soft spot and *riposte*.

Surprisingly, after not showing the least sign of interest in him, Margaret had suddenly set her cap at the handsome Lord Graybrook. Thus far, he had failed to acknowledge her existence, which was probably best for both of them. Olivia wasn't blind. She had noticed a touch of falseness in her sister's interest in the man and wondered about her sister's intentions. If she didn't know Margaret so well, she'd say she was only interested in the man's title, and not the man himself. But Margaret wasn't generally fascinated by status and titles, so Olivia couldn't account for her feeling that something was not quite as it seemed.

However, Margaret did show distinct signs of frustration. Her dimpled smiles that used to be so common were becoming increasingly rare, and her temper worsened by the day. Olivia was beginning to fear that her sister would try something desperate, such as hiding in his carriage after a ball to surprise him. Others of Margaret's acquaintance had done similar things, and she couldn't eliminate it as a possibility if her sister failed to catch Lord Graybrook's attention.

So while normally Olivia would never have mentioned Graybrook, the need to divert her sister's attention from her own difficulties drove Olivia into forbidden territory.

Margaret studied her for two seconds before the anger and disappointment in her eyes overwhelmed her self-control. "Lord

Graybrook has been exceedingly busy. It is hardly surprising that he has not visited recently." Her eyes sharpened, and a small half smile curved her mouth. "What do you hear from our dear Mr. Bron? He seems to have forgotten us since he became Lord Milbourn. And you had developed such a *tendre* for him, too, when he was teaching our brothers fencing." She dropped her gaze to admire her fingernails, resting on the book in her lap. "It must be quite painful when he avoids us now."

"I outgrew my affection for him years ago, if I ever had any. And if you will recall, I am betrothed—"

"Not precisely betrothed," Margaret pointed out helpfully.

"I have an understanding with Lord Saunders. Our father arranged it before he died," Olivia answered frostily, although saying the words always made her feel uncomfortable.

Nonsense. There is nothing awkward in my situation. It is quite normal.

She ought to be proud that Lord Saunders intended to fulfill his and her family's expectations that they would marry. Perhaps their understanding wasn't precisely romantic, but Lord Saunders was a gentle, sweet man. He would make a good husband. So she ought to be pleased with the match that was her mother's last wish.

And as Margaret was fond of pointing out, Lord Saunders was much sought after. He had the wealth and social position that would make her life very comfortable after they wed, and his appearance was quite pleasant in a plump, brown rabbity sort of way.

Everyone said it was a brilliant match. *Everyone.* She should be happy, glowing with triumph to have walked away with the catch of the Season.

"An understanding," Margaret repeated thoughtfully. "Yes. However, forgetting that minor detail, it remains most disheartening that Lord Milbourn ignores us. Why, he could hardly be bothered to wave when he drove by in his curricle the other day."

"He drove by? When?" As soon as the words left Olivia's mouth she regretted them. Warmth crept up her cheeks.

Margaret watched her with a slight smile. "Yesterday. Not that it matters, of course." Laughter bubbled through her words. "Since you are practically betrothed."

"Of course," Olivia agreed hastily.

"You know I hate to keep raising this point, but I suspect that if Lord Milbourn does not agree to teach, many of your ladies may not attend your school after all. It is not nearly so interesting to fence with another lady, is it? And Lord Milbourn has such an air of danger about him. He makes one want to cross swords with him, does he not?"

"I confess you see him in a much different light than I do, and I see nothing unfortunate about the situation. I shall not mind in the least if Lord Milbourn ignores us. He is merely a baron, after all, and Lord Saunders is an earl, so I am content—"

Margaret's sharp hoot of amusement interrupted her. "When did you start chasing titles, Livie? You are not the least interested in such things. If you were, you would be more anxious to accept Lord Saunders and marry him forthwith."

"I have never been anxious to marry anyone. And I believe we may both forget Lord Milbourn without the slightest regret," Olivia continued relentlessly. "I am quite good enough to manage the school alone, thank you. I am sure the students and their parents will be reassured that the academy is all female, including the teacher."

Her heart twisted, but she would never admit that her love of fencing was not her sole reason. In some distant and dark part of her soul, she harbored the hope that Lord Milbourn might be interested in the academy. He might even agree to teach, and she might see him more frequently. She pushed the wistful thought back into the darkness where it belonged.

Nonetheless, in her memory, his dark eyes danced with sardonic amusement. Margaret was right; he had always seemed exotic and dangerous. Tall and slender, with the black hair and dark eyes he'd inherited from his Spanish mother, he'd moved with grace and power when he parried with her brothers during their fencing lessons.

Dangerous.

Yes, that was a good word for him; dangerous but also coldly indifferent.

Thankfully, she was sure she'd outgrown her childish fascination with him — she was almost sure of it, except when some thought strayed out of that dark corner in her mind.

"Reassuring for the parents, but boring for the students," Margaret quipped. "Your ladies shall have no one with whom to flirt. Deadly dull."

"Oh, there is no reasoning with you, Margaret."

"I am not the one scandalizing the Ton with fencing schools and thoughts of young ladies in breeches."

"They won't be in breeches, as you very well know. We have special split skirts, rather like those wide trousers some Cossacks wear, although they are much wider and fastened around the ankles. They are quite proper, I assure you."

Margaret threw her hands into the air and sighed heavily. "Must you remove any hint of excitement? No male teachers and quite proper uniforms? Honestly, I am surprised you have any students at all."

"The ladies must be able to get permission from their parents and guardians, and if the school is too scandalous, I would have *no* students," Olivia replied triumphantly.

She refused to admit that, like her sister, she knew she would have an overabundance of students if she had at least one male teacher. Assuming that male were as attractive as Lord Milbourn.

"Well, I wish you luck of it." Margaret glanced at the slanting beam of watery morning sunshine coming through the window and stood, brushing off her woolen skirts. "I am going for a walk this afternoon. It has finally stopped raining, and I shall go positively mad if I stay inside another minute."

"You are not going alone, are you?" Olivia asked, rising from the gold and ivory striped silk settee and glancing out the window. The sunbeams might have been feeble and more blue than yellow, but they were welcome after so much sleet and rain. She had the urge to get some air herself, although she wasn't enthusiastic about accompanying her sister and listening to her far too astute questions.

Margaret shook her head. "Edward and Hildie are accompanying me. We are going to walk around Hyde Park." She grinned. "We might even catch sight of Lord Milbourn riding by. Don't you want to join us?"

"I won't go as far as Hyde Park, but let me know when you leave. I will accompany you to the school. I must make sure everything is ready for the first class tomorrow afternoon."

"You could do that tomorrow. You do not have a class until four, unless you have so many students you must have an earlier class as well." Margaret watched her with bright, bird-like eyes.

Olivia shook her head. "No. I must do it today. If there is anything amiss, I can correct it before the first class."

"You sound so responsible," Margaret murmured, wrinkling her nose. "And stuffy."

"I *am* responsible. Now if you will excuse me, I need something from the library." Olivia strode to the wide door and hesitated, glancing over her shoulder at her sister.

"Go on." Margaret waved her hand before she walked past her to the wide, colonnaded gallery leading to the wide staircase. "You have my permission." She smiled sarcastically as she headed for the branch of stairs leading up to the second floor. "I believe I shall help Hildie with her sewing."

Olivia sighed as she watched her younger sister ascend quickly and disappear above her into the shadows of the second floor. She had to admit that she was nervous about her fencing class tomorrow, and she wanted to review Edward's copy of fencing master Domenico Angelo's *L'Ecole des Armes,* published in London in 1763. If she didn't at least glance through it again, someone would undoubtedly ask her some esoteric question and embarrass her on her first day. After all, it wasn't all just the thrill of crossing swords; there was technique and an underlying philosophy as well.

Locating the leather-bound volume in the huge library was easier than she anticipated. Book in hand, Olivia ensconced herself in one of the huge green brocade chairs by the fire to escape the icy drafts wafting past the heavy green and gold silk curtains over the windows at the rear of the room. Warmth gradually vanquished the chill, and

Amy Corwin

as she skimmed through the book, her hands slowed. The words on the page in front of her blurred. Her head drooped to her chest, and she sunk into a light slumber.

The rumble of men's voices awakened Olivia. She jerked her head up and glanced around. The fire in front of her was still burning merrily, so she hadn't been asleep for long. Her eyes stung as she focused on the book lying on her lap. She rubbed her right eye and almost stood when she heard her brother, Edward, speak.

"I don't know how to advise you, Underwood," he said. His voice sounded strained and slightly angry, as if he were being asked to assist in something with which he wanted no involvement.

"You *must* help me," Gregory Underwood said, his voice rising in desperation.

Olivia squirmed in her chair. The two men sounded as if they were standing near the windows behind her, but the high winged back of the chair hid them from view. Clearly, they had not seen her when they entered the library. She desperately wanted to leave, but she sensed that the tense discussion was intended to be private, and she didn't want to embarrass either her brother or poor Mr. Underwood.

Mr. Underwood, in particular, struck her as a shy, intensely private man, and she often felt the urge to pat him on the dome of his egg-shaped head and reassure him that he had no need to worry so. His pretty, fair-haired wife was even more retiring and seldom attended social events. Olivia had rarely seen Mrs. Underwood without her small, nervous hand clinging to her husband's arm, and she often wondered if Mrs. Underwood would simply collapse into a quivering puddle of skirts without her husband there to support her.

However, despite their exasperatingly shy dispositions, Olivia had always liked the pair. They were both kind and always too happy to receive a last minute invitation to a supper — if there were not too many other people attending — to even up the numbers. And Mrs. Underwood had a delicious sense of humor when she relaxed enough to display it.

The last thing Olivia wanted to do was to cause Mr. Underwood embarrassment.

"How?" Edward asked again, impatient.

Olivia could hear the muted thuds of her brother's firm tread as he paced over the thick green, crimson, and gold carpet. Even without seeing him, she knew he would have his hands clasped behind his back and his dark brows drawn down in a frown.

"Grantham...some sort of journal...claims to have a letter...." Mr. Underwood's voice faded in and out as he talked, and she only heard half of his words. "You must help me, *please.*" His voice grew louder as he pleaded with Edward. "My wife is in a delicate condition...." Again, he dropped into the low murmur of a whisper. "... lost two infants already...will kill her. Just speak with him."

Mr. Grantham? What did he have to do with Mr. Underwood?

Olivia couldn't help but wonder at Mr. Underwood's agitation. She didn't realize the two men knew each other, much less imagine what Mr. Grantham might have done to upset him so much. Mr. Grantham had been a friend of the Archer family for years, and he'd always been so respectable. He was not the sort to do anything disagreeable, at least not on purpose.

Although she strained to hear, the conversation at the other end of the room dropped in volume until it was just a low rumble of voices as the two men moved closer to the window. A few minutes later, footsteps padded closer to her and then passed behind her as Edward escorted Mr. Underwood out of the library.

Olivia remained seated for several minutes, her gaze fixed on the crackling yellow and orange flames, troubled by what she'd overheard. She sighed. It would gain her nothing to question Edward. He was unlikely to confide in her whatever he'd been discussing with Mr. Underwood and would probably lecture her about the evils of listening to private conversations. Sometimes, her brother's sense of honor was annoyingly inconvenient.

Flipping through the pages of the book in her lap, she tried to focus on the fencing treatise. Unfortunately, her thoughts kept returning to Mr. Grantham and Mr. Underwood. She frowned and massaged the skin between her brows. Poor Mrs. Underwood. Clearly her husband had been worried about her and her delicate condition. He'd said she'd lost other babes, and Olivia's heart went out to her. The shy lady's lovely, pale face and shadowed eyes seemed to stare at Olivia from the shadows. What should she do? Worrying would surely make matters worse for the Underwoods.

If only Edward would confide in her. Olivia was sure she could find a way to help them if she knew what the difficulty was. If there was one thing she detested, it was a problem with no clear resolution. It was like the constant itch of a flea bite between the shoulder blades where she could neither scratch nor ignore it.

When she glanced at the clock, she realized she'd been in the library longer than she'd thought. If she hoped to visit her academy while it was still daylight, she had to leave soon.

Chapter Two

Olivia put the fencing book back on the lower shelf between two other volumes on the subject and left the library. She walked thoughtfully to the grand staircase, which rose in a broad sweep to the first floor where it bifurcated into two galleries, one on either side, set off by beautiful marble Corinthian columns. On the right, the staircase ascended again to the second, third, and fourth floors. Works of art, mostly English pastoral scenes, lined the red-painted walls of the gallery, and high above was a domed ceiling painted with rosy clouds floating in a pale blue sky and cherubs peeking down at those using the staircase.

A smile tugged at her mouth. How many times had she, Margaret, and Hildie hidden behind the columns in the gallery and then peered through the railings to watch their mother, glittering in diamonds, silk, and frothy lace, glide down the stairs to join their father for a ball somewhere in London? She could almost smell her mother's lovely rose perfume and feel the effervescent pride every time she climbed the stairs.

The broad staircase was exquisitely designed to allow anyone in the gallery to view those ascending or descending the marble stairs, or simply walk along the colonnaded space to view the paintings on the walls. And the long gallery had been the perfect place for children to surreptitiously watch the adults in their magnificent finery leave for the theater or a ball.

Halfway down the stairs, Margaret halted to frown at her as she stood in the hallway. "Are you not going with us after all?"

"Yes, I am," Olivia replied hastily, stepping onto the first stair. "I won't be a minute. Please, wait for me."

"Very well, but don't take too long. You know how impatient Edward can be." At the sound of footsteps clattering down the marble staircase, Margaret raised her head. "There he is." A lighter, faster pattering echoed the first set. "And Hildie. Do hurry."

Olivia nodded and ran up the staircase, meeting her siblings halfway. Edward and Hildegard were already dressed for the brisk February weather, wearing warm clothes and stout boots for walking.

"Are you going with us, Livie?" Hildegard asked, adjusting the tilt of her new bonnet to a saucy angle. The cherry-red ribbons brought out the color in her rounded cheeks, and her gray eyes sparkled with enthusiasm, her face charmingly framed by the soft, pale blue brim of her bonnet.

"I'm not going to Hyde Park. I'm going to the academy. I must make sure everything is perfect for tomorrow."

A little of the sparkle went out of Hildegard's eyes. "Surely, you could go tomorrow?"

Edward turned to frown at Hildegard. "Your sister's notion to run an academy may be ludicrous, but she is, at least, behaving with a great deal of sober maturity in her handling of the matter. Do not annoy her, Lady Hildegard." Edward nodded at Olivia, and then his glance slid past her. Frowning slightly, his gaze drifted to the window above the door. "If we wish to walk, we must do so soon. The weather appears unsettled."

Olivia's gaze was drawn to follow his. "Yes, well, don't let me delay you." The weather hadn't improved since morning, and the sky looked heavy with thick banks of gray-tinged clouds that hid the afternoon sun. She shivered and decided she didn't need her academy ledger at that moment. If she were going to the academy, better to leave now before it started to rain again.

She followed her brother and sister down the staircase and gladly accepted her warm poke bonnet with the blue velvet lining and curling white plumes from Latimore, their butler.

His arms were full of hats, gloves, and coats for them to choose from, and he handed the items around briskly. Latimore had been with them since before Olivia's birth and seemed almost fatherly to them, particularly after their papa's death. He stood now with one white-gloved hand on the doorknob, studying all of them with an indulgent smile barely curving his mouth as he made sure they were all dressed for the uncertain weather. He was so careful in his duties to the family that Olivia sometimes wondered if he would simply refuse to open the door if she didn't don the appropriate bonnet or wear her gloves.

Edward questioned her about the school as he took his hat from Latimore, making Olivia increasingly nervous that she had forgotten something that would embarrass her tomorrow when she faced her first students.

No, no, I am prepared, she thought. She just needed to make sure the charwoman, Mrs. Adams, had swept out the rooms adequately and that there were sufficient split logs and kindling to keep the front sitting room warm. While the ladies would certainly be warm enough while practicing in the ballroom, they would most assuredly want a place to rest, and it wouldn't do to let them grow chilled.

Simple enough. So why did ticking off each item in her mind make her so nervous, as if there were one more line on the list that remained invisible? She rubbed her hands together, her fingers feeling cold and damp even though she had yet to leave the warmth of the house.

"You can't go by yourself, Lady Olivia," Edward protested when he finished adjusting his hat at a rakish enough angle to satisfy him.

"I certainly can," Olivia replied, pulling on her gray kid leather gloves and wriggling her chilled fingers. Her hands didn't feel much warmer, even encased in the gloves.

"Nonsense. It just isn't done," Edward said firmly, as if the matter were settled now that he'd pronounced judgment.

"Shall I send for the maid, sir?" Latimore asked in sonorous tones.

"Yes."

The butler glided forward and yanked one of the bell pulls.

When a flustered maid appeared, wiping her reddened hands on her apron, Edward said, "Notify my brother, Mr. Peregrine Archer, that his presence is required." He paused to consider this for a moment before adding, "And he should be prepared for a brisk walk."

"Yes, sir," Mary, an extraordinarily tall and gangly maid, replied before dashing off in the direction of the library. Her limbs were so long and thin that in her black and white uniform, she looked like a loose-legged stork flapping her way down the hallway.

"Peregrine?" Olivia asked her brother in a dry voice. "Are you quite sure his attendance is better than going alone?"

"He is nearly an adult. It is about time he acted like it." Edward dismissed her questions with a flap of his gloved hand.

While she had nothing against her younger brother, he was only one and twenty, and most of the time, if one were unaware of his age, one might think he was almost thirteen. So while he was a male as required for a proper escort, she felt uncertain about his usefulness if they should meet footpads or other violent individuals. Peregrine was far too "Hail, fellow, well met!" to be any danger to a criminal. In fact, he reminded her of a big-eyed, curly-haired spaniel just thrilled to meet anyone new, regardless of social status or threatening appearance.

Despite that, she had to smile. Of all her brothers, he was her favorite. His relentlessly cheerful demeanor always managed to scare away her worries, even when she had a strong case of the dismals. It was just too bad that his speech was marred by a severe stutter they seemed unable to cure.

Peregrine was definitely better company, though, than her far too serious and staid brother Edward, or the sharp-eyed Margaret. At least Peregrine was enthusiastic about her endeavor and had tried several times to convince her to accept him as a teacher to lend a little color and interest to the academy.

He didn't quite understand that she was trying to avoid color, or anything that would make the parents of her prospective students decide against allowing their daughters to apply. Olivia had to avoid anything too improper or scandalous, and took pains to describe fencing as an invigorating exercise that would only be conducted in the company of other ladies. Her fencing academy would be a place for wholesome health and conversation, nothing more.

Olivia smiled as Peregrine came flying down the hallway toward them, heels clattering on the marble, and his coat tails flapping behind him. As he catapulted toward her, she held out a gloved hand to stop him from ramming into her. He gripped it, whirling her around and smiling as if a simple walk were the most enticing prospect imaginable.

Laughing, she shook her head, resigned and relieved to his boisterous company. He was just what she needed to lift her mood on such a dull and dreary day, and in truth, she didn't particularly want to visit the empty academy alone.

The fencing academy was set up in an elderly townhouse owned by her brother Harnet, the Earl of Wraysbury, and while it had lovely, large rooms and was more than adequate for a school, it had been abandoned for several years. As a result, the dusty, echoing rooms often unnerved her for no reason except that she heard the rustling scurry of rats in the walls more times than she cared to, and she'd had the persistent feeling of being observed. The only eyes present were those painted on elegant ladies and gentlemen sauntering through the Roman murals adorning some of the walls, but she couldn't shake the feeling that someone else — someone very much alive and not overly fond of her — observed her.

Of course, her nervousness was sheer nonsense. The building was in the middle of a block of similar structures and only had windows at the front and the back. No one was interested in the old house, and there was very little chance of being observed. It was only the dingy walls, the scarred wooden floors, and the general gloom that bothered her.

The dingy walls were to have been painted a lovely pale yellow yesterday, so the rooms she intended to use should be much brighter and more cheerful.

Peregrine released her hand with a bow, and she finished buttoning her pelisse. Her brother took his beaver hat from Latimore and set it at a jaunty angle on his brown curls, his gaze fixed on the front door. His gray eyes danced with excitement at the prospect of accompanying Olivia to her school, a destination she'd previously denied him based upon the fact that he was likely to be a nuisance and would make far too many nonsensical suggestions about her plans.

Now it no longer seemed so terrible to have him wandering around the empty building, opening doors, thrusting his head into cupboards, and staring up chimneys.

"W-well, so I get to see t-the famous fencing academy, after all," he stuttered in excitement as he pressed his hat more firmly on his head. He caught Olivia's right hand, threaded it through his elbow, and dragged her in the direction of the front door.

Latimore opened the door as they approached and bowed solemnly.

"I'm not sure this is necessary, after all." Olivia grinned as she tried to tear her hand out of her brother's grasp.

"Of c-course it is necessary," Peregrine countered. He pulled her down the front steps and through the black wrought iron gate to the busy sidewalk. "A w-woman c-cannot w-wander around London on her own, you know. You w-would be accosted by the v-vilest sorts imaginable, Ollie."

She laughed at his use of his special pet name. "Ollie" was the one word he could say without stuttering, and he never failed to accompany it with a wide grin. The gleam of triumphant pleasure in his eyes brought another giggle and lingering smile to her lips. The name was like some charming childhood secret the two of them shared.

"We won't be gone long. I simply want to ensure everything is prepared for tomorrow," she said as he held the black wrought iron gate and stepped aside for her to pass onto the walkway.

"T-tomorrow is the day, t-then?" He dragged her forward at a faster rate, as if he were even more anxious to inspect the school than she was.

"Yes." She tugged on his arm. "Will you please walk at a reasonable pace? I refuse to *run* all the way to Cavendish Square."

"Of c-course, yes," he agreed hastily. He moderated his long stride for two steps before pulling her forward again. He was obviously in a good mood and feeling confident, since his stutter had nearly vanished as he chattered about a pair of grays he was considering acquiring for his high-perch phaeton.

She sighed, took a deep breath, and rushed forward at a rapid walk that was really more of a run while he changed topics to the weather, horse racing, and any other topic that passed through his mind.

At the corner of Mortimer Street, Peregrine jerked to a quivering halt like a Spanish pointer spotting a pheasant in the field. "Isn't that your friend, Miss Denholm, ahead of us?"

Sure enough, the majestic form of Miss Denholm strode forward at a clipping rate, the fluffy white plumes on her green silk bonnet waving well above the hats of the other pedestrians as her long stride carried her past them.

Rude though it might be, Olivia didn't want to spend the afternoon providing Cynthia with a tour of the academy. She needed to make sure the rooms were clean and prepared for students, and she simply didn't want the distraction of her friend's boisterous presence.

"Yes—"

"If w-we hurry, we can catch her." He yanked her forward a step.

She pulled back and stood flatfooted on the walkway, resisting her brother's efforts long enough to see Miss Denholm disappear around the next corner. "There — she is gone now. No point in galloping after her."

"We would have c-caught up with her if you'd hurried." He flicked her a curious glance. "I thought she was your friend — one w-would think you didn't even want to greet her."

"Yes, one might think that," Olivia answered sweetly, applying a gentle pressure to her brother's arm to encourage him to proceed. She glanced at the gray sky above. Beneath the ever-present city odors of smoke and horses, she thought she could smell the crisp scent of snow on the moist, chilly wind that whipped past them. "However, I am sure Miss Denholm is as anxious to reach her destination as we are. There is snow in the air — I am sure of it." She glanced sideways at Peregrine and grinned. "And I thought you were anxious to see the academy for the first time."

"Certainly — just forgot about it for a minute." His pace increased once more until she was trotting again to keep up with him.

When they finally turned onto Mortimer Street, she was breathing heavily, although she refused to give in to her breathlessness and kept her mouth clamped shut.

"You need a sign, Ollie," Peregrine said as he opened the creaking gate for her. "Something with lots of gold and such."

"A discreet bronze plague next to the door is quite sufficient. Once the academy is flourishing, that is." She went past him to climb the three steps to the doorway and pulled a large keyring out of her silk damask reticule.

"You will never get students t-that w-way!" he exclaimed. "Here. Let me." He grabbed the clanking ring of keys from her hand, pushed her aside, and opened the creaking door. He waved his right hand with a flourish. The leather soles of his boots crunched on the marble floor, and he glanced down briefly. "Enter at w-will, Ollie. All is w-well except for a bit of d-dust."

Olivia entered, took the keys from his grasp, and returned them to her reticule. Despite the thick soles of her walking boots, she could feel the grit on the floor. Apparently, Mrs. Adams hadn't been there to clean yet. That would have to be corrected before tomorrow. If she had to, she'd send Mary and a few of their maids first thing in the morning to at least sweep the floors and dust the furniture in her office, the sitting room, and the ballroom where lessons would be held.

"W-what now, Ollie?" Peregrine walked over to the staircase, and with his hand on the newel post and his right boot on the bottom step, he craned his neck to peer up into the shadows of the first and second floors.

While the staircase was wide and sturdy, no one could really call it grand. The right wall supported one side, and a long, curving wooden banister swept up on the left. Although there were no draperies on any of the windows, the townhouse seemed dim and gray. The air was musty. As they stood there, Olivia heard the splatter of rain hitting the stoop and windows.

Peregrine hastily ran to the front door and slammed it shut. "No sense letting the rain in, eh, Ollie? D-damp enough as it is." He stared at the palms of his gloved hands and then rubbed off the dust he'd collected from the newel post before removing his gloves and shoving them in his pocket. He started to take off his hat only to stop when he found no handy table to lay it upon.

"I'm going up to my office." She pulled off her own gloves and put them in her reticule, feeling slightly overwhelmed.

Was she really ready for this new endeavor? The notion sounded so exciting when she'd first envisioned it two years ago. Then her brother, Harnet, acquired the townhouse, and one thing led to another, and she was swept up in bringing her dream to reality.

All that time and she still hadn't managed to get the floors swept and polished. The townhouse looked abandoned and dismal. Uninviting. And ladies were so particular. This was clearly unacceptable. She would definitely send Mary and at least one other maid to clean tomorrow morning. The charwoman could hand over the key Olivia had entrusted to her, and she'd find another woman to take care of the place.

Decision made, she squared her shoulders and strode to the staircase. "Do you want to come with me or explore?"

"Lead on, my d-dear sister. I am at your c-command." He followed her and waited at the base of the staircase for her to precede him.

After a moment's thought, Olivia went up the stairs, removing her bonnet and shaking off the rain as she ascended to the first floor. She paused at the landing, shrugged her shoulders, and strode to her office. After all, she had three students, so she needed to make sure she had sufficient supplies for them. She could not expect the ladies to bring their own foils, even though she had suggested it.

"D-do you need me? I want to look around," Peregrine said, already heading for the third floor.

"Go on." She waved him away. "I will call if I need you."

She opened the wide door and stepped inside. Even though there were no drapes to block out the sun, shadows filled the corners, and the room seemed damp and dark. Unpleasant. The air smelled terrible, and she crinkled her nose as she glanced around, trying not to breathe.

Metallic — the taste of old, dirty coins. She sneezed.

Her office was originally a large drawing room with windows overlooking the busy street below. The small panes of glass let in what little watery light there was, but it was not enough to make the room cheerful or inviting. Her brother, Wraysbury, had provided her with a large mahogany desk, several chairs, a wardrobe, and a huge cabinet to furnish her office. She kept her fencing costume and several foils locked inside the wardrobe and hadn't decided what to do with the cabinet yet. The bulky thing seemed more suitable to hold brooms or gardening implements than grace an office, but she had so few items of furniture that she was glad to obtain anything she could use for the school.

Her income, while generous, was not sufficient to allow her to fully furnish the entire townhouse with the elegant pieces most ladies would be accustomed to seeing. So she'd happily accepted any discarded or castoff items her relatives saw fit to offer, including an absolutely repulsive marble angel with a simpering expression and broken wing that Peregrine had given her to use as a paperweight on her desk. She suspected he'd found it on a rubbish heap somewhere but wisely decided not to object as it was heavy enough to be useful.

She went to her desk, vaguely uneasy. The odd smell made her sniff and look around again. Maybe there were dead rats in the walls. She dug out a handkerchief from her reticule and held it to her nose. The faint odor of lavender clung to the fabric, but it couldn't keep the unpleasant odor of decay from catching in her throat.

The townhouse had been vacant for far too long. No wonder she felt as if something were wrong. There were probably a great many things wrong with the structure itself, as they would most likely discover if the rain continued.

There were probably mushrooms sprouting in the cellar and wood rot eating the eaves.

After tucking the acceptance letters from her students into the top drawer of her desk, she selected the key for the gigantic wardrobe where she kept her small hoard of fencing appurtenances. She unlocked the wide double doors and threw them open.

The first thing she saw was the marble cherub staring at her, sitting atop a mound of clothing. A strange pile of clothing, complete with boots. And hands.

She choked and slammed the door shut. Rapidly blinking, she pressed her hand to her pounding chest as she worked to slow her gasping breaths. Then she turned and eased open one of the wardrobe doors again. She peered through the crack.

The cherub's blank eyes stared back. Below the statuette was a dark jacket, gaping open to reveal a red brocade waistcoat and fawn breeches ending in boots. The clothes weren't empty, either, as evidenced by the grayish hands.

There is no head!

The marble statuette sat, smiling merrily, atop the shoulders.

She stifled a scream and stepped back, glancing down when her heel slipped. A sticky puddle of blood oozed around her boots. She hopped away, and couldn't help another muffled shriek at the sight of the crimson footprints she left behind. Panic tightened her chest.

"Ollie," her brother called. "D-did you c-call me?"

She glanced up to see him grinning at her from the doorway. Her mouth worked, but she couldn't seem to speak.

"Olivia?" He stepped into the room, frowning. "W-what is it? D-dead mouse?"

She made a few inarticulate sounds before pointing a shaking hand at the wardrobe.

Peregrine strode forward but glanced down in time to halt before stepping in the puddle of gore. "Good Lord!" he exclaimed, before flushing. "Sorry. Apologies."

Olivia finally found her voice. "The watch — we must send for the watch."

"But w-who is he? W-what happened? D-did he attack you?"

"I didn't murder him! He was dead when I opened the wardrobe."

"How c-could he be? T-the blood is w-wet."

"I don't know." She stared at her brother. If he didn't believe her, who would? She wanted to scream and be sick. Her throat constricted. "I don't understand it. I found him this way."

Peregrine glanced around the office and poked his walking stick into the shadowy corner behind the wardrobe. "T-there is no one here. Have you seen anyone?"

"No. Whoever did this must have gone out the servants' entrance when we came in the front. It is the only answer."

"W-what was he doing t-there? D-did you ask him to meet you here?"

"Of course I did not! I don't know why he was here." She walked over and shut the wardrobe, careful to avoid the poor man's blood.

"W-who is he?"

"I don't know!" Her voice rose shrilly. "How could I possibly know?" She swallowed and took a long breath.

He shrugged.

"We must send for the watch," she repeated.

"I'll go," Peregrine said. His gaze flicked around the room uncomfortably.

"You cannot. I will go." Now that she'd had time to collect herself, she realized that sending Peregrine by himself might not be the best course of action.

Her brother would try valiantly to tell the authorities what had happened, but his stutter would make that difficult task impossible. Strong emotions always made him worse, and if he couldn't speak properly, it would only upset him further and anger the watch.

"No." He scowled at her. "You c-cannot go alone."

"Well, I will not stay here alone." Let him think she was terrified of remaining here with a dead body if he wanted to. At least it would prevent him from going.

Peregrine tried to swear, but his words came out as a staccato burst of incoherence, while his face grew redder and redder with frustration.

"Never mind." Taking pity on him, Olivia went to the window and threw it open. The street below was still busy, and within seconds a well-dressed man in a black greatcoat walked rapidly along the walkway leading in front of the building.

"Sir," she called. "Sir! Please, we need your assistance."

30

The man glanced up, frowning. "Madam? I apologize, but I am in a hurry — I cannot stop."

She stared down at his face, stunned.

Mr. Underwood looked up at her, his face pale with tension and eyes sunken in dark pools. "What is it?"

"Mr. Underwood!" she exclaimed. "What are you—"

"Lady Olivia — I apologize — I must go. I must fetch the doctor — it is urgent." He took a step forward before she could stop him.

"Wait! Mr. Underwood — there has been a terrible accident," she called to him, stretching out a hand as if she could grasp one of his greatcoat's capes and bring him to a halt. "We need assistance."

He glanced up again. "I cannot stop!" His voice was hoarse with urgency. "My wife — I must fetch the physician." Despite his words, he stepped back and put a hand on the black gate, obviously torn between his frantic mission and basic politeness.

"I understand, but could you please send for the watch?" She paused, desperately wanting to request a physician as well, but it seemed cruel to force him to find two.

She couldn't quite accept the fact that the man in the wardrobe was dead. She clung to the possibility that there might be a chance to resuscitate him if they obtained help for him.

"The watch?" The area around his mouth whitened as he pressed his lips into a thin line. "I must find a physician. There is no time."

"Please. If you would send for the watch, I would be grateful."

"If I find the watch, I will send him here." He gripped the top edge of the black wrought iron gate briefly before he pushed himself forward. Head down against the buffeting of the wind, he strode forward, the black tail of his coat flapping behind him.

Olivia turned back to her brother. "Well, it should not be too long." She glanced down at the scuffed wooden floor. "I spoke to Mr. Underwood—"

"Underwood!" Her brother stared at her, mouth agape.

"He looked terrible — he was in a panic." She swallowed and took a deep breath. "He said he was going for a physician." She remembered the bits and pieces of conversation she'd heard in the library and Mr. Underwood's concern for his wife. "I hope Mrs. Underwood has not become ill."

Peregrine nodded absently, a thoughtful frown on his face. The toes of his boots were less than two inches from the pool of blood. The thin red liquid was already turning dark as it dried.

She couldn't bear to remain in the room another minute. "We should wait downstairs." She held out her hand to her brother.

He moved with alacrity into the hallway and stared at her in surprise when she stopped to lock the door behind them.

"Surely you d-don't expect him to get up and w-walk away," he said, watching her with a critical eye, his mouth drooping with unhappy frustration.

"I did not expect him to die in my wardrobe, either, but it appears our expectations are doomed to disappointment."

"Speak for your own expectations, d-dear sister. T-that poor d-devil in there is not w-walking anywhere." Despite his words, he followed her down the stairs.

They waited in the gloomy entrance hall, pacing back and forth, before a loud knock rattled the door. Olivia and Peregrine exchanged nervous glances. Peregrine yanked open the door.

Several men stood crowded together on the stoop. The burly man in the center with a thick, bullish neck and glum expression stepped forward and glanced around. His small, black eyes cut from Peregrine to Olivia. His frown deepened.

"I received a report that assistance was needed at this residence. An accident of some sort." His deep voice seemed harsh and unnaturally loud in the silence of the old townhouse. He swept his shabby black hat off his head and bowed. "Constable Fred Cooke, Madam."

Olivia nodded. "I am Lady Olivia Archer. This is my brother, Mr. Peregrine Archer."

Mr. Cooke bowed again and brushed past Peregrine before gesturing to the men accompanying him. "This here is Mr. John Idleman, the coroner. And behind him are Mr. Andrews, Mr. Frome, and Mr. Jeffers."

The coroner was a rail-thin, solemn man with hazel eyes and sparse gray-brown hair. He nodded and stepped into the hallway. "The physician, Dr. Campbell, was unavailable. I hope we may assist you in his stead, my lady. I have brought several men to assist, if it is necessary to move a gentleman."

Olivia and Peregrine exchanged glances. "I don't know. That is, there is a man — I fear he may be deceased."

"And where is this individual?" Mr. Cooke eyed Peregrine as if suspecting the young man were amusing himself with a joke at the constable's expense.

"Uh-uh," Peregrine choked, unable to break through his stutter. He flushed a deep red, and his brows jutted out in angry ridges.

Cooke's gaze hardened, and he stepped forward, his hands fisted at his sides. "Well, sir? Where is this individual? I would hate to think you have wasted our time for your own amusement."

"Uh, up..." Peregrine struggled to get the words out as his frantic gaze caught Olivia's.

Snickers whispered through the group of men, and several raised their hands to hide their laughter.

Peregrine's flush deepened. His choking grew worse until Olivia stepped forward, inserting herself between the chuckling men and gripping her brother's shoulders. "Peregrine!" She gave his shoulders a shake. "Look at me."

He looked at her before his gaze drifted past her shoulder to the man behind her. His eyes flashed with anger and frustration.

"Peregrine!" she ordered. "Take a deep breath." She desperately wanted to speak for him, to take command, but she knew that would only make matters worse for her brother and take away whatever shred of pride he had left.

Even when she tried to help him by insisting he breathe deeply and remain calm, his stutter choked him. Any words starting with T, V, W, P, D or C stuck in his throat like so many rocks.

The men sniggering behind her only made it worse. She winced inside, guessing at his anger. This was not the first time he'd faced others who delighted in making him the object of derision and sport.

His years at school must have been a torment she wished her parents had spared him.

After a long minute, he straightened his broad shoulders and gazed firmly at the men in the hallway. His frown silenced those who had been laughing behind their hands.

"Uh." He paused and swallowed. "Upstairs. Follow me, if you will." He turned on his heel and ascended the staircase.

Olivia had never been so proud of him than she was at that moment. She nodded at the cluster of men and gestured for them to follow her brother.

Then she trailed after them, wishing she had gone with Margaret instead. No wonder irresponsible people always seemed to be so cheerful. They left it up to the dutiful to uncover all the unpleasant things in life, such as the dead man in her wardrobe.

Chapter Three

When they reached her office, they clustered around the door, waiting for her to unlock it. She caught Peregrine's eye as she fitted the key in the lock, and he nodded to her reassuringly. As soon as she opened the door, the stout constable, Mr. Cooke, walked past her and entered.

"Well, my lady," Constable Cooke said, glancing around from the center of the room. He crossed his arms over his barrel chest, and his upper lip curled with disdain. He obviously still believed he'd been called there for their amusement or as part of a wager. "Where is this injured party?"

Olivia took a step toward the wardrobe and her gaze fell once again to the dark stain on the floor in front of it. Her small footprints painted a trail in brownish red, pointing in her direction. A cold sweat prickled down her back, making her shiver. The thought of opening the door and exposing the man within made her stomach clench.

She didn't want to see the body again. She flung a beseeching glance at her brother.

"Quite," Peregrine said without the hint of a stutter. He stepped forward, opened the double door, and backed away, carefully avoiding the bloody stain on the floor.

Cooke's round face grew pale, then flushed, and finally settled into a sickly gray that made the dark shadow of his beard stand out like coal dust on his lower face. "Mr. Idleman," he said in a strangled voice. He gestured toward the wardrobe.

The coroner stepped around Constable Cooke, took one look at the contents of the wardrobe, and frowned. "Mr. Andrews, if you please, we must have our twelve men. This poor soul is past our help." He waited while one of the men hurried out before he faced Peregrine. "Mr. Archer, explain if you will. What is the meaning of this outrage?"

Peregrine took a deep breath and answered slowly, "W-we found him as you see him now."

"Found him?" The coroner's thin, long face grew longer still, and vertical lines carved deep grooves from the edges of his narrow lips to his nose. He looked around. "Who owns this house? It appears abandoned. Why were you here, sir?"

Before Peregrine could answer, Constable Cooke interrupted. "As a member of the local constabulary, I must warn you, sir. If this was one of them wagers gone wrong, the law shall look very harshly on those involved." He studied Peregrine with hard eyes before casting an equally critical glance at Olivia. "Now, why is this man in your wardrobe, sir?"

"It is my wardrobe," Olivia answered hastily. The firm, noble expression on her brother's face hinted that he might believe she had something to do with this terrible situation and was prepared to sacrifice himself to keep her safe. "And this is my townhouse. We are renting it from my brother, the Earl of Wraysbury."

"This house?" Mr. Idleman looked around, his gray brows raised in disbelief as he took in the dusty furniture and gray cobweb dangling near the ceiling in the far corner.

"As I indicated, the owner is my brother, the Earl of Wraysbury. I am renting it from him," she continued hurriedly. "I am starting an academy for ladies on the premises."

The curl in Cooke's lip grew more pronounced. He clearly didn't believe either her or that ladies had need of an academy of any sort.

Olivia studied him, relieved that she'd had the foresight not to mention it was a fencing academy. She could just imagine his reaction to that information.

Not that she was ashamed of her school, of course. Quite the opposite. But the last thing she wished for was to engage in an esoteric argument on the merits of fencing as a form of beneficial exercise for women with a man like the constable. He clearly had a stubborn, bulldog character which might be wonderfully suited to his job, but made him particularly dismissive of new ideas.

A quick peek at the window only increased her desire to leave. The sky outside was glowing with crimson streaks, and the room was gradually growing darker. She glanced at her brother and then again at the gloomy, dirt-streaked panes of glass.

"Ladies?" Mr. Idleman asked in disbelief, focusing his attention on her.

"We have not opened yet. My brother and I were simply here to determine if the building had been cleaned and readied. Clearly, it has not," Olivia said.

"So I noticed, my lady," Constable Cooke said. He clasped his hands behind his back and thrust his head forward to stare at her from under lowered brows. "I also noted that the door to this room was locked."

"Yes, I locked it before we went to find assistance," Olivia answered.

He looked from her to the wardrobe. "And this?" He waved at the gaping piece of furniture.

"It was locked, as well. It is always locked. The academy's supplies are kept there."

"And what was the condition of this room and that wardrobe when you arrived, my lady?"

"Locked," she answered impatiently. Lightning crackled outside the window, followed by a boom of thunder. She jumped with a shiver and rubbed her arms. "I kept them locked, of course."

As she spoke, her brother rummaged through the top drawer of her desk and withdrew a phosphorous box. He carefully lit the lamp sitting at the edge of the desk and moved it closer to cast its golden glow over the wardrobe and its terrible contents.

"And who, may I ask, has keys?" Cooke asked with a satisfied smile and the smug air of someone who knows the answer to his own question. He obviously expected a swift conclusion to his investigation.

"I naturally have keys, and the charwoman has a key to the house." Olivia caught her brother's gaze.

He frowned at her and shoved his hands into his pockets, his shoulders hunching slightly. Concern wrinkled his forehead, and he was beginning to look like a turtle slowly withdrawing into his shell as he stepped closer to the window and out of the wavering circle of light.

"Does the charwoman's key fit the door to this room? Or the wardrobe, my lady?" Cooke continued his questions.

Olivia stiffened, hugging one arm around her waist. Her other hand rose, and her fingers fastened on the top button of her pelisse, twisting it. "N-no." She cleared her throat. "Her key only fits the door at the rear of the house."

"So you were the only one with keys to this room and the cupboard, and both were locked when you arrived, my lady?" Constable Cooke's knowing grin widened. He looked almost gleeful at the thought that he might be staring at a murderess.

"Yes — no." Olivia laughed nervously as she remembered entering the room. "That is, the door to this room was unlocked. However, the wardrobe was locked. It is a mystery, to be sure. I cannot imagine how he entered without our knowledge."

How could someone have locked the wardrobe without a key? She could understand that someone might have picked the locks on the door and the furniture, but how did he lock it again?

"That is indeed a mystery, to be sure," Mr. Idleman said in a dry voice.

Before she could think of a response, she heard the clatter of heavy footsteps coming up the staircase. A straggling group of men entered, and the foremost, the man Mr. Idleman called Mr. Andrews, nodded to the coroner.

"Here are the jurymen, Mr. Idleman," Mr. Andrews announced, stepping to one side of the door. As the somber group filed into the room, he called out their names, "Mr. Hanks, Mr. Bulwer, Mr. Samuels, Mr. Wright, Mr. Thompson, Mr. Oakdale, Mr. Thorne, and Mr. Chesterton."

Counting the men who'd remained with the coroner, there were twelve, in addition to Mr. Idleman and Constable Cooke.

The room suddenly felt crowded, and the previously cold and musty air was thick with strange odors of beer, cabbage, sweat-dampened wool, and the metallic smell of drying blood. Olivia coughed and raised her handkerchief. The faint scent of lavender still clung to the material. She held it to her nose and pressed the cool, soft folds to her mouth.

"Take heed of the floor, Constable," Mr. Idleman cautioned him. He pointed to the pool of blood. "There are footprints here, small prints made by a lady's boot, if I am not mistaken. And made before the vital fluid dried." He looked at Olivia. His gray brows rose high on his forehead as he eyes grew hard.

"They are mine," Olivia admitted. Her fingers tightened around the handkerchief. "I did not realize... That is, I did not notice the stain when I arrived."

"It was daylight, was it not?" Mr. Idleman asked.

"Yes, but I was not expecting — that is — I was not looking at the floor." Olivia's gaze locked on the stain and the wobbly line of footprints leading from it to the doorway. Her face burned. When she glanced up, she found her brother standing next to her. Her hand crept into his, grateful for the warmth of his fingers.

"The blood was sticky," Constable Cooke pointed out, ending his statement with a damp smack of his plump lips.

"I was only here for a moment before my brother followed me into the room."

Peregrine squeezed her fingers and nodded. "Not long. I heard nothing untoward."

"Of course not," Constable Cooke murmured softly. "Did either of you see an intruder?"

Olivia and Peregrine exchanged glances. Peregrine answered, "No. T-the building appeared t-to be empty."

"It would only take a moment to hit a man and push him into this wardrobe," Mr. Idleman said as he examined the door's lock. "And this mechanism has a spring that could have locked the door when it was shut." He clasped his hands behind his back and leaned forward to peer at the dead man. "What is that object?"

"A marble cherub," Olivia answered hastily. "It was on my desk." She gestured at the massive desk behind the men standing in a semicircle, staring at her. "My brother gave it to me." As soon as the words left her mouth, she felt her stomach contract. Why had she said such a thing? Her neck stiffened as she struggled to avoid glancing at him.

Peregrine once again tightened his clasp on her hand to reassure her. She squeezed back. *Sorry.*

"Then who, other than you two, knew that weapon was here?" Cooke asked, his small eyes glinting in the growing shadows.

"It was not a weapon," Olivia protested. "It was a paperweight. And it was sitting on that desk, in plain view of anyone who entered this room."

"A locked room, and you with the only key." Constable Cooke rolled from heel to toe and back, his gaze moving from Olivia to the dead man and back to Olivia. He frowned at her. "I regret the necessity, my lady, but I must point out that apparently, you were the only one with access to this here locality, and the only one, other than your brother, who had knowledge of the fatal weapon. You have as much as admitted that those are your footprints in the victim's blood."

"My good man!" Peregrine stood straighter and took a deep breath. His face assumed the cold, distant expression they'd all seen on their father's face when he'd confronted them with their youthful misdemeanors. Speaking very slowly and distinctly, he said, "You forget t-to w-whom you speak. W-we sent for you w-when we d-discovered t-this horror. Your implications are impertinent and d-distasteful in the extreme."

Olivia gazed at her younger brother in awe. Illogical though it was, she was relieved not to be the one incurring Peregrine's ire at that moment.

"Yes, well, gentlemen, we must do our duty. Please view the circumstances and ask any clarifying questions before we, ah, touch the deceased," Mr. Idleman said.

The men silently walked forward to peer at the body, stepping carefully around the stain. None of them seemed inclined to ask any questions, and in fact, no one even dared to look at Olivia or Peregrine. They all kept their gaze resolutely directed toward the floor as they edged past the brother and sister.

When the last man filed past, Constable Cooke positioned himself in front of the wardrobe and gingerly picked up the marble statue. He carefully wrapped the cherub in a large, red handkerchief liberally sprinkled with round yellow spots. With the weapon removed, they bent forward, but the victim's head leaned back into the dark rear corner and was so besmirched with gore that it was impossible to recognize his features. Cooke glanced at the coroner, who nodded.

Taking a deep breath, Cooke gripped the body's superfine wool jacket and pulled him forward. The corpse toppled out of the wardrobe to sprawl awkwardly on the floor. The constable rolled the victim over to reveal the face.

"Do you recognize him, my lady?" Mr. Idleman asked.

Olivia's clasp tightened on her brother's hand as she raised her free hand to press her handkerchief against her mouth with icy fingers. She caught Peregrine's startled gaze.

"Mr. Grantham," she said in a shaky voice.

Mr. Underwood! Had he come here and murdered Mr. Grantham when Edward wouldn't help him? He'd been on the street below and might have been running away. That would account for the panic straining his pallid features. Her thoughts whirled chaotically, but she kept her lips firmly pressed together. She refused to implicate him until she knew for certain the nature of his conversation with her brother and the reason for his presence so near the academy.

"He is known to you, then," the constable confirmed with satisfaction.

"He is an old friend of our family. We all knew him." She looked to her brother, too shocked to think clearly. Should she mention Mr. Underwood after all?

No! She couldn't do that to him. *But what had Mr. Grantham been doing here?* He hadn't seemed that interested in her school the last time he visited them.

Peregrine nodded. "An old family friend."

"Was he assisting you with your, em, academy?" Mr. Idleman asked. He cast a glance at Cooke that seemed to indicate the two men were in accord regarding their scorn for her endeavor.

"No. I have no notion of why he should be here," Olivia said.

"You did not arrange to meet him here, in your office?" Cooke asked.

"No, I did not," she answered.

"Then how was he able to enter your office and open the cupboard? Did he have a key?" Mr. Idleman asked as Cooke studied her.

She was beginning to feel like a mouse snagged by the sharp claws of a cat. She glanced around. All the men were staring at her with varying degrees of curiosity and sympathy in their eyes. Mr. Underwood's name hovered in the back of her throat, pushing forward, but she swallowed the words, refusing to throw suspicion in his direction until she felt more sure of his guilt. "I have no notion how he entered, or why he was here. I certainly did not invite him here."

Cooke shook his head before turning back to the wardrobe. He pulled out one of the fencing foils that had been behind the body. "What is this?" He faced her, holding the thin sword with the tip pointing up at the ceiling. "There are swords here. What sort of ladies' academy is this if these are your supplies?"

"If you must know, it is a fencing academy." Olivia's chin rose. "It is a most invigorating sport, and quite proper."

Frowning with disapproval, the constable and coroner looked at each other as if trying to decide if teaching ladies to fence could possibly have anything to do with the death of Mr. Grantham.

"If t-there is nothing else, Lady Olivia and I will leave you t-to your investigation. T-there is nothing more we c-can t-tell you, and my sister has had a severe shock." He drew out his slim, silver case of calling cards and handed one to the coroner. "Good day, gentlemen."

Before anyone could react, he drew Olivia's hand through the crook of his arm and drew her along with him out of the room.

Olivia took a deep breath in the hallway and drew her brother closer to touch her lips lightly to his cheek. "You were splendid, Perry dearest. Thank you so much."

He shook his head and walked faster, descending the staircase ahead of her. He clearly wanted to get out of the musty townhouse as quickly as possible. It wasn't until they were outside that he paused to jam his hat on his head and give one last glance up at the tall building.

Icy sleet stung their faces, and Peregrine blinked repeatedly. "I did not t-think t-they would let us go so easily." He shot a quick, curious look at her. "You d-did not arrange to meet old Grantham, d-did you?"

She stopped and dragged her hand away. "I did not! How could you possibly think I would do such a thing?"

"Well, he c-could fence," Peregrine answered lamely.

A hot surge of frustrated tears burned her eyes. "Most men of our acquaintance can fence. I had no reason to make an assignation with him here. Why, he is — was — at our townhouse nearly every day. If I wanted to speak with him, I could have done so there." Her voice shook, and she swallowed, walking faster. The sleet burned her cheeks and throat. "Of everyone, I would have thought that you would have faith in me."

"Oh, d-don't be a ninnyhammer, Ollie," he replied testily, grabbing her hand and dragging her forward at a faster pace. "I know you d-did not kill him. There is not a d-drop of blood on you. Except your shoes, of c-course."

"And that's the only reason you believe me? Because I am not besmirched with his blood?"

Peregrine chuckled, although he still looked pale, and the cold had made the tip of his nose red. "No. You c-could not harm a fly, Ollie. Everyone knows t-that."

Slightly mollified, she stopped trying to pull her hand away. "Maybe so, but I am afraid Mr. Idleman and Constable Cooke are not so sure. We have not seen the last of them."

Her brother chuckled uneasily, not bothering to disagree. They both knew there were going to be some unpleasant events unfolding over the next few days, and the future of Olivia's academy seemed as bleak as the weather.

Chapter Four

W hen Olivia and Peregrine entered their townhouse, Margaret, Edward, and Hildie were already in the hallway, shedding hats, gloves, and coats. Sparkles of ice flew around them and spattered against the marble floor as they shook off their outerwear and stamped their feet.

Margaret took one look at Olivia's face and frowned, almost dropping one of her gloves. Ever vigil, Latimore caught the item before it hit the floor and added it to the bundle of clothing draped over his arm while a footman hurried forward with a broom and rag to wipe up the mud and melting ice.

"What is it, Olivia? Has something happened?" Margaret asked.

Suddenly, everyone was watching Olivia as she undid the ribbons of her bonnet and handed it to the butler. "We found…" She glanced over her shoulder at Peregrine, but he was busy with his jacket. "Mr. Grantham was, well, I fear he has had an accident."

"An accident?" Edward repeated in a stern voice that suggested disbelief.

Margaret gripped Olivia's wrist. "What kind of accident? Was he hurt?"

Olivia stared into her younger sister's eyes, searching for a way to make the news less stark and terrible. Margaret had always been so fond of Mr. Grantham, particularly after their father died. He supplied tolerant, amused snippets of guidance when she required it and a sympathetic ear when she needed to pour out her woes to someone. Mr. Grantham had been gentle and kind to all of them, but there was no doubt that Margaret was his favorite. He never failed to

44

bring some trifle with him when he visited, whether it was a ribbon or a favorite confection.

"I am sorry, Margaret," Olivia said. "He passed away."

"He is dead?" Margaret's fingers tightened on Olivia's wrist, and her mouth quivered as her eyes filled with tears. "How? He was not that old — how could he have died? Was it a carriage accident? This weather is so dreadful."

"No. I am sorry," Olivia repeated. She gathered Margaret into her arms, despite her sister's rigid back, and held her.

Margaret's wrenching sobs fell in a burning trickle against Olivia's neck. And Olivia felt tears spill over her own cheeks as she clasped Margaret closer and whispered random endearments into her soft hair. She jerked when Hildie threw her arms around the two of them, clutching her older sisters and crying noisily against their shoulders.

Even Edward glanced away and had to clear his throat several times.

When their tears slowed, all of them turned away, hunched, and their gazes fixed on the floor as if looking at each other would only bring forth a fresh wave of grief. Murmuring apologies, they drifted apart, trudging upstairs to the privacy of their bedchambers. That evening, they all had trays in their rooms, too wearied with sorrow to endure a more elaborate meal in the formal dining room.

The next morning, the post brought a couple of brief but politely worded apologies from two of the ladies who were to be Olivia's first fencing students. She read the notes blearily, through red-rimmed, itching eyes.

That just left one lady. Olivia sighed and refolded the letters and slid them into the drawer of her writing desk. This afternoon's post would undoubtedly bring apologies from her last student, Cynthia Denholm.

Well, perhaps it was for the best. No one would wish to set foot in the townhouse so soon after yesterday's tragedy, especially not Olivia. She kept seeing Mr. Grantham huddled in the wardrobe with the cupid statuette sitting on his shoulder.

Last night, she had barely slept, and this morning, she still felt numb with shock and grief. When Mary came into the room to clean the ashes from the fireplace, Olivia realized she'd forgotten to send Mary, or any of the other maids, to the building to clean the rooms properly.

Although given what had happened, it seemed unlikely that the maids would be willing to go there unless one of the larger footmen went with them. And Olivia couldn't blame them. She would be uneasy going there alone as well.

Olivia rubbed her forehead. Her head felt achy and stuffed with wool.

What should she do? No doubt the constable had also confiscated the foils and other wardrobe contents. They'd had nothing to do with Mr. Grantham's unfortunate death, but she knew she would be wise to anticipate Constable Cooke's actions.

The thought seemed like one more obstacle, and she was so tired she could scarcely think.

She would have to start all over again, and she didn't know if she had the energy to do so. Belatedly, she realized that Margaret had been correct; there was very little to tempt a lady to enroll. The ladies could easily meet for ices at Gunther's if they wanted to get together to gossip. And a walk or a ride in one of the parks would suffice as exercise. No need to scandalize Society and risk censure for engaging in such an unladylike activity.

They didn't know how exhilarating it was to fence, to hear that whisper of steel against steel as one tested the foil of one's opponent. They had never experienced what she had, never knew the thrill of matching swords and wits and winning against all odds.

But now, she almost regretted her impulse to start a fencing academy. Her back stiffened. Now that she had begun down this path, she'd appear idiotic and lackadaisical to halt at the first difficulty. She was made of sterner stuff than that.

Her fingers brushed over a fresh sheet of the creamy paper she used for letters. Ladies might not enroll to fence with Olivia, but they would certainly do so if Lord Milbourn were one of the teachers. His dashing, faintly exotic presence would easily overcome the sordid scandal of finding a dead man in her office. The notion brought a hectic flush to her cheeks.

She had to stop thinking of him. He was not the answer to all of her difficulties.

A frown grew, wrinkling her brow. But she needed assistance. Why not him? He had tutored all of her brothers in the fine art before he'd inherited his title and accompanying fortune. Perhaps he would see it as an entertaining lark. Even if he only attended a few sessions, it might be enough.

She dipped her pen in the crystal inkwell and wrote quickly, begging Lord Milbourn for assistance. It wasn't until she signed her name that she had second thoughts. She couldn't ask him. It was too forward. What would he think? No doubt, he would believe she'd never outgrown her childish fondness for him.

How embarrassing.

And what would her betrothed, Lord Saunders, say? Probably nothing. The thought was demoralizing. She rested her chin on her fist, staring glumly out the window. Lord Saunders never said anything about any of her notions, no matter how outrageous they were. He was too kind to hurt her. And she ought to respect his feelings. Her schemes had already embroiled her in a murder, and she knew she would see disappointment and concern in his soft eyes the next time she saw him. He would stand by her, no matter how scandalous her behavior, and he'd never say a word. He'd just look at her with his huge sad eyes, heave a sigh, and carry on bravely.

Nothing could be more sure to make her feel positively cruel and thoughtless than the sound of his soft little sighs.

She folded the letter.

"Olivia? Olivia!" Margaret's voice rushed through the open door behind Olivia like a summer storm. "Oh, there you are." Sniffing into a handkerchief, she walked into the room, followed by a short, plump man with large blue eyes and a receding hairline. "Lord Saunders is here, Lady Olivia."

"How charming to see you, my lord." Olivia stood and stretched out one hand.

"I came as soon as I heard. My deepest sympathies to you. I understand Mr. Grantham was a good friend to your family." Lord Saunders caught her fingers and obligingly bowed over her hand.

When he straightened, his wide-set blue eyes roved over her face, and his mouth pursed with concern. "You are looking well, Lady Olivia. I had expected, that is, er, I am relieved you appear so well."

"Yes. I am well," she answered more sharply than she meant.

Margaret turned her shoulder to them and held her wrinkled linen handkerchief to her nose. "I don't know how we shall bear it," she whispered in a muffled voice.

"Of course, my dear Lady Margaret." He patted her forearm awkwardly. "Your grief is only proper and right, given your loss. It does you credit."

Olivia studied him. Did he mean to imply that because she was not sobbing, she was not exhibiting the proper sentiment?

He'd obviously rushed over, expecting to find her locked in her bedroom, prostrate with shock. His mournful eyes played over her face, and she thought she could detect disappointment in their depths. Perhaps he didn't think it was right that she was wandering around the house as if nothing had happened.

Her head rose. Once again, she'd failed to live up to his expectations of frail, sensitive womanhood, and although he was too kind and respectful to voice any criticism, she felt just as crushed when she saw the disappointment in his eyes.

"I told you, finding poor Mr. Grantham in her cupboard did not bother her in the least," Margaret interjected, her eyes swollen and red. "She is quite hard-hearted."

"I am not completely heartless," Olivia protested. "I was horrified. It was a terrible thing, and we will all miss Mr. Grantham."

"Of course you will," Lord Saunders said. "Your sentiment is only proper. I would have expected nothing less. I am just sorry that you were ever exposed to such a thing." He drew himself up like a pigeon puffing out his breast and strolled over to a nearby couch, politely waiting for the ladies to be seated. "At least you can bow out, now, from this ridiculous notion of a fencing academy. No one could possibly criticize you for ending the affair. In a sense, this may prove to be the best thing that could have happened." When Olivia's eyes widened in surprise, he hastily added, "Of course, Mr. Grantham's death could never be considered a good thing. Oh, no, that was not my meaning at all, you understand. I simply meant that out of every tragedy, some good may come. Well, of course, we are all quite upset, and it is a terrible thing."

"Of course it is. You are so kind to understand, Lord Saunders." Margaret gave Olivia a stern look before she sniffed and waved to the couch near Lord Saunders. She wandered through the room, stopping briefly at the writing table, before joining Saunders. "Will you not have a seat, my lord? Lady Olivia, why don't you ring for some tea? I'm sure Lord Saunders would like some refreshment after his long walk. We must think of others, despite our grief."

"Oh, no, I did not walk. I took a hack. But if you ladies would like some tea, I should, of course, be pleased." He hesitated in front of the sofa, half-sitting before standing again and waiting for Margaret to take a seat before he smiled and sat beside her.

Olivia yanked on the bell pull in the corner of the room. She was about to lower herself into the wing chair next to their couch when there was a burst of clicking noises in the hallway, growing louder as they headed for the sitting room. Leaping in front of her betrothed, she faced the door.

Yapping and frenzied clicking whooshed into the room as a pack of joyful beagles galloped toward Olivia. Her beagles! Somehow, they had escaped from their room just off the kitchen and, happily making the most of their freedom, had come in search of her.

Two dogs jumped on her skirts, tongues lolling from their mouths in glee.

"Down, Caesar, Brutus." She forced them down, scratching their long, soft ears with a smile before she turned.

An alarmingly pale Lord Saunders was standing on the seat cushion of the couch while Margaret stood in front of him, pushing back Justinia, Octavius, Titus, and Bathsheba. The dogs bayed at him, and Lord Saunders's mouth worked. He moaned incoherently, his eyes cutting from one dog to the other as they leapt up in their efforts to reach some part of his anatomy to lick.

"Get down," Margaret ordered, her tear-stained face growing flushed. "How could you, Lady Olivia? You know how your dogs affect

Lord Saunders. How could you do this after Mr. Grantham? Have you no heart — no sensitivity — at all?"

"I am sorry, they must have escaped from their room." Olivia caught several of the dogs and dragged them away by their leather collars, only to have them roll over on their backs in an effort to entice her to rub their bellies. "Naughty little doggies."

Caesar gazed up at her with huge brown eyes, pink tongue hanging out, and rolled a little closer to expose his tender belly. She couldn't resist his blandishments and stopped to rub him. With a laugh, she petted them all and made them sit at her feet in an orderly group. Their happy expressions lifted her heart for what seemed like the first time in days.

"Perhaps you could take Lord Saunders for a walk, Lady Margaret," she said. "I'll keep the dogs here until you are gone."

"But I am expecting Lord Graybrook—" Margaret broke off, casting a glance at Lord Saunders obliquely through her thick lashes. "Well, perhaps he has decided not to call after all. I shall be pleased to have your company, Lord Saunders."

"Delighted," Lord Saunders mumbled, eyeing the dogs.

Margaret raised her hand to help Lord Saunders descend from the couch. With amazingly nimbleness, he skirted the wing chair, putting the furniture between him and the dogs. The animals eyed him with bright, curious eyes and wagging tails, clearly hoping this was the start of some new game.

"Honestly, Lady Olivia, I shall never understand why you even brought those dogs with you. They are of no use whatsoever in London," Margaret chided her as she followed Lord Saunders out of the room.

"They wanted to come," Olivia said lamely.

How could she explain that when she'd climbed into the carriage, Caesar had run out and jumped in, terrified of being left behind. And then the others had begun baying and escaped from the groom to make a mad dash for the carriage. Once they jumped inside, she couldn't bring herself to force them out or see the look of disappointment in their brown eyes. It would have felt too much like betrayal to leave them after that.

Margaret took Lord Saunders by the arm and drew him into the hallway. When they'd gone, Olivia stooped to rub all the dogs, trying to be serious and chide them for upsetting her betrothed. But when Caesar and Titus rolled over onto her feet, waving their paws in the air, she couldn't help laughing. The others soon pushed forward in their efforts to dominate her attention, and she felt a little of her grief and worry fade.

She should have felt badly about upsetting her betrothed, but somehow, when she saw the gentle remonstrance in his gaze, she only wanted to take the dogs and escape to the small grassy area behind the townhouse. Some of her grief returned, however, when she remembered poor Mr. Grantham.

What had happened to him? He'd been such a quiet, gentle man, and a cherished friend. Why had he gone to the academy? Her brow wrinkled. How had he entered without a key? Had he been meeting someone? Had he met Mr. Underwood?

The thought made her queasy, and she pressed a hand against her stomach. She didn't want to believe Mr. Underwood had been involved, and yet his conversation with her brother and his presence near the academy haunted her.

So many questions. And worse, Mr. Grantham's death seemed so senseless. How could anyone be angry enough with him to hit him with the first object that came to hand? He had been so inoffensive that it was impossible to imagine the circumstances that must have led to his death. The picture of the stained marble cherub resting on Mr. Grantham's shoulder, obscuring his head, and the stickiness of his blood on the floor beneath her boots would not leave her. It spoke of brutal, senseless rage.

Uncontrollable anger.

Mr. Underwood had been angry. He'd seemed desperate when she overheard his conversation with her brother. Even more damning, he'd been near the academy soon after Mr. Grantham had died.

Should she report it?

No. If anyone reported it, it should be Edward. He alone knew precisely what Mr. Underwood had said to him.

Amy Corwin

Once the motive was clear, she would feel more comfortable telling the authorities that he had been in the vicinity of the townhouse that afternoon.

Undecided, she did nothing, and even the dogs couldn't brighten the rest of her day. She moved through her social duties in low spirits, writing letters, and accepting callers. As the afternoon wore on, she began to realize that the delicate questions of the ladies who visited could not mask the excited curiosity in their eyes. While they were quick to offer their sympathy, they all asked the same questions about the academy and Mr. Grantham's state when Olivia discovered him.

How dreadful, they simpered behind gloved hands, their eyes bright with excitement.

Olivia was almost relieved when the beagles escaped from their quarters twice more while ladies were visiting. Excited by the prospect of strangers in the house, the dogs bayed and dashed up the stairs and along the gallery with the footman running after them in close attendance.

Olivia calmly sipped her tea to cover her laughter.

"What is the meaning of this outrage?" Mrs. Roberts shrieked, jerking to her feet as Brutus sniffed at her overly ruffled hem. She stood quivering as the other dogs encircled her, sniffing and pawing at her dress. "I came here to lend a sympathetic ear and support, despite the evils of your situation, and I must say, I expected better of you, Lady Olivia."

"I *am* sorry, Mrs. Roberts, and I fully appreciate your kindness. Perhaps you could overlook the dogs as simply evidence of my evil situation." Olivia picked up the teapot. "Would you care for some more tea?"

"Tea? *Tea*? Surrounded by those brutes? I should say not, and I am sorry to say that your frivolous attitude does you no credit, Lady Olivia." She swished her skirts away from Octavius's inquisitive nose. "I am afraid I have another engagement. Good day, Lady Olivia."

"Good day. I hope I have not made you late." Olivia stood and gestured to the dogs.

For once, they obeyed her, and trotted calmly over to the fireplace. In a rare display of obedience, they sat in an orderly line in front of the hearth, wagging their tails in anticipation of another caller.

After Mrs. Roberts left, the few other visitors she received only stayed long enough after meeting Olivia's beagles to plead other appointments and beat hasty retreats.

Olivia had never been so pleased to have her dogs nearby than she was that afternoon. Perhaps she ought to request their presence in the drawing room every day between one and three in the afternoon.

Her relief increased when the clock on the mantel chimed and she realized she could finally stop receiving guests. She took the beagles for a brief and well-deserved walk outside and then retired upstairs to change for dinner.

As their gloomy supper drew to a close, Edward carefully folded his serviette, placed it next to his plate, and said, "I propose we attend *Harlequin and the Magic Rose* at the Adelphi as we intended. What say you?"

Margaret shook her head, her eyes fixed on her plate. She had scarcely eaten a bite.

Olivia studied her with sympathy, wishing she'd sat close enough to give her sister's hand a squeeze.

"I will stay with Lady Margaret," Olivia said. After all the curious visitors she'd received that afternoon, she had no wish to meet even more inquisitive acquaintances at the theater.

Hildie and Peregrine, however, smiled, exchanged glances, and Hildie said, "Perry and I will come with you. I'm sick of this moldy old townhouse."

"Before you go, may I speak to you, Edward?" Olivia said.

Her sisters eyed her curiously, but they didn't comment as the two girls left together. Peregrine studied her, let out a long-suffering sigh, and exited as well, clearly exasperated by Olivia's desire for privacy.

When they were alone, Olivia faced Edward. Her hands knotted together as she studied him, trying to think of a way to explain how she happened to overhear his conversation in the library.

"Well?" Edward prompted. "We must leave soon for the theater — can this not wait?"

"No — I..." Olivia halted, took a deep breath, and then plunged on. "I fell asleep in the library, earlier — the other day. When I woke up, you were conversing with Mr. Underwood."

Edward's chest expanded as he frowned at her. He was clearly unhappy about her admission.

Before he could say anything, she held up one hand. "I did not intend to overhear anything, truly, but I did not want to embarrass Mr. Underwood, either. He sounded so upset and serious." She leaned across the table to lay her hand on her brother's forearm. "And I did not hear everything. I only heard him mention Mr. Grantham."

"And now you are wondering if he murdered him," Edward said brutally.

"Well, I just..." She winced at her words. She just what? Thought that the soft-spoken Mr. Underwood had lost his temper and killed Mr. Grantham?

"Just what?" Edward's eyes glinted with anger.

She sat back, shrugged, and shook her head. Her fingers twisted together so tightly that her knuckles were white.

"Do you truly believe Mr. Underwood would kill anyone?"

"There is no need to be angry with me," she said in a small voice. "I just thought if Mr. Underwood were desperate enough.... Well, it might have been an accident. And you should inform the coroner — at the inquest."

"I am well aware of my responsibilities, Lady Olivia," Edward responded stiffly. "And if I believe my conversation with Mr. Underwood is relevant, I will notify the appropriate authorities. Now is that all?"

"Yes. I am sorry — I did not mean to interfere."

His anger faded as quickly as it had arisen, and he smiled before he leaned forward to give her shoulder a squeeze. "You never *mean* to interfere. You simply do." His expression grew serious again, however, as he studied her face. "Promise me you will not involve yourself in this matter. One man is dead — I would not see anything happen to you."

"I will not." Her smile twisted ruefully. "But I believe the coroner already thinks I stand right at the heart of the tragedy."

"But Peregrine was with you." Edward's frown deepened.

"Not every minute, no." She tried to sound confident, but her voice sounded plaintive even to her ears. "I was alone in my office several minutes before he joined me."

"How long?"

She shrugged. "I'm not sure. Perhaps only one or two minutes. I went into the room, opened the wardrobe to check the equipment, and saw Mr. Grantham. I screamed, and Peregrine ran in just a few seconds later. That is all I remember — not very helpful, I fear."

"No, it is not." Edward's dark brows drew down as he stared at her with a combination of aggravation and anger. Finally, he shook his head and turned away. "Cannot be helped now, however. I wish you had never started that ridiculous academy" — he held up one hand — "but as you did, we must do what we can to keep your name out of this matter. Just try to avoid any further difficulties."

"I will, I promise," she agreed with such a meek voice that Edward's eyes twinkled.

His lips twitched, but he refused to smile. "Why is it I do not trust your promise?"

"Because you are wise beyond your years," Olivia said before she slipped past him and retreated to the library.

An hour later, Edward, Peregrine, and Hildegard left for the theater, while Margaret retired to her room, pleading a headache. Olivia explored their library, picked out a book, and spent the evening ensconced in her favorite wing chair next to the fireplace. She couldn't concentrate on reading, however, and kept thinking about Mr. Grantham and Mr. Underwood. Was Edward wrong? Was Mr. Underwood involved? Her thoughts swam in useless, repetitive circles. It was not long before she developed a tired headache like Margaret had and went to her bedchamber.

She had half-expected Constable Cooke to appear with additional questions that evening. As she prepared for bed, she had the uncomfortable feeling that their quiet day had simply been the lull before the storm.

Chapter Five

Olivia was once again seated at her delicate white writing desk in the corner of the Ivory Drawing Room, writing a reply to the Duchess of Peckham's kind letter, when Latimore rapped gently on the doorframe of the open door.

He cleared his throat.

"Yes? What is it?" she asked, sprinkling sand over her missive.

"Lord Milbourn, Lady Olivia," Latimore announced.

She glanced at her desk, suddenly reminded of the note she'd written to him the day before. She pulled open the slim center drawer. It was gone.

What? The picture of Margaret standing next to the desk yesterday filled her mind. *How could she take it upon herself to post my letter?* A sense of betrayal warred with her embarrassment.

Flustered, Olivia stood just as Lord Milbourn strolled around the butler.

"Lady Olivia," he drawled. "I felt sure you wouldn't mind an impromptu visit. Your surprising letter seemed a trifle urgent." One dark brow soared in query.

"Thank you, Latimore." Olivia nodded at the butler.

Latimore bent forward slightly as he gripped the doorknob. His bland expression couldn't quite hide his concern at leaving Olivia alone with Lord Milbourn.

"Leave the door open," Olivia said. "That will be all, Latimore." One hand touching the curls of her loosely arranged hair, she glanced around and gestured toward a primrose-colored silk couch. "I apologize, I had not expected...." her voice trailed off as she smoothed the gray folds of her dress. Her cheeks felt warm.

Why hadn't she worn something more flattering? Her morning dress was an old gown of her mother's that Olivia had found in one of her trunks. The fine silk was too good to give to her maid, so Olivia industriously remade it into a more modern gown to wear in the mornings. However, it was far from modish, and the muted color was not particularly flattering. For once, she regretted her thrifty impulse to save an old-fashioned gown most women would have given to their servants.

She looked up at Lord Milbourn, her breath fluttering.

Tall and well-built with wide shoulders and long, lean legs, Lord Milbourn's tanned, saturnine face was as handsome as ever, with the black eyes and olive skin he inherited from his Spanish mother, and a strong, square chin. He looked like a dangerous Spanish lord, striding like a wild storm, whipping through the ivory and gold confines of the drawing room.

He smiled and waved away her apology as he wandered toward the couch.

Her beagles' yapping echoed through the house in response to the sounds of a visitor's arrival.

"Oh, no, not again." Olivia sighed. "This is becoming a dreadful habit."

Before she could say more, the beagles rushed into the room, baying with glee and searching for anyone willing to play with them. Bathsheba leapt up on Lord Milbourn, pawing his black trousers and leaving behind streaks of dust and dog hair.

He chuckled, rubbed her ears, and sat on the couch while Titus and Justinia sniffed at his trousers and tried to push their heads under his hand. Bathsheba immediately took advantage, jumped on the sofa, and laid her head in his lap. She stared up at him with adoring brown eyes as he smoothed her ears.

"Down, Bathsheba! Oh, don't allow her to sit on the furniture. She knows she's not supposed to do that," Olivia said, trying to keep the other dogs from jumping up onto the opposite couch to join her. "Latimore!"

Lord Milbourn laughed and shook his head. "At least Bathsheba is pleased to see me."

"We are all pleased. Oh, do push her down." Olivia swept the other dogs out of the room just as the butler arrived, followed closely by the footman. "Latimore, how did they escape again?"

"I apologize, Lady Olivia." Latimore grabbed Bathsheba bodily and carried the wriggling dog to the door. He glanced at the footman who was busy fastening leads to the rest of the animals. The butler cleared his throat. "It seems Caesar has learned to open the door to their quarters."

The footman flushed and appeared unable to meet Olivia's gaze as he accepted Bathsheba from Latimore. "Sorry, Lady Olivia," he mumbled.

"Well, if he can open the door, I suggest you lock it. And don't let him have a key," she said with a bland expression.

The footman gaped at her before hurriedly dragging the dogs away. Latimore might not think it proper to laugh, but his eyes danced as he bowed his way out of the room.

"So, *mi niña bonita,* why have you sent for me?" Lord Milbourn asked.

My pretty girl. She wished she felt flattered instead of annoyed.

"I am hardly a child at eight-and-twenty, my lord," she answered. "And I didn't send for you."

He caught her gaze. One of his dark brows rose.

She felt her cheeks warm again. "I never meant to send that note. It was a mistake."

"A mistake?" He seemed amused at her embarrassment as he leaned back and stretched one long arm along the back of the couch.

"Yes, a mistake. My sister —" she broke off and wriggled on the gold brocade couch opposite him. "It is unimportant. The point is that I apologize if we have inconvenienced you."

"It is of no importance." He waved away her apology again. "So this academy, how does it fair?"

"It is very successful," she said. She glanced at the ornate clock on the mantelpiece and suppressed a sigh. The first class was scheduled to have begun a half hour ago, if there had been any students to attend.

"*Muy bien*," he said, congratulating her with a small smile.

She smiled in return and studied him, sensing sarcasm and not completely trusting his benign expression. He was far too fond of irony and too keen on testing her mettle, as if he were always engaged in a subtle duel with her.

At least he would never kill her with kindness, she thought, suppressing a long sigh.

Another soft knock interrupted them. "I beg your pardon, Lady Olivia," Latimore said from the doorway. He bowed, and when he straightened, his face was set in grave lines. "There are two gentlemen asking for you." His voice, when he intoned "gentlemen," indicated that in his opinion, the visitors were anything but gentlemen. His mouth thinned into a narrow line.

Olivia exchanged glances with Lord Milbourn. He remained relaxed on the couch, a glimmer of amusement in his dark eyes, completely unhelpful.

"I will see them here, Latimore."

The butler disappeared and a few minutes later returned with two men. One man lagged behind the other, and Olivia immediately recognized the stout, bull-necked man as Constable Cooke.

"Mr. Matthew Greenfield, inquiry agent, and Constable Frederick Cooke, Lady Olivia," Latimore announced sonorously, his head tilted slightly up with silent disapproval.

Olivia nodded. "Lord Milbourn, may I introduce Mr. Greenfield and Constable Cooke?" She performed the introductions mechanically, her hands already turning cold with anxiety.

"My lady," Mr. Greenfield bowed. "I hope we have not intruded at an inopportune time."

"Not at all," Olivia answered.

At first, Mr. Greenfield's wizened appearance made Olivia think he was quite elderly, until she caught the bright, inquisitive light in his blue eyes. He was small, particularly in comparison to his stocky companion, and his drab, dark green jacket with frayed cuffs and worn black trousers added to his well-aged air. His sparse gray hair fluffed around his narrow head like the downy feathers of a newly hatched chick, and his lined, gray-tinged skin wrinkled even more deeply when he smiled at her.

He bowed again, making him seem even more birdlike than ever. "The coroner's inquest is tomorrow, my lady." He glanced over his shoulder at Constable Cooke.

Cooke shifted from one foot to the other, frowning and staring at the back of his associate's head.

"It would be kind of you to attend," Mr. Greenfield continued. "The coroner would be most grateful for your statement."

Olivia stiffened. The last thing she wanted to do was to relive her experiences at the academy. However, she knew her duty. "Certainly," she said at last. "Give the information concerning the inquest to Latimore. He shall ensure I arrive at the appropriate time. Is that all?"

Mr. Greenfield tilted his head to the left. "How is it you arrived at the Cavendish Square townhouse when you did? It did not appear much used when I examined the premises."

"I am opening an academy at that location. I wanted to make sure it was prepared for students." Her throat tightened, and she paused. "It was purely by chance my brother and I arrived when we did." She stared at Constable Cooke's broad face. A smear of some greasy substance shone at the left corner of his plump mouth. Something about it made her suddenly feel queasy. "I believe I went over this already with Constable Cooke."

The constable kept his gaze fixed on the back of Mr. Greenfield's thin neck.

Mr. Greenfield didn't turn to look at him. He smiled and nodded. "Yes, certainly. If you don't mind a few more questions, my lady?"

"I thought these matters would be covered at the inquest." Olivia locked her hands together in her lap. The couch's back pressed against her, trapping her between the armrests. She moved restlessly and sat forward a fraction. When she glanced at Lord Milbourn, his sharp eyes were fixed on Mr. Greenfield intently, although the negligent lines of his body might lead one who didn't know him well to believe he was disinterested.

"They will, indeed," Mr. Greenfield concurred agreeably. He studied her thoughtfully for a moment and pulled a small black book from his pocket. Several pieces of paper had been shoved inside, although they didn't precisely fit, and their ragged, crumpled corners stuck out. "But I have been hired by Mr. Grantham's relatives to look into the matter, and I feel it important to provide them with a full report." He cleared his throat and glanced at her. "What time did you arrange to meet Mr. Grantham at the academy?"

Olivia's back tightened. She straightened. "As I already stated, I did not arrange to meet Mr. Grantham there, or anywhere, for that matter."

"This is not your handwriting?" Mr. Greenfield extracted one small piece of creamy notepaper from his book. He held it out to her between two fingers.

"What is that?" Olivia's heart fluttered, pounding against her breastbone. Her clasped hands remained locked together in her lap. She recognized the small sheet as a piece of paper from the private stock she kept in her writing desk.

He waved the note and nodded to her. "Please, Lady Olivia, perhaps you should examine it."

She reluctantly took the note and unfolded it. One quick glance was enough to warn her of the contents. She held it in her lap and gazed at Mr. Greenfield in silence.

"Is that not your handwriting?" he repeated the question.

"Of course it is my handwriting," she said. Her chin rose.

"It says —" Mr. Greenfield started to say before she cut him off.

"I can read it quite well," she said. "It says, *Wednesday, Academy*. What of it?"

"We found it in Mr. Grantham's pocket, Lady Olivia." Mr. Greenfield held out his hand for the note.

Lips compressed, she handed him the piece of paper, proud to see that her hand did not shake.

"If you did not intend to meet him at the academy, why did you send him that note?" Mr. Greenfield asked.

Behind him, Constable Cooke's grin widened. He rocked from heel to toe, gazing at her with all the pleasure of a hangman viewing a job neatly done.

"I did not send him that note — it was on my desk." She gestured toward the escritoire. "It was a note to myself. I meant to add more to it, but I forgot." Olivia rubbed her temple and then, aware of all the men watching her, she slowly lowered her hand. "I was distracted. There was a great deal to do for a project of that sort."

Mr. Greenfield nodded. The sympathetic, thoughtful frown on his face and soft expression in his pale blue eyes were obviously meant to reassure her, to convince her to confide in him. But he was slowly and cunningly leading her into a trap.

She could sense the noose dangling in front of her, just waiting for her to slip her head through it.

"How do you suppose he got that note?" He carefully tucked the paper back into his black notebook.

She watched him with a growing sense of desperation. "I have no idea." A sharp pain behind her right eye jolted her. She started to raise her hand to rub her temple again before she caught Mr. Greenfield's gaze. She clasped her hands together. "I started that note, as I indicated, and left it on my writing desk." She gestured at the desk again. "As I stated."

"When was that?" Mr. Greenfield asked.

"Several days ago."

His cold blue eyes sharpened. "How long ago? Do you remember?"

"I — I believe I started the list Monday. That would have been the eleventh, would it not?" She glanced at Lord Milbourn.

He nodded, but he offered her no assistance. She could read nothing from his bland expression.

"Then you have no explanation for the presence of your note in Mr. Grantham's pocket?" Mr. Greenfield's question could not hide the implication that she had sent that note to Grantham to arrange a meeting with him.

"It certainly appears, sir, as if the poor man got that note all unsuspecting and met *someone* in that office," Constable Cooke interjected his opinion, watching Olivia all the while with a knowing grin. "He must have forgot himself, them being alone and all. And that unknown person hit him on the head with that marble statue. And when she saw what happened, she shoved him into that cupboard, along with the weapon, before she was interrupted by her brother. Or some such." He rocked back on his heels and then forward again to his toes, hands clasped behind his back. "And she never noticed she left her shoeprints in his blood, fresh blood, mind you, as was still flowing as it were. Or that her note was still in his pocket."

"Thank you, Constable Cooke," Mr. Greenfield said, never glancing at his associate. "The circumstances are indeed clear to see. Now, the note, Lady Olivia? Have you an explanation?"

"I cannot enlighten you, Mr. Greenfield," she replied coolly. "I imagine anyone could have picked it up from my desk after I wrote it Monday morning." She smiled at him. "It complicates matters, of course, and inquiries will have to be made. I am sorry I can't offer more assistance."

"Did you have a great many visitors Monday and Tuesday, Lady Olivia?" Mr. Greenfield persisted.

"There are always a great many visitors when we are in town, Mr. Greenfield. You might ask our butler, Latimore, for a list. If he remembers."

"How many guests would you have entertained those days?" Once again, Mr. Greenfield seemed intent on maneuvering her into a corner.

She lifted one hand in a vague gesture. "A few, certainly. We generally use this drawing room. However, anyone may have come up here — visitors often enjoy coming up to the second floor to admire the paintings along the gallery, even briefly while waiting to be announced. Anyone could have come in here and seen the note. I am afraid it may not be easy to trace the path that missive took on its way to Mr. Grantham's pocket."

Mr. Greenfield studied her for a minute before opening his little book to write something in pencil on one of the pages. "Did any of your visitors have any reason to harm Mr. Grantham?"

"I am unware of any reason to harm Mr. Grantham. None of us argued with him. He has long been a friend of our family," she stated firmly, feeling more confident. They couldn't possibly think she had a reason to murder such an old and dear friend. The idea was ludicrous, and once they interviewed other members of the family and servants, they would understand just how ridiculous their suspicions were.

At least, she hoped so.

Her thoughts fluttered around the image of Mr. Underwood again. Apparently, he'd had reason to be upset with Mr. Grantham. Had Edward already spoken to Mr. Greenfield about it? Should she say anything?

No. Best to let her brother handle that matter. She didn't know the context or content of the discussion between Mr. Underwood and Edward, so she couldn't really give them a full report, only her impressions.

Mr. Greenfield's thoughtful expression suggested he was unconvinced. "You had no argument with him?"

"No," Olivia replied impatiently. "As I stated, I had absolutely no reason to wish him ill. No one in this family had any reason to have wanted such a terrible thing to befall him." She stood. When Lord Milbourn followed suit, she nodded at the corner of the room. "Would you be so good as to ring for Latimore, Lord Milbourn? I believe we have answered all of Mr. Greenfield's questions, have we not?" She stared at him, daring him to disagree.

"Very good, my lady." Mr. Greenfield tucked his notebook back into his pocket and bowed. "Any additional information we require may be obtained at the inquest. Thank you for your patience with us, Lady Olivia. We are in your debt." He bowed again and began the process of backing out.

Latimore arrived so quickly that Olivia suspected he had been waiting nearby in the gallery. He waved for Constable Cooke and Mr. Greenfield to precede him down the hallway, clearly determined to keep both men under his keen scrutiny.

Their footsteps had barely faded when Lord Milbourn returned to stand in front of the fireplace. A small frown creased his dark eyebrows. "You did not indicate you were in such a difficult position, Lady Olivia."

She flushed and looked back at the open door. She didn't need him to bring the awkwardness of her position to her attention. She could not have been more uncomfortably aware of it than she already was.

Chapter Six

Before Olivia could reply to Lord Milbourn's comment about her awkward position with regards to Mr. Grantham's murder, Latimore returned. He cleared his throat gently in the doorway and waited for Olivia to notice him.

Unfortunately, the woman following him was far too impatient to wait to be announced. She breezed past him, saying as she entered, "That will be all, Latimore. No need for introductions."

Oh, no, not Cynthia Denholm! I cannot manage — I can't talk to her — not right now. Olivia felt the strong urge to break into tears and run from the room. There was only so much bracing encouragement she could tolerate.

While Olivia and Cynthia had been friends since they were old enough to slip out of their leading strings and escape from their hapless nannies, Cynthia had always been, to put it mildly, overwhelming.

And she had grown from an energetic child into an impressive woman. At six feet tall, she towered over most men. She was broad-shouldered and strapping enough to be mistaken from the back for a healthy lad if her skirts were hidden and she was only seen from the waist up. From the front, her well-endowed figure was the epitome of the Amazonian warrior women. All she needed was a bow and quiver of arrows slung over her muscular shoulder.

When Cynthia took a deep breath and opened her mouth, Olivia quivered and prepared for the worst. From experience, she knew that Cynthia's booming voice could be heard quite clearly from the street outside, no matter which floor she occupied.

Nonetheless, it was difficult not to like her. She was so cheerful, and her florid, round face, with its snapping blue eyes and red cheeks matching her flaming hair, were vibrantly attractive. It was just that her boisterous manner simply crushed any quieter personages nearby, and today, Olivia felt very quiet.

"Lady Olivia, Miss Denholm," Latimore intoned from the doorway, refusing to concede control until he had completed his duty.

Cynthia threw her head back and barked out a laugh that hurt Olivia's ears. "Oh, Latimore, as if Lady Olivia does not know me. At ease, man, and be gone. We will rub along well enough without you." She laughed again and shook her head at Latimore's pained expression.

Latimore caught Olivia's gaze. His face remained carefully bland, but the pinched skin around his eyes made Olivia think he disapproved of Cynthia's highhanded maneuverings.

"That is all, Latimore," Olivia said. "You may go."

When she glanced again at Cynthia, her friend was staring at Lord Milbourn with an avid, hungry look on her face. Cynthia's plump, red lips hung open, and her eyes glittered as if she were contemplating a particularly scrumptious cake.

"So." Cynthia chewed her lower lip and stepped closer to Lord Milbourn. Her gaze traveled from his smart boots up to his well-tailored jacket. "Where were you, Lady Olivia? I went to the school, and it was locked up tighter than a nunnery at night. Must not be late, eh? Not on the first day. Though I cannot complain if you have used the time to recruit Lord Milbourn." She stepped forward as if to give him a playful hit on the shoulder, but he managed to sidestep her and ease behind the couch Olivia had previously occupied.

When he glanced at her, his face wore a lopsided grin.

Olivia clasped her hands together in front of her to keep from throwing the small china shepherdess sitting on the occasional table next to her at Cynthia to draw her attention.

"Lord Milbourn is not one of our teachers," Olivia stated firmly.

Cynthia frowned. "Well, that is too bad, is it not? Might have managed to attract a few more students." She waved a hand, dismissing the topic. "Too bad, really, but we must make do. Come on, then. There is still time for our first session."

"First session?" Olivia gaped at her. "Have you not heard?"

"Heard?" Cynthia frowned, her ginger brows jutting out over her blue eyes. Her plump red lower lip thrust out in a near pout, preparing to quiver at the first sign of cruel disappointment. "Heard what?"

"Why...?" Olivia stumbled to a halt and glanced at Lord Milbourn.

He shrugged unhelpfully, his dark eyes glinting with sardonic amusement.

"Well?" Cynthia prompted. "Surely it is not this murder nonsense."

A stifled snort came from the direction of Lord Milbourn.

Olivia frowned at him, but his bland expression didn't help in the least. "A man was killed at the academy," Olivia said.

"They don't usually leave them lying about forever — I'm sure his body has been removed by now." Cynthia glanced in the direction of the door with impatience. "And bloodstains don't worry me." She laughed. "Might add a few drops ourselves."

Olivia looked at Lord Milbourn, feeling overwhelmed at the thought of conducting lessons now, after everything that had happened.

He merely shrugged and smiled cruelly.

"It would not be right to continue with fencing lessons at this point," she objected lamely, unable to think of a better excuse for avoiding the academy.

Apparently, Cynthia couldn't understand the sheer horror of returning to the place where Olivia had found a good family friend murdered.

Her last view of Mr. Grantham returned unbidden. She shivered, the musty smell of the old building laced with the sharp, metallic scent of blood caught at the back of her throat. She remembered her last view of him, his body, slumped in the corner of the wardrobe with the marble cherub peering up at her from his shoulder, and his blood leaking onto the worn, dusty floor. And her small footsteps tracking across the floorboards from the crimson puddle.

Her stomach clenched at the thought of returning to her office.

Cynthia guffawed. "What is it? Public opinion? Don't give in, my dear Lady Olivia. What does public opinion matter? One must be above such things. Ignore it," she advised in a loud, bracing voice. "Get on with it, post haste. It is the only thing to do."

"But the authorities," Olivia said, trying one last objection to Cynthia's determination to receive her first fencing lesson at the agreed upon time and place. "They may not wish to have us there. After all, the inquest is tomorrow." One last notion struck her, and she flung it at Cynthia. "And the place has yet to be properly cleaned. I was going to send Mary to clean —"

"Dust?" Cynthia threw her head back and laughed loudly enough to interrupt Olivia and make her wince as the windows behind her rattled. "Come now, Lady Olivia. We have an agreement, do we not? Time for my first lesson, and proprieties be damned. If I were interested in such paltry things, I would never have subscribed to your academy in the first place." Her bright blue eyes flicked from Olivia to Lord Milbourn and back to Olivia, daring her to offer any further objections.

"Very well," Lady Olivia said, surrendering to her friend's overwhelming force. She straightened her slumped shoulders, exhausted but determined not to give in to her desire to run upstairs to her bedchamber, lock the door, and crawl into bed. "Will you join us, Lord Milbourn?"

He nodded, his dark eyes glinting with amusement. "Of course, *mi niña bonita*. I would not miss this for the world."

Chapter Seven

Alexander Bron, the Baron Milbourn, cast quick glances at Lady Olivia's pale face as they threaded their way through the crowded streets. He found it difficult to see her as anything other than the awkward young girl of eighteen she'd been when he first saw her, hanging about the doorway as he attempted to teach her even younger brothers the rudiments of fencing, the dance of death.

Her brothers had found it amusing to include her in the lessons, expecting her to give up after the first grueling hour. She had not, and Alex had found it much less diverting when he saw the innocent devotion glowing plainly in her wide gray eyes each time she glanced at him. It was inappropriate, and she was the daughter of an earl. At the time, he'd been poor and had no expectation of inheriting a title, so he could not expect her parents to be pleased.

They didn't seem to object however, even when he was sure they knew she was more fascinated by the teacher than with fencing. All he could do was keep her at a distance and hope she would grow bored. However, she didn't, and she certainly tried valiantly enough to learn the art. But her heart was too soft for the sport. She had no instinct to discover an opponent's vulnerability and exploit it, and ultimately, he feared she would only be harmed.

Thankfully, the lessons had ended, and she had gone out of his life like the glow of a candle blown out on a dark night.

That she was still unmarried at eight-and-twenty and still stubbornly pursuing the art of fencing only proved that his initial fears about her had been correct. She should have outgrown her puppy love for him, should have found a worthy man, married, and had a passel of children clinging to her skirts instead of a pack of dogs, no matter how beguiling the dogs were.

And now, his failure to exclude her all those years ago, or put an end to her interest in fencing, had exposed her to murder. While her position as the older sister of an earl offered some degree of protection, it was clear to him that it would not grant her complete impunity from prosecution if the evidence were strong enough.

At the moment, the evidence appeared very strong, indeed.

The faint, worried V between her brows and dark shadows under her eyes showed that she was as aware of this vulnerability as he was. Whether she meant to send it to him or not, her note to him also betrayed her fears. She would never have written to him otherwise.

However, while any man would be flattered to receive her missive, it only rubbed salt into the old wound that should have healed by now. She needed to find another man to champion her. Not him.

Never him. He might be a baron, but he wasn't the man for her.

And yet, he couldn't find it within himself to ignore her plea for aid. Nor could he ignore the fact that Greenfield, while appearing to be intelligent enough, seemed interested only in scraping together enough evidence to furnish a higher court with reason to prosecute her for the murder of Grantham. Greenfield had closed his mind to other possibilities.

That was clearly unacceptable, and regardless of his feelings in the matter, Alexander could not let that happen to Lady Olivia.

Miss Denholm set a cruel pace, and they soon arrived at the townhouse in Cavendish Square. He halted for a moment, contemplating the desolate, abandoned air of the Georgian building. Two of the shutters on the second floor were hanging loosely, their top hinges no longer supporting their weight. Alexander's gaze followed the roofline, which sagged toward the middle and appeared almost crushed between the two taller building on either side of it.

While the Earl of Wraysbury would never allow his sister to use a building that was unsafe, and therefore the bowed look of the roof must be an illusion created by its position between two taller structures, Alexander was uneasy. He saw a building that needed a great deal of maintenance, not to mention several quarts of paint.

Lady Olivia deserved something better than this wreck.

"This is your academy, *mi niña bonita*?" he asked.

Already on the stoop, Lady Olivia fumbled with the large brass key. The lock protested with a rusty squeak before finally grinding open. She pushed the door inward before finally glancing over her shoulder at him.

"Yes. This is the Fencing Academy for Ladies." Her footsteps on the marble entryway crunched from the sand and debris filming the pale stone. She held the door and waved Miss Denholm and Alexander inside.

"It could do with a bit of dusting, eh, Lady Olivia?" Miss Denholm cast an avid glance around, walking past Lady Olivia to the staircase.

"Yes. I believe I mentioned that," Lady Olivia answered with a grimace.

Miss Denholm placed one stout half-boot on the bottom step and stared up at the first floor landing. "Well, you will get it straightened out eventually, and it does not bother me. Where do you hold lessons?"

"The ballroom." Lady Olivia cast an uncertain glance at Alexander, her forehead wrinkled and her eyes shadowed in the dim hallway. "That is the largest room. And there are mirrors to check your form."

"Distracting," Alexander murmured, clasping his hands behind his back.

Lady Olivia straightened. Her brows tightened into a frown as she shut the door behind him. "We can cover them if they prove too distracting."

With the door closed, the air reeked of mildew and dust. Alexander took a deep breath and tasted something else in the back of his throat. The iron odor of death lingered in the house. He glanced at Lady Olivia.

She cast a puzzled look around the hallway. "That odor —"

"Unpleasant, eh?" Miss Denholm's gaze roved avidly around the hallway, her mouth hanging slightly open. "Blood, I suppose. Well, it can't be helped. We will simply have to open windows, Lady Olivia." She drew off her gloves, untied her plain poke bonnet, and yanked it off her head. "We shall need rapiers, of course. Let us get on with it, then."

"There was not that much blood." Lady Olivia stared at Alexander.

He lifted his head and took a deep breath, smiling crookedly as he remembered Lady Olivia's beagles sniffing his trousers. "There does seem to be a touch more to that scent than one would expect from blood." He walked past the staircase to a discreet baize door that stood ajar. The putrid smell was stronger near the door.

"It is terrible here," Lady Olivia said, stepping closer to him. The light scent of lavender that clung to her clothing couldn't mask the rank odor of decay. "Mr. Grantham died upstairs, in my office. Not in the servants' hall."

"Dead rats," Miss Denholm said with brisk finality. She shouldered her way past Lady Olivia and reached out a long arm to push the door open further. "Must be in the kitchen. Well, never mind. Let's get on with it, shall we?"

"One minute, if you please, Miss Denholm," Alexander said. "Wait here. I shall return shortly."

The servants' hallway was dim, and the soles of Alexander's boots scraped and crunched unpleasantly on the filthy wooden floor. The boards creaked and complained, and when he trod on something soft, he grimaced. There were certainly dead mice, if nothing worse.

Two large windows in the rear wall provided better light for the kitchen, but being able to see more clearly didn't improve matters. An old, scarred oak table stood in the center of the room, and the walls were lined with various cupboards and cabinets, some of which gaped open to display downy gray puffs of cobwebs and dust.

A deep breath burned the back of his throat. He gagged. Something was indeed dead, and it wasn't a rat.

A more careful scrutiny revealed a pair of worn black boots on the floor on the far side of the oak table. The laces were broken and were roughly knotted, too short to be properly tied. And the boots were still connected to a pair of thick ankles, exposed under the tattered hem of a gray skirt.

The body of a middle-aged woman lay on the slate floor, partially twisted to one side. She faced away from him, with her right arm draped over her stout body. Graying brown hair straggled out from beneath a black bonnet, and an old, gray shawl covered her shoulders. Below that peeped a black pelisse so old that the wool was worn through in patches to expose a red striped lining.

"Mrs. Adams," Lady Olivia whispered in an appalled voice. She stood at his right shoulder, her hand pressed to her mouth. "Is she … dead?"

"Yes." He walked around the table and knelt on one knee to examine the body.

The floor beneath her, although gritty with dirt, lacked bloodstains. He moved her head gently. Under the brim of her stout bonnet was an ugly wound on the right temple.

He glanced around the room again. The kitchen was cold enough to prevent too many insects from infesting her, but from the puffy slackness of her skin, she had been dead for several days.

The lividity of the cheek facing up, and sheer logic, suggested she had been moved. Certainly the constable would have found her had she been in the kitchen when they examined Grantham in Lady Olivia's office upstairs.

"How did she — what happened?" Shock strangled Lady Olivia's soft voice.

"It appears she was hit on the head." He stood and pulled on the hems of his gloves, although they were already snug on his hands. "We must notify the authorities."

"Again?" Lady Olivia pulled out one of the ladder-backed chairs and sat abruptly, touching her temple with one hand. She took a long, shuddering breath and stood again abruptly, swallowing. Her pale skin turned greenish in the poor, afternoon light. "I am sorry, I can't stay here."

"Go back to the hallway. Explain to Miss Denholm. I must find a constable," he ordered. He gripped her elbow and turned her toward the hallway. "Go on."

She stumbled at the doorway, and he caught her arm to steady her. "I am quite well. There is no need to treat me like a child." She shook her arm to free herself.

"*Si.*" He let her go with a nod. "In this place, death must seem quite familiar to you, *mi niña bonita.* An old friend."

She whirled around to face him, her cheeks flushed and her eyes snapping with clear anger despite the poor light. "What do you mean by that?"

"*Nada.*" He brushed her cheek with his knuckles and smiled. "It is good, however, to see the color back in your face, even if it is merely anger at me."

"You are impossible. And stop speaking Spanish. You only do it to annoy me."

He chuckled. His teasing distracted her, and he would rather see her irritated with him then ill with shock. "No doubt, *mi niña bonita.* Now go back to Miss Denholm and wait for me. I shall not be long."

With an annoyed flick of her skirts, she walked away rapidly. He watched her go until the shadows swallowed her. Finally, even her quick, light step faded from hearing.

He went to the kitchen door, noting that while it was latched, it was not locked. With a final glance at the woman sprawled next to the table, he strode outside and threaded his way through the narrow alley running between the academy's outer wall and the house next door.

The street in front of the townhouse thronged with pedestrians, carriages, and numerous riders on horseback. He hesitated at the wrought iron gate in front of the academy, reluctant to leave the women alone for too long. Even the brawny Miss Denholm was human and therefore vulnerable.

When he spotted a lad with a raggedy brown cap pulled down low over his forehead, he called to him and waved a sixpence.

The boy recognized the gesture with sharp blue eyes and, dodging the traffic with alarming swerves and short dashes, ran over to Alexander. His gaze locked on the coin and remained there as he panted to catch his breath. Under the dirt on his face, he appeared to be about twelve years old, though he was scrawny and small for his age.

"What do you be needing, my lord? A woman?" The lad winked lewdly and smacked his thin lips.

"I need the constable and coroner. Inform them there has been an accident here, and we require their assistance."

When the boy reached for the coin, Alexander held it out of reach.

"You may have this sixpence now." He placed the coin in the lad's hand and caught the thin wrist before the child could run away. "And another when you return with the men I requested. Do you understand?"

"Aye, my lord." The coin magically disappeared before the boy tilted his head like a robin eyeing a likely worm. "And another when I return."

"With the constable and the coroner. Agreed?"

The boy nodded and slipped away, leaving Alexander unsure if the lad would return or simply disappear into the back streets of London.

With a shrug, Alexander went back inside.

The women were gone. He listened for a moment and heard footsteps and the echo of voices above him. He found them in one of the rooms on the first floor. The two ladies were standing in front of several épées, foils, and rapiers laid out on top of a large desk. Beyond them, a wardrobe yawned open with a dried, black stain painting the base of the main compartment and a small area of the floor in front of it. Footprints meandered to the right in a short path four feet away from the stain on the floor.

"Lord Milbourn," Lady Olivia said, glancing up at him. Her face was tense and pale. Small, worried wrinkles pressed between her brows, crushed the skin around her lovely eyes, and pinched her mouth. "Is the constable here?"

"Not yet. I sent for him. He should not be long."

Miss Denholm picked up one of the rapiers and held it up, pointing the tip at the window and staring down the length of the blade. "We should have plenty of time for a lesson, then."

"I don't think —" Lady Olivia protested.

Miss Denholm cut her off with a snort. "Well, he shall want to speak to us, and I, for one, have no intention of simply standing about, awaiting his indulgence. No point in that, eh?"

Lady Olivia flicked a last glance at Alexander before she shrugged. "Very well." She picked up one of the épées and walked around the desk to find corks to place on the sharp tips of the weapons.

"Where are your masks?" Alexander asked sharply.

"They…" Lady Olivia sighed. Her gaze strayed to the wardrobe.

Alexander went to the wardrobe and after searching several drawers, he pulled out several wire mesh masks. He placed them on the desk next to the remaining two rapiers. "Wear them."

"They — there is blood on them." A look of distaste wrinkled Lady Olivia's nose. She held her épée down at her side, pointing the weapon at the floor, and thrust her other hand behind her back, clearly unwilling to touch the masks.

Alexander drew out his handkerchief and wiped off the dried flakes of blood. "There. Your academy will not do so well if you are disfigured, *mi niña bonita*. Wear it."

Miss Denholm picked up one of the masks and turned it over, studying it. "Do men wear these things? I have never seen one before. A bit awkward, are they not?"

"It may be awkward, but you cannot fence without it. And yes, men do wear them." He didn't add, "on occasion." He frowned at Lady Olivia until she flushed and picked up one of the masks.

"Awkward," Miss Denholm repeated, her lower lip thrust out.

"Then let this start your lesson." Alexander picked up one of the masks. "You have heard of Texier De La Boessiere, the French master, have you not?"

Lady Olivia obediently nodded, but Miss Denholm just stared at him with blank, blue eyes. With her red lower lip still protruding, she looked like a large, frustrated child about to have a tantrum.

"He developed these to assist the fencer maintain his position and neither advance nor retreat. That should appeal to you, Miss Denholm. Stand your ground and fight." He reached over and gently wrested the rapier from her hand. "Épées, *por favor*. If you please." He picked up the remaining épée and, holding it up with the blade resting on his left forearm, he examined the weapon.

The balance and workmanship were excellent, and he thought he recognized the collection of swords as those used by Lady Olivia's brothers when he tutored them.

Miss Denholm smiled, tucked the mask under her arm, and picked up an épée. "Lead on, Lady Olivia!"

With a sigh, Lady Olivia picked up a mask and led the way to the ballroom on the ground floor, to the rear of the house. They barely entered the huge, empty room before Miss Denholm was fastening the mask over her face and waving her épée back and forth in front of her.

Alexander dropped his blade on the floor and moved swiftly toward her.

Once more, he gripped her wrist to hold Miss Denholm's arm still. "If you please." He held his hand out to Lady Olivia, palm upward.

She eyed him and Miss Denholm's naked blade and handed him one of the corks. While he protected the tip of Miss Denholm's épée with the cork, Lady Olivia removed her bonnet and pelisse, placed a cork on the tip of her own blade and donned her mask.

Miss Denholm moved away from him and pointed her sword at Lady Olivia, as if she were about to charge.

"Relax, *por favor*," Alexander said, picking up his own épée from the floor.

Lady Olivia's face was hidden by her mask, but her movements were hesitant as she walked out into the center of the room. She moved into a semi-profiled position, and although her chest expanded and contracted with a long, deep breath clearly intended to steady herself, her overall stance suggested uncertainty, rather than the cool confidence she should exhibit.

On the other hand, Miss Denholm strode with alacrity to face Lady Olivia. She was at least six inches taller than Lady Olivia and seemed to be vibrating with energy and confidence.

"Now," Lady Olivia said, her masked face turning briefly in Alexander's direction. "Think of a circle around you, drawn by the furthest reach of your arm and sword." She demonstrated by holding out her épée and slowly turning. "Each of us has such a circle that moves as we move. When we face our opponent, our circles may overlap, and when they do, that presents an opportunity for attack." As she spoke, she turned without thinking to face Miss Denholm.

Leaving herself open.

Alexander stiffened and moved closer, although staying well out of the way of the two women.

The tension in Miss Denholm's shoulders and arms increased until she seemed to quiver with anticipation. Her masked face followed every gesture, every move made by Lady Olivia. She looked like a muscular tiger keyed up to attack.

Miss Denholm suddenly touched the side of her sword to her mask in a salute and lunged forward, hacking the air from right to left and then backhanded, forcing Lady Olivia to defend herself and retreat as best she could. Sharp barks accompanied each slashing motion by Miss Denholm, and as Lady Olivia retreated, Miss Denholm pressed forward harder. Her motions were crude, and at one point, she threw herself so close that she punched Lady Olivia's shoulder with her free hand to force her to stumble back far enough to give her room to hack at her shocked teacher.

While Lady Olivia managed to defend herself, Miss Denholm's superior reach and strength, combined with her aggressive attack, forced her to give way. Her back hit the wall. She pushed forward one foot, then two, her blade sliding up Miss Denholm's and dislodging the cork.

"Halt!" Alexander ordered, racing forward.

Miss Denholm plunged forward, pushing Lady Olivia's blade aside and punching her in the shoulder again to jolt her against the wall. Instead of stopping, Miss Denholm stepped back to grant Lady Olivia room to maneuver and raise her épée.

"Halt!" He grabbed Miss Denholm's wrist and whirled her away from Lady Olivia, inserting himself between the two ladies and trusting Lady Olivia to obey his command to stop. The icy calm of cool indifference slipped over him as he held the blade in his hand.

Miss Denholm, good sense overcome by the excitement of the moment, slashed at him, entirely without grace or form. It was easy to slip in under her guard, and in a few strokes, he disarmed her. Her blade went clattering with dull thuds across the wooden floor.

"I say! Excellent sport!" Miss Denholm exclaimed, her massive chest rising and falling rapidly. Her breath whistled through the mask as she panted and paced back and forth in a tight path in front of Lady Olivia. "Again?"

When she moved in the direction of her épée, Lady Olivia stepped forward. "That is enough. We must work on form first, not leap into a duel."

"But I was winning!" Miss Denholm laughed and made a dash to circle around Lady Olivia and Alexander to retrieve her weapon.

He held his blade out, blocking her path. When she slipped her forearm under it as if to push it out of her way, he stepped back to flick her épée further away with the tip of his sword.

"I was winning, was I not?" she complained. "I want to try again."

"No. Not now. You must learn proper form and not behave like the bull charging the red cape," he said.

A movement from Lady Olivia signaled that she had removed her mask. She pressed her forearm against her forehead and pushed up some dislodged curls. "We must be more methodical in our approach."

"Methodical." Alexander chuckled and strolled over to collect Miss Denholm's épée and remove temptation from her greedy grasp. "Beware the novice for he will attempt maneuvers an expert would not."

"She," Olivia corrected distractedly. "*She* will attempt maneuvers and so on."

"*Si, mi niña bonita* — she. Perhaps your brother, Edward, can assist you. He has the form and proper attitude for the sport."

Of all the Archer boys he had tutored, Edward Archer was by far the most promising. He might appear quiet and staid, but when he held a sword, his calm silence transformed into the cool indifference that inspired both fear and mistakes in his opponents. At times, Alexander had wondered if Edward, the student, would eventually surpass Alexander, his tutor.

It seemed ironic that Lady Olivia, who lacked the instincts for the fight, desperately wanted to excel, while Edward, who had the instincts and talent to become a master swordsman, had no wish to do so.

"Edward?" Lady Olivia stared at him, her cheeks flushed and gleaming with perspiration. A long curl of rich brown hair had escaped again to hang over her brow, and she kept pushing it back with her wrist as she exclaimed, "*Edward*! I am sick to death of having Edward held up to me, as if he were a master fencer rivaling the famous Domenico Angelo himself. He hasn't fenced in ages, and I daresay he is entirely incapable of teaching anyone the first thing about it."

"*Lo siento*." He bowed at her, hiding his grin. "I regret, I spoke without thought."

"Yes, you did," Lady Olivia agreed.

Before she could continue, they heard the unmistakable sounds of booted feet in the hallway.

A deep male voice echoed down the hallway into the ballroom, "Anyone here?"

A staccato burst of light footsteps dashed toward them, growing rapidly louder. The young lad Alexander had sent for the constable ran into the room and came to an abrupt halt. His eyes widened like a startled rabbit as he glanced from Lady Olivia, to Miss Denholm, and finally, to Alexander.

Alexander dug into his pocket and extracted another coin, which he flipped to the boy. "I trust you had no difficulties."

"No, my lord. They's in the hallway." He rubbed the coin between his grubby thumb and forefinger, scrutinized it anxiously, and slipped it into the pocket of an ill-fitting, tattered waistcoat he wore below his jacket. With a grin, he touched the brim of his cap. "Thank you kindly, my lord. Ladies...." He winked and ran back out as if he feared they might try to stop him and demand the return of the coins.

Chapter Eight

Olivia collected the fencing accoutrements and carried them quietly upstairs to her office, hoping to avoid the constable and his men as long as possible. The action also allowed her to escape from Cynthia and Lord Milbourn for a few precious minutes so she could think.

Cynthia's vigorous attack had rattled her. She'd completely overwhelmed Olivia to the point where all she could do was to defend herself and try to maintain some space between them.

It was not a particularly admirable start to her lessons.

Olivia's shoulder ached where Cynthia had hit her, and she suspected a lovely dark bruise was forming. Her thoughts swayed between aggravation and anger. She'd thought she was prepared to teach. Apparently, she was mistaken.

And Lord Milbourn's comments only undermined her confidence further.

Edward! Always Edward! What made him so much better than the rest of them? He wasn't even interested in fencing and only went to lessons when his tutor discovered him in some corner reading a huge, boring book about English law and forced him to join his brothers.

So why was he the one with the talent? A man who only wanted to be left alone to peruse dusty jurisprudence tomes and argue arcane points that no one cared about. Why couldn't Lord Milbourn see how many hours she'd spent training, or how much she wanted to excel? She ought to be several times better than Edward by now, and yet she struggled to maintain a middling proficiency that was more novice than expert.

If only *he* hadn't been there to witness her floundering defeat at Cynthia's Amazonian, muscular hands.

She locked the wardrobe and rubbed the side of her jaw. The muscles ached, and she realized she'd been gritting her teeth.

By the time she descended to the ground floor, Constable Cooke and his band of exceedingly morose men were standing in the hallway, talking to Lord Milbourn and Cynthia. Even though Olivia stepped as quietly as she could, Lord Milbourn glanced her way and nodded at her, dragging her into his interview with the stocky constable.

She took a deep breath and hung on to etiquette to save her. "Miss Denholm, have you met Constable Cooke and Mr. Idleman, the coroner?" Olivia clasped her hands at her waist.

"Oh, yes." Cynthia grinned with delight and rubbed her palms together, creating a rasping noise like a pile of dead leaves caught by the wind. "I have never met a constable before. Or a coroner. Quite exciting."

"Undoubtedly," Olivia said and clamped her lips together to avoid sighing.

One day soon, she was sure to get a visit from Cynthia's formidable parents, demanding to know why their daughter was meeting such people at all. When they did, Olivia would only be able to assure them that she had no desire to meet such people, either. Too bad she had very little choice in the matter.

Constable Cooke turned to face her, his pudgy fingers crushing the brim of his hat. "Another sad day, Lady Olivia, very sad."

"And sadder still for Mrs. Adams," Olivia replied tartly.

Constable Cooke's brown eyes stared at her with a blank look.

"The charwoman," Olivia added. She gestured toward the baize door. "The misfortunate woman lying in the kitchen."

The coroner, Mr. Idleman, nodded and added a note in the small book he carried. His jurymen stood in a ragged cluster behind him, and Olivia thought she recognized most of them from their first visit to the academy. Several nodded and touched their forelocks respectfully when they caught her glance. Their somber, pious air reminded her of the groups of men she often saw lingering outside a church on a Sunday, waiting to gossip, discuss local business, and ogle the ladies.

Mr. Idleman looked up when he finished writing, his pencil poised over the open book. "When was the last time you saw," he glanced down at his notes, "Mrs. Adams?"

Olivia frowned in thought. When *was* the last time? The woman had certainly been good about keeping out of sight and out of the way. So good, in fact, that it appeared she hadn't actually been to the academy to do her job, either. The floors and furniture were just as dusty as they'd been the first time Olivia walked through the townhouse.

"Lady Olivia?" Mr. Idleman prompted her.

"Well, I met her when I engaged her, of course. That was sometime in January. I'm not sure of the exact date. And I saw her again when I gave her the key to the townhouse." When the coroner frowned, she hurried to add, "There was no one here to let her in. She needed a key to clean. I could not possibly be here every morning to let her in."

Mr. Idleman pulled out a thin, ragged piece of linen that was looped through several keys and tied in a knot. "Is your key one of these?"

She accepted the bundle of four keys and studied them. They were all large brass keys, well-worn and dented from heavy usage. They clanked together with a dissonant clatter, held by the knotted piece of fabric. None of them had the elaborate scrolls at the top like either her key, or the one she'd given to Mrs. Adams. A chill caressed the back of her neck.

A key to the academy was missing.

"No. I don't recognize any of these keys." She shook her head as she handed the pathetic collection back to the coroner.

"Were the doors to this townhouse locked?" Mr. Idleman asked, deep lines of disapproval bracketing his mouth.

Once again, the walls seemed to move inward, imperceptibly closing in on her, inch by inch, squeezing all the air out of the room.

She took a deep breath and forced a calm expression, remembering Lord Milbourn's comment about maintaining an air of cool indifference to disconcert one's opponent. The excitement and triumphs of his lessons seemed distant and unattainable.

"Yes. I unlocked the front door myself. When we arrived this afternoon," she said at last.

Cynthia nodded. "I watched her unlock the door. You can take my word for it."

"Thank you, Miss Denholm," Mr. Idleman said.

"The kitchen door was locked too, sir," one of the men behind the coroner said in a low voice. "We checked."

"What fun!" Cynthia exclaimed, grinning and clapping her hands. "A true mystery!"

Several other men nodded, although their gazes seemed to be locked on their feet, and they were positively crushing their hats between their plump hands.

"It is indeed a mystery." Mr. Idleman's pursed lips indicated he had no love of such mysteries.

"Gentlemen," Lord Milbourn said. "Logic would suggest that Mrs. Adams met her fate elsewhere and was moved here."

"I beg your pardon, my lord," Mr. Idleman interrupted. "I see no reason to make such an assumption. The kitchen door, as we said, was locked."

Lord Milbourn's dark brows rose. "Did you not search the kitchen when you were here two days ago? How remiss of you."

Constable Cooke's red cheeks puffed out and deflated as he sucked in air and released it in aggravation. "We searched every inch of this domicile. *Every* inch. She wasn't here Wednesday, I will swear to it."

"Her, er, accident was more recent, then," the coroner said, although his voice quavered with doubt. He stared at the constable as if seeking his support.

"What is your conclusion based upon?" Lord Milbourn asked with an interested smile though his eyes danced with amused cynicism.

"Why..." The coroner glanced around at his men. He cleared his throat several times. "Why...?"

They continued to study the floor.

"Why, the poor woman was not here on Wednesday. She must have been…" He cast a quick glance at Lady Olivia and cleared his throat. "She must have perished after that date."

"Interesting conclusion." Lord Milbourn caught Olivia's gaze. She could read nothing in his dark eyes except a kind of detached intelligence. "I suggest that whoever struck Mr. Grantham needed a key to open the doors. It seems reasonable that he got that key from Mrs. Adams, and that she did not survive the encounter. After Mr. Grantham was discovered here, the same individual used said key once again, more recently, to gain entrance to the house. He then left the charwoman in the kitchen."

"It is one theory," Mr. Idleman admitted grudgingly. "However, the evidence —"

"The evidence leads me to suppose Mrs. Adams has been dead for several days." Lord Milbourn bowed at Olivia. "I beg your pardon for my crudeness, Lady Olivia. However, there is a redness to Mrs. Adams's cheek that indicates she was lying in a different position soon after she died. She must have been moved later, exposing the blood that had previously settled in her cheek. I feel sure you will see it if you examine her again." He studied the fingernails of his right hand, already bored with the situation.

"It may be as you say, my lord," Constable Cooke said, his brows jutting out so far that they left his eyes in angry pools of shadow. "Or maybe not."

"Of course, we will certainly examine the body again," Mr. Idleman said. However, the smug set of his mouth and the upward tilt of his nose indicated that he had no real intention of doing so. He'd made his decision, ill-judged though it might be.

Even Lord Milbourn's sharp stare at the coroner suggested he was aware of the incongruence between the coroner's statement and his attitude.

"Is there anything else you require?" Olivia asked. "I would like to return home, and I'm sure Miss Denholm would like to depart, as well."

"Not at all," Cynthia said with a laugh. "All the time in the world. Carry on, men."

"It is getting late." Olivia's jaw clenched, sending another shooting spasm of pain through her head.

"Please allow me to escort you, Lady Olivia. We can then leave these gentlemen in peace." Lord Milbourn bowed and gestured toward the door. When he caught Olivia's gaze, his face remained impassive, but his eyes twinkled in the dim, grainy light of the hallway.

Olivia slipped a hand around Cynthia's elbow, determined to drag her out with her, if need be.

"We may be a while longer, Lady Olivia." Mr. Idleman held out a hand. "We would be obliged if you would leave the key with us. So we may lock the doors."

"It hardly seems to matter, does it?" Olivia objected. "It seems perfectly simple for hordes of murderers to come and go as they please. Locking the door seems quite useless."

"Nonetheless." Mr. Idleman didn't withdraw his hand. Instead, he shook it slightly in a silent demand for the key. "We would be obliged, my lady. And I will return it this evening."

With a sigh, Olivia fished the ornate brass key out of her reticule and handed it to him.

"Thank you, Lady Olivia." Mr. Idleman bowed. "May Constable Cooke make a copy of the key?"

"A copy? Why?"

"So we may return your key to you while we continue our investigation."

She didn't like the notion of the constable having a key, but she supposed she could have the locks changed when the matter was settled. "Very well. Now, we really must go."

"Thank you. I trust we will see you at the inquest tomorrow," Mr. Idleman said, executing another bow. "I will return your key to you at that time."

"Inquest?" Cynthia's eyes sparkled. "Where will it be held?"

Olivia grabbed Cynthia's elbow and forcibly turned her toward the front door. "It will be terribly boring, I'm sure. In fact, I may send a written statement instead and have one of my brothers obtain the key." She nodded at the men and threw open the door.

Protesting and trying to return inside to watch the jurymen perform their gruesome task of inspecting the deceased woman and her environs, Cynthia managed to escape from Olivia's grasp.

Following them closely, Lord Milbourn blocked her path. "Enough for one day," he commented as he set his hat on his head and studied the passersby.

The pale gray February light was rapidly fading, although there seemed to be an endless stream of pedestrians despite the dreary close of the day. The air felt noticeably cooler with a crisp edge and a bite like a tart apple, although the freshness was dulled by the smoke of innumerable fires.

They had only walked three blocks when Miss Denholm halted. "Well then, I'm off," she announced.

Olivia traded glances with Lord Milbourn. He said, "We shall escort you, Miss Denholm."

"Nonsense. I walked to Lady Olivia's house alone. I can certainly walk the last four blocks without your assistance." She snorted and strode around the corner before they could stop her.

Lord Milbourn watched her go, then looked down at Olivia and shrugged. "An interesting young lady."

"I felt sure you would find her so." Olivia gave his arm a gentle tug as she took a step to proceed forward.

The ghost of a chuckle whispered past her cheek.

"She does show a great deal of enthusiasm for fencing. Very impressive, *mi niña bonita*," Lord Milbourn replied in a bland voice. "Energetic."

A tiredness seeped through her, dragging at her limbs and encasing her feet in lead. After two slow steps, she felt obliged to protest once more, "I am not a child. I wish you would remember that. And the way you seem to forget how to speak English when it suits you is exceedingly annoying."

He pressed a hand over his heart in an exaggerated gesture, and laughter shook his voice when he replied, "You wound me, *mi niña bonita*." He paused before adding, "Promise me you will not return to the academy alone. If you must go, take one of your brothers with you." After a thoughtful silence, he added, "Or send for me."

"Should I ask Edward, perhaps? You seem to admire him so much."

"Yes." His curt reply startled her. "He would do very well." He cast her a sidelong glance, a faint, mocking smile curving his mouth. "And he would be an excellent tutor for your more energetic students."

"I am capable of teaching my students."

"*Si*. And you did so well today, *mi niña bonita*. I was quite in awe of your expertise."

She jerked his arm, bringing them to a halt outside her townhouse. "I —" She stopped and stared into his eyes. "I realize I was surprised and did not maintain my guard as I should have. I am not quite the fool you think me."

"You are not a fool," he murmured. "Though, hardheaded? *Si, mi niña bonita*, that much is true."

"Hardheaded — fool — I don't see much difference between the two."

"Then perhaps I have overestimated you, after all."

"I don't see how that is possible," she said, feeling aggrieved. She was tired and though she hated to admit it, she was frightened. Lord Milbourn's words only added to her sense of ill-usage.

Why could he not be kind to her, just this once?

The inquest was tomorrow, and although the verdict would undoubtedly be an unlawful killing by person or persons unknown, she feared Mr. Greenfield and Constable Cooke were viewing her as the most likely suspect. Most likely, Edward hadn't spoken to them about Mr. Underwood, she thought bitterly. Why wouldn't he do so? He knew how important the matter was. Her social position might protect her from an accusation and subsequent prosecution for now, but she couldn't rely on it forever. The authorities seemed extremely industrious in collecting sufficient evidence to condemn her. She had no faith that her innocence would ensure her safety.

Edward *had* to talk to them about Mr. Underwood, he just had to. The man had been in the vicinity of the townhouse — he had more than sufficient opportunity. The thought made her feel ashamed though. She remembered the panic in his face and his concern about his wife. Olivia didn't wish him ill, and when she considered it, she couldn't believe he would do such a thing.

But the fear that she might be accused drove her to search for a way to cast the blame elsewhere, and she couldn't forget looking down into his pale face as he stood on the walkway in front of the academy.

She expelled a shaky breath. Perhaps it *was* a person or persons unknown. Perhaps the killer was a complete stranger who would forever remain nameless. That would be so much better than discovering it was someone she knew.

She didn't want to discover that one of her dear friends had committed murder. Surely she had better judgment than that.

She glanced at Lord Milbourn and discovered him studying her with a concerned frown puckering his brows. His dark eyes warmed with sympathy for one brief moment, before his mouth twisted into a lopsided grin.

"Never fear, Lady Olivia. I will not abandon you." His grin widened and a glint of amusement lit his eyes. "I may even cut out the estimable Edward and assist you in tutoring your young ladies myself if I am sufficiently persuaded."

"How reassuring," she drawled, wishing she didn't feel quite so lightheaded when he smiled at her that way. "I am sure we shall be positively *overflowing* with students now."

"Undoubtedly." He escorted her up the steps to the front door, which magically creaked opened just as they set foot on the stoop. Lord Milbourn bowed to Olivia. "I will leave you here, *mi niña bonita*. Try not to find any more dead bodies. I fear Constable Cooke may not understand."

Olivia frowned at him, but bit off a sharp retort when she noticed Latimore holding the door open. "And I suggest you do the same. After all, there is only so much we can expect from our constabulary, and Constable Cooke does indeed have his hands full." She stepped over the threshold and untied the gold ribbons of her bonnet. "You must be busy, Lord Milbourn, so I thank you for your escort and bid you good day."

Although the butler's lined face remained suitably impassive, she feared they had already shocked him with the news about yet another corpse at the academy. She dreaded the inevitable gossip about Mrs. Adams's death. She had barely known the poor woman, but a grim sadness filled her at the memory of her sprawled untidily on the dirty floor of the kitchen. She'd hired Mrs. Adams and in doing so, she'd exposed her to the danger that had ultimately claimed her life. Queasy guilt churned through her stomach.

No matter how she studied it, she felt responsible for the charwoman's death. Mrs. Adams may have been lazy and utterly useless as a maid of all work, but she didn't deserve to die, and especially not simply to furnish a murderer with a key to the academy.

"Ah, there you are, Lady Olivia," Crispin Belcher strode forward to nod at Olivia. He stretched an arm through the doorway to shake Lord Milbourn's hand. "Lord Milbourn. I was about to leave a note for you, Lady Olivia." He crumpled a piece of paper and handed it to Latimore. "No need to now."

Mr. Belcher was a close friend of all of her brothers, and one of the quartet of fencing *aficionados* consisting of her brother, Wraysbury, Lord Milbourn, and Mr. Grantham. The group had been a burr under Olivia's saddle for as long as she could remember as they gently, but firmly, excluded her whenever they went to a fencing match or met themselves to practice the art.

She might have been able to thrust her way into her brothers' fencing lessons, but she'd never managed to scale the high walls surrounding the quartet, and she couldn't help but view Mr. Belcher with a touch of aggravation.

There was no possible reason for him to leave a note for her — at least not one she was interested in reading — so as far as she was concerned, he'd have been better off to ask to see Edward.

Oblivious to her irritation, Mr. Belcher held his fashionable silk hat in the crook of his left arm, his gray gloved left hand holding his other glove and a Malacca walking stick. The ornate gold knob on the end of the cane gleamed in the mellow candlelight of the hallway like his golden curls. The tall collar of his black coat framed his face, and his striped trousers made him seem even taller, although he was an inch shorter than Lord Milbourn. His clothing could not be faulted. He was impeccable, as always, which only served to annoy her further as she brushed a recalcitrant curl off her forehead.

Studying Olivia, Mr. Belcher's wide blue eyes softened with concern, and once again, she was struck by the perfection of his regular features. A straight nose, square jaw, and firm mouth, now compressed with grave concern, gave him the appearance of a benign angel offering heavenly sympathy.

Strangely, despite Belcher's golden perfection, her breath and heartbeat were quite regular when he examined her. He failed to make her feel as giddy as a glass of champagne did, as when she gazed at Lord Milbourn. Where Milbourn often seemed coldly indifferent or rude, Belcher was warm and as sympathetic as any woman could want. In fact, Belcher struck her in the same way that Lord Saunders often did: with all the appeal of a soggy breakfast bun.

How shameful of me. They are both kind men, and I should feel honored to be engaged to one and friends with the other.

"I hope I am not intruding." Mr. Belcher's glance flicked from Olivia to Lord Milbourn. "However, when I heard the terrible news, I felt I had to offer my condolences." He touched her wrist with his fingertips.

"Heard the news?" she faltered. Surely Mr. Belcher hadn't heard about Mrs. Adams so soon!

She looked at Lord Milbourn. He was studying Mr. Belcher, and she couldn't read anything from his expression except polite interest. Somehow, she'd expected more evidence of their friendship. Although Mr. Belcher and Mr. Grantham were several years older than Lord Milbourn, who was only five years older than her brother, they were still members of their privileged quartet.

A flicker of amusement danced in Belcher's blue eyes for a second and was gone. She stared at him, wondering if she had imagined it. She was tired, upset, and frankly longed to retire to her room and do nothing except stare out the window.

"Grantham," Mr. Belcher replied. "I heard, well, I am sure you are well aware of the rumors since you were unfortunate enough to be the one to discover his ... passing." He touched her wrist again, his brows pinching as he frowned with sympathy. "I am truly sorry. We shall all miss him. He was a true friend."

She glanced again at Lord Milbourn, before she said, "Yes."

Mr. Belcher caught the direction of her quick look and studied first Olivia and then Lord Milbourn. His frown deepened. "You were surprised — I apologize — but has something else occurred?"

"You will hear soon enough," Lord Milbourn replied, cutting off Olivia.

"Hear? Hear what?" Mr. Belcher's gaze traveled from Lord Milbourn to Olivia and back. "Surely nothing else could have happened?"

"A woman has been found as well. At the academy," Lord Milbourn said curtly.

"Woman?" Mr. Belcher's forehead wrinkled with confusion, and his sharp blue eyes searched her face. "What woman?"

"A woman hired to clean," Lord Milbourn answered for Olivia as he followed her into the house. "She apparently died several days ago."

Olivia let out a sigh, relieved not to have to explain matters. A slow headache was beginning to wrap tight bands around her forehead. It was everything she could do not to rub her temple and weep.

"How awful for you, my dear Lady Olivia." Mr. Belcher threw his hat, glove, and cane on a nearby occasional table and grabbed Olivia's right hand. He pressed it under the warm fingers of his bare hand, staring at her. "I cannot imagine how shocked you must be. And to have your affairs exposed to public scrutiny this way, well, I can only offer you my sympathy and support. Whom do the authorities suspect? Is the madman in custody?"

"I fear they suspect me," Olivia said abruptly, her mouth twisting with the bitter admission.

"You?" His grip on her hand tightened as he stared into her eyes. "They must be fools to suspect you. You must be mistaken."

"I cannot argue with that, Mr. Belcher. However, I am not mistaken," she said, wriggling her hand out of his clasp. Part of her wanted to step closer to Lord Milbourn and lean on him for just a moment, just long enough to ease the bands compressing her temples.

"It does look bad, of course," Mr. Belcher said slowly, gazing thoughtfully at his belongings on the nearby table. "However, I am sure there must be some evidence, something to prove your innocence, despite any suspicious circumstances."

Suspicious circumstances! She winced. If a family friend like Crispin Belcher thought the situation raised questions about her involvement, then what hope did she have of convincing the authorities that she was innocent?

Oh, why hadn't Edward talked to the authorities about Mr. Underwood? Or had she misunderstood the conversation between the two men and jumped to the wrong conclusion when she'd seen him on the street? If so, she was the only suspect left.

A chill breezed past the nape of her neck, lifting the soft curls and making her skin itch.

"Anyone applying sufficient logic to the course of events would conclude that Lady Olivia could not possibly be involved," Lord Milbourn interjected smoothly. "As I'm sure the authorities will eventually recognize."

"Of course." Mr. Belcher's frown of concern lifted away as if it had never wrinkled his brow. An expression of smiling, sunny confidence replaced it. "And I trust they shall soon make an arrest and put an end to your worries, Lady Olivia."

Or give her something new to worry about. She wished she had the confidence in Mr. Greenfield that these two men had. As it was, she felt fortunate not to be arrested already.

Chapter Nine

A soft knock at the front door distracted Olivia. Lord Milbourn, Mr. Belcher, and she all turned to watch Latimore open the front door. He bowed in greeting and waved the newcomer inside.

A bolt of pain shot up Olivia's neck to her throbbing temples as she watched her betrothed take a few hesitant steps over the threshold into the hall. His nervous gaze flicked past them from one door to the next, the tension in his face revealing his fear of another assault by her dogs. He gripped his walking stick at its midpoint and held it in front of him, prepared for the worst.

"Lady Olivia, Lord Saunders." Latimore bowed before closing the door.

"Lord Saunders," Olivia greeted him. She forced a polite smile and nodded. "You know Lord Milbourn and Mr. Belcher, I believe?"

"Indeed, yes. Gentlemen." He nodded, but didn't stop glancing around until Lord Milbourn strode up to him and offered his hand.

"Good afternoon, Saunders," Lord Milbourn said, waiting patiently while Lord Saunders shifted his cane to his left hand and shook hands.

Mr. Belcher walked forward to greet Olivia's betrothed and ask after his health.

Olivia gestured for Latimore to join her and whispered, "Where is Margaret? Or Edward for that matter?"

"I beg your pardon, Lady Olivia." Latimore glanced at the three men exchanging casual comments about the weather and the prospect for snow before morning. "Mr. Edward left twenty minutes

95

ago with Mr. Peregrine and your sisters." The corners of his mouth creased ever so slightly in as much amusement as he would allow himself to display. "They took your dogs with them, Lady Olivia. Mr. Edward felt they needed exercising."

As usual, she couldn't rely upon any of her siblings to rescue her from an increasingly awkward position. What was she going to do with three gentlemen callers?

Mr. Belcher picked up his gloves, cane, and hat. "Excuse me, Lady Olivia. Gentlemen. I am afraid I must bid you good day."

She bit her lower lip to keep from expressing her relief.

"I should leave, as well," Lord Milbourn said. He caught Olivia's gaze with his dark eyes.

"When —" She halted, aware of Lord Saunders's gaze. When she looked up, Mr. Belcher was also watching her, his golden brows raised in gentle curiosity. She fought against the flush she felt rising over her cheeks and took a deep breath. "There are some matters I must discuss with you." Lord Saunders's gaze burned her face, but she refused to look at him. "About the academy."

A slow smile curved Lord Milbourn's mouth. "Of course. Tomorrow —"

"Tomorrow is the inquest," she pointed out.

"If I may, I will escort you there. We can then discuss the academy." He bowed politely.

"You shall not go to the inquest, Lady Olivia." Lord Saunders stepped forward abruptly. "A lady of your rank — it is not done." He glared at Lord Milbourn as if challenging him to disagree.

This was the first time she'd ever heard him express his opinion forcefully. Olivia stared at her betrothed in surprise before she recovered sufficiently to say, "I really think I must go, Lord Saunders. I'm very sorry, but I think it best." She glanced at Lord Milbourn. "One of my brothers will accompany me, there is no need to inconvenience yourself."

"Very well." Lord Milbourn gave her a shallow bow.

"But — but..." Lord Saunders stumbled over his objection. He clearly felt strongly about the matter, but his diffident nature made it impossible for him to maintain his position firmly. "You must see, you must allow me to advise you. Why, we are nearly betrothed, surely, you must see the wisdom...."

Nearly betrothed. But not quite. An interesting choice of words. Olivia examined him, unable to stop herself from thinking that if Lord Milbourn didn't want her to attend, he wouldn't have the least difficulty in telling her so. But then again, he cared very little what anyone thought and was unlikely to advise her to avoid the inquest simply because of fears about what others might say.

"Thank you, Lord Milbourn. Your support is reassuring," Olivia said, ignoring Lord Saunders's mumbled protests.

"It is my pleasure. Good day." Lord Milbourn bowed to each of them.

"I will join you," Mr. Belcher said, already standing near the door. "Good day, Lady Olivia, Lord Saunders."

Latimore held the door as the two gentlemen strode out, leaving Olivia facing her betrothed.

Hectic color flushed Lord Saunders's plump, gentle face. He sputtered under his breath, walking back and forth in a tight line four feet long. "Lady Olivia," he said when he caught her glance. He stopped pacing. Some of the color left his cheeks, leaving him pale and frowning.

"Perhaps you would join me in the sitting room?" Olivia gestured toward the staircase.

"Of course, of course," Lord Saunders stammered. He started toward the stairs ahead of her, halted with his foot on the lowest step, flushed, and stepped back to gesture to her to precede him.

Head throbbing, she sighed, sent one glance at the closed front door, and picked up her skirts to climb the staircase.

They'd barely entered the Ivory Drawing Room when Lord Saunders cleared his throat and clasped his hands behind his back. He stood on tiptoes for a second and gazed at her with a dropping mouth and look of vast disappointment in his pale blue eyes. He blinked several times. His anxious gaze searched the room as if he feared some murderous intruder might be taking a nap on one of the silk brocade covered couches while he waited for them.

"Well. I trust you are satisfied," he said, obviously striving for a firm tone, though his voice quavered over "satisfied," turning it into a question.

"Why should I be satisfied?" She walked over to the two armchairs and couch arranged in front of the fireplace.

The weather had once again grown icy as the sunlight faded, and some thoughtful maid had lit the fire. The flames burned merrily within the beautiful fireplace, illuminating the deep, golden Sienna marble Ionic columns that supported the sculpted chimneypiece frieze. The carving depicted a central classical urn, flower-bud festoons, and two flanking classical muses, and just looking at the clean lines and graceful design seemed to calm Olivia.

She stretched out her hands, grateful for the warmth, and gestured to the white-figured damask chair on her right. "Would you care to sit?"

"No, I should not." Lord Saunders frowned at her before stalking closer to the fire. He let out a long breath and then sat on the edge of one of the gold and ivory striped couches. "If you had not lost your senses and attempted to start this dreadful academy, none of this would have happened. Surely, you must see that it is madness! You must end this immediately. It will make us all a laughing stock if you continue."

"I am afraid I disagree," she said coldly.

"Then consider what has happened as a direct result of your actions. You have lost a dear family friend —"

"I had *nothing* to do with his death!" she exclaimed. Her eyes stung, and she wiped them quickly with her fingertips, refusing to give in to tears.

"Nonetheless, he died. I am sorry to speak to you in this way, but I must. As your betrothed —"

"The contract has yet to be signed." His words tightened around her like a noose around the neck. She couldn't breathe — she didn't want to hear anymore, didn't want to think that he might be right. Her hands clenched together in her effort to keep from touching her throat.

Did others believe she was responsible for Mr. Grantham's death? Did Margaret?

She hadn't wanted that to happen, she hadn't wanted any of this to happen. How could they think otherwise?

He sighed. "That is a discussion for another time, Lady Olivia." Then he peered at her, rubbed his nose, and took another deep breath. "Please consider my request. Do not go to the inquest tomorrow."

She nodded and wearily sat in the opposite chair, rubbing her throbbing temple. "I said I was going — I have to go. Surely, you see that."

"You could very well write your statement and hand it to them. There is no need for a lady to attend a coroner's inquest. You have no idea what they are like. It is positively gruesome. I — I forbid you to attend." He cast her a defiant glance before rubbing his hands together in front of the fire. "To be on public display like that." He shook his head and peered at her again, searching her face for understanding. "If you had any decency of feeling, any sensibility, you would not consider such a course of action. I ask you, please, do not go, Lady Olivia. I beseech you to consider your family. Lady Margaret is grief-stricken. Surely you have no wish to hurt her any further by exposing her to sordid gossip."

For one second, she considered mentioning Mr. Underwood in an attempt to shift the blame to him, but she quickly dismissed it as unworthy. She would not throw his name about like pieces of stale bread tossed to the birds. "Lord Saunders, I understand, truly I do. But you don't seem to realize that it is entirely possible that they consider me to be a suspect. I must know what is said, if only to protect myself."

He studied her, his mouth drooping and his eyes shining as if he were about to cry. "I had hoped, well, there it is." Leaning forward, he fixed his earnest gaze upon her. "I understand how it could have happened. A delicate, sensitive lady such as yourself, faced with a gentleman perhaps a bit too forward, too familiar. Anyone would understand how it could have happened. However, you must realize you could never be held responsible for something you did out of fear.

Panic or hysteria — perfectly understandable, you know." He nodded at her. "You are a *lady*. No woman would ever be blamed under the circumstances. You may trust my judgment in these matters. The authorities will dismiss the matter. You shall see. So there is no reason for you to attend and expose yourself to public censure or worse. Write your statement and be done with it." He leaned forward to pat her clasped hands. "Think of your family, and of Lady Margaret. Please."

She jerked away and managed to cover the gesture by bending toward the fire and rubbing her hands vigorously. He believed Mr. Grantham had made improper advances toward her, and she'd murdered him in a state of hysterical panic.

How can he believe such a thing? Is that truly what he thinks of me? That I am just another hysterical woman who would kill a family friend simply because he acted too forward?

Her emotions spun in circles like a child's toy. Anger surged forward at his casual assumption that she would have panicked instead of simply slapping his cheek and calling her brother to her aid.

Instead of believing in her innocence, Lord Saunders had casually dismissed her fears and advised her to confess. Obviously he knew nothing about her or what she would do.

Worse, did others see her the same way? Did Margaret believe Olivia had murdered Mr. Grantham? The thought made her feel as if she'd stepped over the edge of a precipice without a rope or helping hand to keep her from falling to her death.

Once again, she felt as if an invisible ribbon tied her to Lord Milbourn. The silken ribbon gently tugged at her, drawing her to him. She needed to see him, to talk to him. He would never dismiss her worries so lightly or believe she was silly enough to hit Mr. Grantham over the head with a marble Cupid simply because he flirted with her.

Lord Milbourn might tease her with Edward's expertise at swordplay, but he didn't treat her like a fool.

And although he might seem cold or distant, she felt a passion within him, hiding behind that calm exterior. That fire called to her like a beacon in the night, drawing her closer and offering her the reassuring glow of trust. But for now, she needed the icy clarity of his intelligence to review the events and help her prove her innocence. If she could just talk to him alone....

She glanced at Lord Saunders, who was eying her hopefully, as if he thought he might finally have persuaded her of the correctness of his opinion. Letting out a long breath, she stared at the floor. Here she was thinking about Lord Milbourn, wishing she could discuss her situation with him, when she should rightly be talking to her betrothed. She ought to be thinking of him, obeying his requests, and giving him the respect due to him.

He'd been nothing but kind to her, even though they both knew this was no love match. Their two families wanted the alliance. It was a good match, and yet it made her feel desperate to escape.

His request should not have come as a surprise to her. She knew he was shy, painfully so. He had screwed up every ounce of courage he possessed to ask this one simple thing of her: stay away from the inquest and avoid public scrutiny. A lady would certainly do as he requested.

Any other lady would dislike the gossip, the infamy of having not one, but two bodies discovered in her townhouse. A proper lady wouldn't even need to be told to stay away.

But no other lady would have thought of starting a Fencing Academy for Ladies, either.

A soft footstep sounded in the hallway, and Margaret rushed into the room. Her cheeks were flushed pink and her blue eyes flashed brilliantly as she glanced around and noticed Lord Saunders. Elusive dimples appeared to frame her pretty mouth.

"Lord Saunders! How delightful. Latimore said you were here." She walked into the room, barely giving Olivia a nod. "I am so relieved to see you. It has been so dreadful here." She glanced at Olivia. "Lady Olivia must be comforted to have your strong arm to support her, to support us all." She leaned against the side of Lord Saunders's chair, smiling down at him.

Flashing a smile, Lord Saunders flushed as pink as a rabbit's nose with pleasure and sat up straighter, before assuming a properly grave expression. "Well, of course, I have given her the benefit of my advice." He glanced at Olivia uneasily, apparently afraid she would contradict him. "I can only hope she listens to the voice of reason."

Margaret laughed. "Lady Olivia always knows best. Or so she informs us when we beg to differ." She touched Lord Saunders's shoulder and leaned closer. "I, however, would appreciate your advice. Edward gave me permission to decorate the music room, and you have such elegant taste. Would you not help me? I promise not to take too much of your time."

He looked at Olivia and seemed to have difficulties meeting her direct gaze. "Delighted, of course. Um, but what of Lord Graybrook? He might wish you had requested his assistance —" he broke off uneasily, unable to meet the eyes of either lady.

"Lord Graybrook's wishes do not interest me," Margaret replied archly. "And I am persuaded you have much better taste."

"You flatter me, Lady Margaret. But I am always willing to do what I can." Lord Saunders stood with alacrity, his smile matching Margaret's. She slipped her hand through the crook of his arm, and they started for the door before Lord Saunders remembered Olivia.

"I beg your pardon, Lady Olivia. Would you care to join us?" he asked.

Margaret frowned at her, her eyes hard and unwelcoming.

Olivia sighed and shook her head. "No. You go on. Margaret is the musical one, not I. And I would like to rest."

"Very well," Lord Saunders said. "I hope you will consider my advice, Lady Olivia."

"I shall most assuredly give it all the consideration it deserves," Olivia answered without thinking.

She immediately regretted her words, but neither Lord Saunders nor Margaret appeared to notice. They were already discussing the merits of various wallpaper designs and paint as they walked through the door.

Alone again, Lord Saunders's comments about her involvement in Mr. Grantham's death echoed in her ears.

Poor Margaret — does she hold me responsible, too? She couldn't possibly believe that Olivia would do such a thing — not in her heart — not about her sister — but the bitter thought that others might think her guilty remained. Mr. Grantham's death had hurt Margaret so dreadfully that she might be desperate to assign the blame to someone — including Olivia. So it was entirely possible that Lord Saunders was correct, and that Margaret did indeed blame her for Mr. Grantham's death and for her terrible grief.

For some unaccountable reason, she and Margaret had grown apart. Margaret now seemed to actually dislike her, so it would be easy for her to believe the worst of Olivia. The thought was heartbreaking. All their difficulties seemed to begin on the day Olivia agreed to accept Lord Saunders's offer, and she couldn't help but think of that as the last afternoon when they'd all been truly happy. Her sister had grown distant and difficult, and she'd stopped creeping into Olivia's room at night to giggle and share secrets as they had done since girlhood.

She blamed Olivia for even the most trivial setback, and instead of focusing on her own future, Margaret had failed to find a suitable interest or a match of her own, despite three London Seasons.

Olivia had almost lost patience with her and given up on ever recapturing the warm relationship they'd once had. But she hadn't stopped trying, or hoping that Margaret would see that her older sister still loved her and longed for their previous closeness.

Her stomach cramped, and she pressed her cold fingers to her mouth. What had she done? More importantly, what should she do?

Chapter Ten

As they walked away from the Archer residence, Alexander glanced at Belcher and then turned at the corner in the direction of the academy.

"May I join you?" Belcher asked as he matched his step to Alexander's. Before Alexander could respond, he chuckled and shook his head. "I was surprised to see you with Lady Olivia, although I suppose I should not have been. She has always been mad about fencing — just as you and I have been — though I confess I had thought one of her brothers would have made her see sense. It seems to have led her into a great deal of difficulty. Ah, well, she was always a willful and contrary chit." He sighed and glanced around. "My club is not far. I daresay a drink would not be amiss."

Alexander shook his head and contemplated a cutting remark. Finally, he simply said, "I have other matters to attend to."

Belcher chuckled. "I don't suppose that includes checking on our remarkably astute constabulary and their progress in this terrible affair of Lady Olivia's?"

"I am considering it," Alexander replied coolly.

"Let me join you, then." Worry settled on Belcher's brow, wrinkling it into deep furrows. "I confess — willful or not — I am concerned about Lady Olivia. I dislike believing she could ever have killed Grantham, but I don't know what other conclusion one can come to. And although we have all been friends for years, I have always thought Grantham a bit highhanded. If he found Lady Olivia alone, well, he could have acted the cad toward her. She might have been provoked enough to hit him with that statuette."

Alexander shot him a thoughtful glance. "I had not noticed any tendency in Grantham to take advantage of any of the ladies in the Archer family."

"Perhaps I am mistaken." Belcher shrugged. "But Grantham did appreciate the ladies, and the Archer females are remarkably attractive."

"Perhaps," Alexander murmured, irritated with Belcher's company.

He wanted to speak with Cooke and Idleman, and didn't want someone else interfering or asking irrelevant questions. Belcher had a way of addressing oblique criticisms to others that got people's backs up. He'd certainly set Alexander's teeth on edge enough times. However, Wraysbury and Grantham had found him amusing, so Belcher had remained a member of their quartet.

Now, it was a trio.

The academy came into view as they rounded the corner of Mortimer Street. Alexander's pace quickened as his thoughts raced ahead.

Idleman and his jury seemed competent enough, however they were focusing too closely on Lady Olivia. Alexander was not so naïve as to assume that she could never kill anyone, but he didn't believe she'd killed Grantham or her charwoman. If Grantham had bothered her, she would have called for her brother to throw him out. Or she would have done it herself. She was no shrinking wallflower, afraid of her own shadow.

A slow grin touched his mouth, but he instantly sobered. Bloodstains and footprints interested him. If she had lost her temper and hit Grantham, she was too intelligent to leave her footprints in the man's blood. And from what Peregrine had said, she didn't have any stains on her clothing. After bludgeoning Grantham and shoving him into the wardrobe, she would surely have had bloodstains on her sleeves at least.

Where were the stains? No one had noticed any on her clothing either, and she had not had time to change before Idleman and his jurymen arrived.

Then there was the charwoman to consider. Why kill her? Lady Olivia had her own key. And if she had done so for some inexplicable reason, why hide the body for a day? The victim had been stout, and her body would have been unwieldy and difficult to move. Lady Olivia would have had a great many challenges to overcome in dragging the corpse, and there was the question of where the woman had been kept until she was deposited at the academy.

The simplest possibility seemed to be that Mrs. Adams had been murdered either in her home or near — but not inside — the academy in order to obtain her key. The door to the kitchen seemed the likeliest location. If she'd been murdered in her home, she probably would have been left there. Even if the murderer wanted to fasten the blame more securely on Lady Olivia, it seemed unnecessary to drag her here through the busy London streets.

So she had to have been left nearby. Again, outside the kitchen door made the most sense as the murder location. The killer may have waited there for the charwoman to arrive. Because one only reached that door through a narrow alley, there would have been little chance of being seen. He could then kill her to obtain the key and prevent her from telling anyone that she had seen him or lent him the key. He then hid her body — somewhere close — and used the key to unlock the door for his meeting with Grantham.

The building was obviously unused, and few expected Lady Olivia to really open her academy, so it was the perfect place for a private conversation. Even Grantham had jested in private that she would never succeed — no lady would sign up for a fencing class no matter how harebrained she was. What fair-skinned maid would risk scarring her beautiful face?

The murderer must have agreed and had been confident that they would not be interrupted by anyone.

Except they *were* interrupted when Lady Olivia arrived.

That must have been a bit of a shock for the killer when she arrived with her brother so soon after he'd dispatched Grantham. Whether he had planned to hide the body in the wardrobe from the beginning, or did so in his haste to escape detection when Lady Olivia walked in, was a minor matter. The fact was that he'd shoved the body in a convenient hiding place and left down the servants' stairs before anyone saw him.

It was the only reasonable solution.

Alexander's frown deepened as they approached the front door of the townhouse. Proving Lady Olivia's innocence was not going to be easy. Even if what he suspected were true, there wasn't any proof that she was not involved, except the lack of bloodstains on her clothing.

Blood and keys, blood and keys. Those elements were at the heart of the matter.

Lady Olivia had her own key and had no reason to murder her charwoman. And he refused to believe that the two deaths were not connected.

If Lady Olivia had arranged to meet Grantham at the academy and subsequently murdered him, then there was no explanation for Mrs. Adam's death. Unless the charwoman had walked in on the scene.

No. Impossible. Lady Olivia had been at home before she and her brother had gone to the academy. The two of them had to have arrived at almost the same time that Grantham had met his end. His blood had been fresh enough for her to track it across the floor on the soles of her shoes.

So Mrs. Adams could not have surprised her. Unless Peregrine had been complicit in the two crimes as well.

But then, why hide Mrs. Adams's body while sending for the authorities to investigate the death of Mr. Grantham? Lady Olivia and Peregrine Archer had to be innocent. Simple logic supported their stories.

Unfortunately, the same facts could be seen in quite a different light if one were so inclined, and the authorities appeared to be very inclined in that direction.

"Gloomy old place, eh?" Belcher commented as Alexander opened the front door. He brushed past Alexander and strode inside, gazing around avidly. "I heard the actual murder took place upstairs. Is that true?" Without waiting for Alexander's reply, he strode to the staircase and glanced upward into the gloom of the first floor landing.

"Yes." Alexander walked to the baize door leading to the servants' area at the back of the house. If the coroner and his men were still present, they would most likely be in that vicinity.

"Where are you going?" Belcher called from a point halfway up the staircase.

Alexander didn't answer. He slipped through the doorway, intent on his own investigation. If Belcher wanted to wander around upstairs, he was welcomed to do so.

As he expected, the coroner and his men were milling around the kitchen, mostly engaged in gossip, while four of them wrapped the body in a stiff, weathered piece of canvas. Constable Cooke stood a few feet away, watching their efforts and talking to another man Alexander recognized as Mr. Greenfield.

Greenfield glanced at the doorway as Alexander entered and nodded.

"I would like to look at the body again before you remove it, if you don't mind," Alexander said, walking around the kitchen table. "Have you determined the cause of death?"

"Hit on the head," Constable Cooke said. "Though I don't see what business it is of yours."

The statement verified the observation Alexander had made when they discovered the body. The fact that Cooke's assessment agreed with Alexander's failed to reassure him about the ultimate conclusion of the investigation, however. Sometimes expediency took precedence over the truth, although Lady Olivia's position might shield her enough to make them at least attempt to find the true murderer.

"The manner of death is of interest to anyone wishing to see this murder solved," Alexander answered Cooke's comment with a half-smile. He knelt on one knee next to the corpse and caught the uncertain gaze of one of the men wrapping the canvas over her.

The man looked from Alexander to Greenfield.

Greenfield nodded. "Uncover her head. Her left temple was crushed by a blow, my lord."

The man gently unfolded the canvas and stood back, waiting for Alexander to examine her.

A blow had indeed broken the skin of the left temple, as he had initially noted. He bent closer. A livid gash separated the thin flesh, and a dried line of blood ran across her face, pooling in dark flakes around the eyes, and disappearing into her bonnet.

So he'd been correct. She had lain on her right side immediately after death, causing the blood to spill over her face. The fluid had also pooled under the skin of her right cheek. It had created a purplish-red stain that now seemed to be permanent, for it had not changed position, even though she had been laying on her left side when her body was discovered.

Examining the left temple again, he thought he could see an odd imprint in the center, bisected by the torn skin. A signet ring, perhaps? Had someone wearing a large, heavy ring hit her on the temple and killed her? A ring, or something else round with circular ridges. The knobbed end of a poker, perhaps, or even a candlestick. There were numerous possibilities.

He pulled out a small journal and pencil and drew as much of the pattern as he could make out, along with a note concerning the size of the wound. A small frown pinched the bridge of his nose. *I have seen this somewhere.* The sense of familiarity gnawed at him, but he couldn't place it. Perhaps it was something as inconsequential as the knob on a fire iron.

"What do you see?" Greenfield moved closer to peer over Alexander's shoulder.

"You observed the lack of blood on the floor?" Alexander asked.

"Yes, of course." Greenfield nodded, a deceptively mild, curious expression in his blue eyes. "Her hat caught most of it. You can see where it flowed over her face."

"Precisely. And what do you make of that?" Alexander stood and brushed his hands off on the hem of his jacket as he took a step away from Greenfield.

Greenfield smiled. "What I make of that is that she was wearing her bonnet when she died, and it failed to protect her from the blow that killed her."

"Anything else?"

"If you have noted something we have missed, please enlighten us, my lord," Greenfield answered. His voice remained mild, but his gaze had hardened. He clearly wasn't overly pleased about Alexander's interference.

"In what position did she lie when you arrived?" Alexander asked, guiding them in the direction his thoughts had taken him.

"She was on the floor next to the kitchen table, lying on her left side."

"I have never seen any fluid run upwards," he murmured, watching as the men covered up Mrs. Adams's bloated, gray face again.

"You rolled her over, from right to left," Constable Cooke interrupted, scowling at Alexander.

"No." Alexander shook his head and clasped his hands behind his back. "I tilted her face up, briefly, to see the contusion on her temple. Her body remained lying as we found it."

Cooke's round face grew florid as he stared at Alexander, anger burning in his eyes. His massive shoulders hunched forward, and his hands closed into fists before he exchanged glances with Greenfield. When Greenfield gave a nearly imperceptible shake of his head, Cooke shoved his fists into the pockets of his jacket, pulling the heavy wool fabric down until the hem hung mid-thigh.

In the same calm voice, Greenfield asked, "And what is your conclusion from that, my lord?"

"She was murdered elsewhere and moved to this location. Did you notice the wound?" Alexander asked.

"A single blow to the temple," Greenfield answered cautiously.

"Oh, so this is where you are," Belcher interrupted from the doorway. Grinning, he entered the kitchen, only to turn pale and halt. "What is that infernal smell?"

"Mrs. Adams," Alexander answered sardonically.

"Mrs. Adams? Good Lord, another corpse? This dreary house is positively infested with them."

"Apparently," Alexander said.

"And you are?" Greenfield turned toward Belcher and eyed him.

"Belcher, Mr. Crispin Belcher, at your service." Belcher sketched a bow in Greenfield's direction as his gaze bounced from one man to the other. "Dreadful affair. Never heard of such a thing. Two bodies in one house." He finally focused on Alexander. "What is this about a wound?"

"The deceased died from a single blow to the temple," Greenfield said, although the summary had clearly been addressed to Alexander. "Is that not correct, my lord?"

"As far as it goes," Alexander replied slowly. Although the room was large, it felt overcrowded, and the odor of death turned his stomach. He turned away to face the open kitchen door, grateful for the faint breeze that carried the musty odors of dampness and bricks from the alley. He took a deep breath to clear away the metallic smell of decaying blood from his lungs.

"Well, if you have anything else to say, do so, my lord. There is no need to be coy," Idleman said. He frowned at all of them, clearly irritated by the interruptions. However, before anyone could speak, he continued, "It may be that these two unfortunate deaths are related, or they may not be, but each poor soul shall have his own inquest. Mr. Grantham's shall be tomorrow, and this woman's shall be held on Monday. If you wish to add anything to either proceeding, then I suggest you attend and do so."

"Well, what more is there to say?" Belcher asked with a noticeable lack of gravity. Nothing seemed to affect his cheerful mood for long, and his blue eyes sparkled in the dim light of the kitchen. "The poor lady was hit on the head and died." He glanced down at his fashionable, long-tailed coat and brushed some dust off the sides. "Though it is a pity that whoever did this couldn't have waited until she finished cleaning. The condition of this domicile is execrable."

Alexander studied him before drawling, "Do you by any chance know Miss Denholm? I am persuaded the two of you would have a great deal in common."

"Miss Denholm?" Belcher frowned in concentration. "Should I know her?"

"Yes. Undoubtedly," Alexander murmured. Neither Miss Denholm nor Belcher seemed unduly upset by the specter of death. If anything, they both seemed inclined to view it as nothing more than a minor inconvenience.

"Well, if you gentlemen will excuse us, we must carry out our sad duty," Mr. Idleman said, clearly ready to depart with Mrs. Adams's body. "It is getting late."

Night had already fallen, and the kitchen windows were dark. The men clustered around Idleman appeared tired and dispirited, as if they personally felt the grief of the charwoman's pitiful death. The men were all prosperous looking, well-fed individuals, who struck Alexander as the sort who would normally have worn expressions of smiling complacency. But now they stood with bowed shoulders, and their hats clutched in their broad hands, disliking their gruesome task, but resigned to carrying out their duty as quickly as possible.

Three men appeared to be gentlemen, and wore fashionable coats, top hats, and gloves. They glanced around uncomfortably before donning the fatalistic and lugubrious airs of their more commonplace companions. No one wanted to remain there. Clubs, supper, or simply the warmth of their own hearths were waiting for them.

Alexander nodded to Idleman and Greenfield, ignoring the blustering constable, who seemed to want to stay and argue. As Idleman said, Alexander could always discuss the small details that had caught his attention at the inquests.

"By the by, Idleman, did you send someone to search for the button?" Greenfield asked in a quiet voice as Alexander headed for the passageway leading to the front door with Belcher on his heels.

Halting, Alexander glanced over his shoulder at the coroner.

"Button?" Idleman frowned at Greenfield before the lines on his forehead smoothed out. "Oh, yes. The button." He shook his head. "No. We have not had the chance."

"Then if you will excuse me, I will go look for it." Greenfield edged around the table and glanced into the corridor, his gaze resting on Alexander and Belcher briefly.

The considering look in Greenfield's eyes bordered on a challenge before he gave them a sharp nod in acknowledgement and walked forward. He brushed past them and through the open baize door, heading for the main staircase to the first floor.

That man bears watching. Alexander watched him disappear into the shadows at the base of the stairs. Well, Lady Olivia was innocent — Alexander would stake his life on it — and if Greenfield thought to accuse her, he would find himself in a fight he was ill-equipped to win.

But for now, Alexander needed to see Lady Olivia again and persuade her to send a statement rather than attending the public spectacle of the coroner's inquest. While he didn't agree with anything Lord Saunders had babbled earlier, and had been frankly appalled to learn that Lady Olivia might even consider marrying the buffoon, Alexander did agree with Saunders's advice. No need to step into the inquiry and remind the authorities of her involvement in the affair. It would be best if she could be forgotten, entirely.

If that were even possible.

Chapter Eleven

I cy sleet spattered against the gray windows as Olivia slowly finished dressing in the small dressing room adjoined to her bedchamber. Despite the cheerful fire burning in the other room's fireplace, the heat couldn't penetrate the chill in the small dressing room. She felt cold and shaky with anxiety. Today was Mr. Grantham's inquest.

She didn't want to attend, and yet she had to. She needed to hear the conclusions of the authorities herself, even though she dreaded doing so. If they thought she were involved in Grantham's death, then it was best to know. She didn't want to wait and see the sympathy in her family's eyes when they broke the news to her, skimming over critical facts she might need to know.

Worse, she couldn't bear to consider what Alexander — Lord Milbourn — must think. Did he share Lord Saunders's belief that she'd murdered Mr. Grantham?

She pulled on a demure, dark gray walking dress with a tailored Spencer and after a moment's hesitation, a small jet broach and matching earrings. Her skin was as pallid as the ice forming in the corners of the windows, and her eyes peered out of bluish-black hollows. She looked like a life-long invalid unwisely rising from her sickbed.

When she finally went to the dining room, she was surprised to find only Edward and Peregrine there. Her heart dropped as she skirted the table and headed for the sideboard even though the thought of eating the sulfurous smelling eggs or fishy kippers made her stomach twist. Where was Margaret? She always ate breakfast.

Margaret was always ravenous in the morning. Nothing ruined her appetite.

She blames me — maybe they all do. Olivia's hand shook as she hesitated over the warm slices of bread, smelling of yeast. If Margaret thought Olivia had killed Mr. Grantham, then what would the coroner's court decide? She smoothed some pale, creamy butter on a slice of bread and placed it on her plate, even though she suspected she would never be able to eat it.

"Are you attending the c-coroner's inquest?" Peregrine asked as Olivia sat across from him at the table. His appetite was apparently intact. A few scraps of ham, a bit of egg, and the last inch of a slice of bread — the heel, his favorite slice — graced his plate. As soon as he finished speaking, he crammed the last of his bread into his mouth and took a sip of coffee.

Olivia caught Edward's glance. He stared at her with a stern scowl of disapproval.

"Yes," she said at last. She looked down at her plate and poked at the bread with one finger.

"I thought as much," Edward said.

"T-there you are. T-that's t-two guineas, Ed." Peregrine grinned as he held out his hand toward his older brother. "I knew you w-would go, Ollie."

The worried ruts worn into Edward's forehead deepened as he dug into his pocket, extracted a few coins, and threw them at Peregrine. "If the two of you had any decency at all, you would never consider such a thing."

"But d-decency is not nearly as rewarding," Peregrine answered with a wink at Olivia. "Don't look so glum, Ollie. The inquest should be quite interesting. Never been to one. Have you?"

Olivia tore off a small piece of buttered bread and raised it to her mouth. After catching Peregrine's excited gaze, she lowered it to her plate again. "Why would you even ask me such a thing? Of course I have never been to an inquest. I have never had any desire to attend an inquest."

"Very commendable." Edward nodded as he folded his serviette and placed it next to his plate. "I suggest you avoid this one, as well."

"I would much prefer that alternative," she said waspishly, staring at the torn bread. "However, I cannot do that, as you well know." She forced herself to pick up a small corner and eat it. At least the butter kept the bread from being too dry. She finished the slice, swallowing with difficulty through a tight throat. It would have been unladylike and embarrassing to have her empty stomach rumbling at the inquest.

In a small way, she felt very virtuous when she managed to finish her meager breakfast and rise from the table.

"Shall I go with you?" Peregrine asked hopefully, shoving his chair back and standing.

"Stay here. Or go for a walk," Edward said. He let out a long-suffering sigh as he stood. "I shall go with you, Olivia."

Thank goodness. She didn't want to go alone after declining Lord Milbourn's offer of escort, and while she loved Peregrine dearly, she preferred the calm steadiness of Edward. And he had studied law in preparation to open his own law offices in London, so he would understand the proceedings well enough to offer her sensible advice.

She just hoped she wouldn't need it. She had already sent her statement to Mr. Idleman, and should be able to attend without directly participating. Unfortunately, she had no faith in her luck.

"But I w-would like to go! Ollie?" Peregrine turned to her with imploring eyes. "You want me to attend, d-don't you?"

"I'm sorry, but I think it really is enough if only Edward and I go." She glanced at Edward.

He nodded.

"I doubt it will be very pleasant," she added.

Peregrine frowned and then straightened, an implacable expression smoothing over his face. It was a measure of his determination that he controlled his stuttering by saying slowly and forcefully, "I was there when we found Mr. Grantham. I am attending."

Except he hadn't been there. Not precisely. And that was the difficulty. Olivia and Edward exchanged glances. He nodded and shrugged, raising his hands in a gesture of surrender.

"Very well. Then we shall all three go." She let out a long breath. The single slice of bread she had choked down felt like a ball of lead in her stomach. But it had been the sensible thing to do, and she had the satisfaction of accomplishing that much.

The prisoner dined well. Scratch that. She hadn't dined well, and she wasn't a prisoner. Not yet, anyway.

Peregrine seemed to be the only one eager to leave. He strode ahead of them into the hallway and paced in front of the door.

"Edward, may I speak to you for a moment?" Olivia asked as her brother headed for the doorway as well.

He turned toward her and raised his brows. "Yes?"

"Did you speak to Mr. Greenfield about your conversation with Mr. Underwood?"

"That is none of your concern, Lady Olivia," he said with a heavy, disapproving frown.

"It *is* my concern. They suspect me!"

"So you would rather they suspect Mr. Underwood?"

She flushed and gripped the back of a chair. "No! Of course not. I just —" She halted. What could she say? In truth, she *did* want them to suspect Mr. Underwood instead of her.

Anyone but her.

"Yes?" he asked unhelpfully.

"I am afraid they will not discover the truth, that they will blame me," she said lamely.

"They do not blame you." He dismissed her words with an impatient wave of his hand.

"They do!" Her grip on the chair's back tightened. She could feel the elegant carving on the wood biting into her palm. "They think I killed Mr. Grantham, and I did not!"

"Of course you did not. Don't be a fool."

She took a deep, calming breath. "I only want them to have all the facts so they can discover the truth. Why will you not help me?"

"I am assisting you. Trust my judgment." He smiled ruefully and held out his hand. "I will not let them accuse you, believe me. No one in our family wants that."

"I do trust you, but.... What did Mr. Underwood say to you? He spoke of Mr. Grantham — I heard him."

Edward nodded and moved a step closer to the door. "He did. And his words would only lead to more confusion, not less. I will question him again to make sure, but I don't believe he had ought to do with Grantham's death."

"But I saw him!" she exclaimed.

"You saw him?" Edward studied her with a frown. "Where?"

"I saw him walking past the academy. He was in the vicinity when Mr. Grantham was murdered — it could have been him."

"You must be mistaken." He dismissed her words with a shrug.

"I am *not* mistaken. I spoke to him — asked him to fetch the watch."

The impatient disbelief hardening his eyes faded. He grimaced and said, "I will look into the matter and consider what you've told me. Now if you are planning on attending the inquest — against my advice — then we really should leave."

She nodded and followed him out. As they neared the door, they discovered that Peregrine had already requested their wraps from Latimore. Her brother impatiently paced to the door and back to them, as if trying to shoo them forward.

Apparently Olivia moved too slowly because Peregrine grabbed her pelisse and bonnet from the butler and shoved them into her hands. Before she was ready, she was walking between her brothers, watching their breath puff out in steamy clouds in the chilly February morning air. The untied ribbons of her bonnet fluttered under her chin until she drew her hands out of her brothers' grips and tied them.

Edward strode along on her left, nearest to the curb, while Peregrine walked ahead with a fast, long-legged pace. He kept getting ahead of them and darting back to encourage them to go faster. Edward ignored him, maintaining a thoughtful silence. A tiny frown formed a V between his brows.

Once or twice, he looked so serious that Olivia's nerves jangled in anticipation of some terrible revelation. If Edward was worried, then the situation might be worse for her than she thought. Surely, he didn't think she'd bashed Grantham on the head and shoved him in the wardrobe without Peregrine realizing what was happening? He said he didn't, but could she believe him? He might think Peregrine was protecting her, and that she had really committed the murder.

The fact that she was sure that Peregrine would protect her, even if he saw her murdering a family friend, made his position as a witness unreliable at best. And Edward would obviously know that. No wonder he looked so somber.

If only Lord Milbourn were striding along next to her instead of Edward. He could be so annoying with his mocking *mi niña bonita*, but in some indefinable way, he strengthened her confidence. He made her feel more sharply intelligent when he was teasing her. A worthy opponent — someone to be taken seriously, not simply dismissed with a smile because she was a woman.

All too soon, they arrived at their destination. The inquest was held in one of the larger rooms of an old hostelry, and the allotted chamber was already stuffy and overflowing with people jostling to get a view of the coroner, the jurymen, and most of all, the body, which rested on a trestle table in the corner, behind a hastily erected curtain tastefully drawn halfway around the corpse. After one swift glance, Olivia kept her head turned away from the pitiful remains of Mr. Charles Grantham.

Mr. Idleman was seated at the head of a large table and seemed impervious to the jostling crowd. He had several sheets of paper on the table in front of him, and he was methodically picking up each sheet and glancing over it before returning it to the pile.

Olivia noted that her statement, written on a sheet of her thick, ivory paper, was one of the documents. A cold trickle of unease slipped down her back when he picked it up and studied it. His thin face gave her no sign of his thoughts.

Edward and Peregrine shouldered their way through the people. Peregrine's wide-shouldered back blocked Olivia's view, but he waved at someone and reached back to pull Olivia forward.

"Milbourn is here. Good to see a familiar face, eh, Ollie?" Peregrine asked.

"Yes." Her trepidation eased, and she smiled at Lord Milbourn.

He nodded in her direction as Edward and Peregrine grabbed several chairs and placed them near Lord Milbourn in the corner on Mr. Idleman's left.

When the coroner saw them, he stood. "Mr. Archer, I presume?"

"Yes." Edward's dark brows rose, surprised at the coroner's decision to address him.

"We borrowed Lady Olivia's key for the investigation." He fished a key out of his pocket and handed it to Edward, ignoring Olivia. He obviously preferred to deal with another man. "I am returning it, with our thanks."

"Very well," Edward said as he accepted the key and held it out to Olivia.

As she accepted it, Mr. Idleman looked briefly at her, nodded, and returned to his chair.

"Glad to see you, Milbourn," Peregrine said, leaning toward him. "My sister has been beside herself with w-worry." He shook Milbourn's hand before sitting down and waving Olivia to the empty chair next to Milbourn.

Olivia flushed as she gazed into Lord Milbourn's somber eyes. "Peregrine exaggerates, but it is good to see you."

"I am happy to hear you say that," he drawled. "I had not thought to see you here, Lady Olivia."

Her cheeks grew even hotter. "I wanted to hear, well...." Her voice trailed off before she swallowed and took a deep breath. "I thought it best to discover in which direction Mr. Greenfield was leaning."

His dark eyes searched her face. "You do realize the inquest only deliberates on the manner of death. The coroner is not responsible for assigning guilt."

"But they will go over what evidence they have, will they not?"

"Yes," he replied gruffly. "I merely hope you are not disappointed. It may have been better if you had not attended."

"Well, I am here now, so that is that." She glanced past Lord Milbourn to the coroner.

Mr. Idleman must have seen her out of the corner of his eye. He glanced up and nodded before separating her statement from his other notes and placing it on his right.

Was that a good sign or bad? Somehow, her fingers found Lord Milbourn's hand. He pressed her fingers warmly, and retained her hand as she studied the coroner. What was Mr. Idleman thinking? She tried to read the stark lines of his profile, but except for his bristling brows and appropriately serious expression, she could obtain no clues. He didn't glance her way again after his initial acknowledgement. After going through his documents, his eyes fixed on the door.

Several men entered, followed by Mr. Belcher. Olivia stared at him in surprise, and he seemed to sense her scrutiny. He smiled at her and flipped his hand up in acknowledgement before making his way over to them. After greeting them, he dragged the last empty chair over to sit next to Edward.

The two of them conversed in low voices, preventing Olivia from hearing them. Apparently Mr. Belcher was satisfying his curiosity about the death of his friend, like all the others thrusting their way into the room. Olivia shifted in her chair in irritation, staring at the worn floorboards and regretting her decision to attend.

Then, to Olivia's surprise, Latimore walked quietly through the door, followed by Olivia's personal maid, Alice Farmer. Farmer had her right hand tucked through Latimore's elbow, and she kept her gaze locked on the floor as they threaded their way to the far edge of the room.

Farmer jerked nervously whenever they came too close to any of the other witnesses or visitors, and her grip on the butler's elbow was so tight that her fingers pleated his black sleeve. Her sharp nose, always tipped with pink, was positively red and twitched as anxiously as a mouse sensing a dangerous cat nearby. She fished a worn and wrinkled handkerchief out of her pocket and dabbed her nose, her gaze flashing around the room.

When she noticed Olivia, her sallow skin paled to an unhealthy gray, making her nose an even deeper crimson. Farmer blinked her watery, hazel eyes several times and crowded against the stolid bulk of Latimore, dropping her gaze to stare at her feet.

Why was she here? Idle curiosity? Farmer was so timorous that Olivia couldn't picture her braving the crowds simply to harvest a few seeds of gossip. The maid's presence seemed to bode ill, though Olivia had no real reason for thinking so.

Curiosity, while annoying, could not hurt her.

She glanced at Latimore and remembered that she was probably responsible for his presence here. She'd told Mr. Greenfield to ask their butler for a list of visitors who could have picked up her note in the days before Mr. Grantham's death. With a jolt, she realized it could have been Mr. Grantham, himself, who had accidentally picked it up, perhaps believing it was a scrap he could use for his own note, or for some other purpose.

Latimore's attendance seemed less ominous than the maid's, although it did bother her that he resolutely refused to glance in her direction. He stared straight ahead at the opposite wall, with the air of a man prepared to stand in one place for hours on end with nothing to do but work through math tables in his head.

Finally, Mr. Greenfield arrived and closed the door softly behind him. Silence washed through the room like a wave clearing footprints off a beach.

Mr. Idleman cleared his throat.

The inquest began. Despite Olivia's strained nerves, as the coroner went through his introductory remarks, she began to have difficulties keeping her eyes open. The room was overcrowded and the temperature inside grew warmer and warmer in defiance of the occasional icy draft. Mr. Idleman's voice droned on in a low alto buzz, identical to a honeybee on a drowsy May morning.

The coroner read her statement, and then Peregrine's, before he called on Constable Cooke to give his account. There was nothing startling in any of it, and the only people who seemed interested were those onlookers who weren't directly involved. Several of the jurymen stifled their yawns behind their hands. One portly soul listed to one side and nodded off. He wore a well-made blue jacket with elegant brass buttons, brown trousers, and a brown and white plaid waistcoat that was stretched to near-popping over his plump belly, and his double chin rested on his barrel chest amidst the nest of his white linen neckcloth.

When he started to snore, Mr. Idleman looked his way and frowned. His jurymen were supposed to be listening and making their own inquiries, not napping. The equally prosperous man next to the sleepy fellow prodded him vigorously in the ribs.

The interruption seemed to convince Mr. Idleman to bring forward his additional witnesses. Perhaps that would banish the somnolence seeping through the room. Latimore was first. He stared at the ceiling, his hands clasped behind his back, and recited from memory a list of visitors to the Archer's townhouse.

Olivia stifled a yawn behind her hand. No one on Latimore's list seemed likely to have stolen the scrap of paper from her desk. They were all friends of her brothers or ladies of her acquaintance. None of them held any particular grudge against the Archers.

There was just no reason for the theft — for any of it.

Latimore's impressive feat of memory seemed to satisfy Mr. Idleman and his jurymen. They couldn't think of any questions, and the coroner called Miss Farmer forward.

Farmer paled to a ghostly white. Her mouth worked soundlessly as she tottered forward, her thin, nervous hands clutching the edges of her shawl and wrapping it more tightly around her thin body.

Mr. Idleman performed the necessary adjurations to speak the truth and introduced her, taking care to identify her as Lady Olivia's personal maid.

"Miss Farmer," Mr. Idleman said. He picked up something small from the table and held it in his hand, although Olivia couldn't see what it was. "You recently gave Mr. Greenfield something of relevance to this case. Please explain to this court what you discovered and where you discovered it."

"W-what?" Eyes wide and glassy, she stared at the coroner, tugging her shawl even more securely around her bowed shoulders.

Mr. Idleman held his hand palm upwards.

Olivia leaned forward, but could not see what he displayed to the maid.

"Is this the item you found?" the coroner asked.

"I don't know. Yes. Maybe." Her voice rose shrilly, and her gaze darted around the room. "Is it the button? I don't know, not for sure."

The coroner glanced at Mr. Greenfield. "Is this the button you received from Miss Farmer?"

"Yes, sir," Mr. Greenfield said with a nod.

"Miss Farmer, where did you find this button?" Mr. Idleman asked the maid, impatience turning his face to granite.

"I cannot say, sir!" Farmer covered her bluish, trembling lips with the shaking fingers of one hand, her other hand still abusing her shawl.

"You told Mr. Greenfield that you found the button caught in the ornamental braid on the cuff of Lady Olivia Archer's pelisse," Mr. Idleman stated. "Did you not do so?"

"I cannot say, sir! I dare not say!" Farmer screeched before her eyes rolled up in her head. She collapsed into a puddle of shawls and skirts on the floor.

Olivia leapt to her feet and ran to her maid. She dragged the unconscious woman's shoulders up to cradle in her arms.

When Peregrine joined her, she said, "The smelling salts — they're in my reticule."

Her brother grabbed the pouch hanging from a ribbon around her wrist and struggled with it for several seconds until he withdrew the small bottle. "Here, Ollie. T-though why you should d-do anything for her is beyond me."

When she looked up, everyone in the room was staring at her avidly, as if waiting for the next grand scene.

She felt like a perfect ogre when she realized they most likely expected her to terminate her maid's employment on the spot. It's what most of them would do if one of their servants provided the authorities with evidence of their misdeeds.

But it was not what she intended to do.

The button wasn't evidence of her misdeeds, because she hadn't done anything.

"She was only doing what she thought was right," Olivia glared at Mr. Greenfield. This was all his fault. He'd forced Farmer to confess and give them the button.

Then her stomach dropped. Farmer had found the button caught in the gold braid around the cuff of Olivia's pelisse. How had it gotten there? She hadn't touched Mr. Grantham after she found him.

But who would believe her?

Farmer coughed and sneezed, wiping her pink nose with her wrinkled, grayish handkerchief as she struggled to sit up.

"Allow me, Lady Olivia," Latimore said as he kneeled beside them. He slipped an arm around Farmer's shoulders and gently raised her to her feet.

With impressive gravity, he addressed the coroner, "If you please, sir, I believe Miss Farmer is suffering from hysteria. If she gave her evidence and statement to Mr. Greenfield already, then perhaps the court would be willing to direct its questions to him and allow her to excuse herself?"

"We would prefer to hear her statement from her own lips. However, as you say, she spoke directly to Mr. Greenfield and handed him the evidence. We may therefore excuse Miss Farmer and hear instead from Mr. Greenfield."

"Thank you, sir," Latimore said.

Farmer sobbed into the handkerchief she pressed against her face as Latimore tightened his arm around her shoulders and guided her to the door.

Brushing the dust off her skirts, Olivia returned to her chair and sank down gratefully. Her limbs felt weak. For one second, she feared that she, too, would faint. Lord Milbourn covered her clasped hands with his warm palm, and she glanced at him in gratitude. He, at least, was on her side. For now, anyway.

When the two of them disappeared, Mr. Greenfield faced the coroner. He cleared his throat, and then said, "When I questioned the servants at the Archer domicile in the execution of my duties, Miss Alice Farmer came to my attention. She is Lady Olivia Archer's personal maid, and I felt it worthwhile to question her in light of what had occurred. Miss Farmer was reluctant to speak, but eventually saw the sense in communicating what she knew concerning the state of Lady Olivia's clothing when she returned home after the discovery of Mr. Grantham's remains."

"And what did she say?" Mr. Idleman prompted impatiently. He fingered the button, rubbing it between his middle finger and his thumb.

"She said there was no blood on any of Lady Olivia's clothing, except for some stains around the hem, and on the soles of her walking shoes."

Mr. Idleman's restless fingers moved over the button more rapidly. "And what of the button?"

"Miss Farmer indicated that she had found a button — that button — caught in the braid around the right cuff of Lady Olivia's pelisse." He paused when the murmur of voices rose to such an excited pitch that the hum drowned his voice.

Mr. Idleman pounded the table with a gavel. "Silence!" He glared around the room until the whispering died. "Continue, Mr. Greenfield."

"She did not recognize the button. It did not appear to come from any of Lady Olivia's garments, so I took the button and compared it to those on the jacket the deceased was wearing at the time of his, em, accident."

"And what was your conclusion, Mr. Greenfield?"

"The third button down from the collar on Mr. Grantham's jacket was missing, sir. The button Miss Farmer handed to me matches the remaining buttons on his jacket."

"Buttons often look alike," Mr. Idleman commented.

Mr. Greenfield nodded. "Indeed, sir. However, these buttons were fairly unique in that they were brass and had the letter G pressed into their centers. The button Miss Farmer found also has the letter G pressed into its center."

The coroner held the button between his index finger and thumb and raised it so all could view the evidence.

A bold G was clearly stamped into the center, with a ridge encircling it.

G for Grantham.

But she hadn't touched him. She gripped Lord Milbourn's hand.

His broad shoulder brushed hers as he leaned toward her. "Steady, *mi niña bonita*. All is not lost, though it be as dark as night," he whispered.

No wonder Edward had been so vehemently against her attending. If she had simply sent her statement, she would not have so many eyes fixed on her, and she would not be in a position to be questioned again. She cast an apologetic glance in his direction.

He caught her gaze and shook his head, giving her a half-smile to show he understood and didn't wish to dwell on her error.

A wave of thankfulness surged through her. He was such a good brother — he rarely held her mistakes over her head. He, at least, didn't seem to blame her.

When she looked at Mr. Idleman, considering what her maid had said, another thought struck her.

Someone is attempting to make me appear guilty of murder.

She was sure she had not touched Mr. Grantham. There was no simple way to explain why the button was caught on the braid of her sleeve, unless someone put it there. And the only conceivable motive for that was to make her appear guilty.

For no logical reason, the image of Cynthia Denholm, insisting on her fencing lesson, arose to mind. No one would dare accuse *her*. They wouldn't dare.

What would the indomitable Cynthia do?

She was still considering the point when Mr. Idleman looked in her direction and said, "Lady Olivia, if you do not mind, we would like to address a few more questions to you."

"You have my statement." She clasped her shaking hands together in her lap. Although she was aware that Lord Milbourn and her brothers were watching her, she kept her attention focused on the coroner.

"Indeed we do, and I thank you for it," he replied politely. "However, as you must have heard, other questions have arisen that must be addressed." He studied several of his jurymen before focusing his hazel eyes upon her.

How could she ever have thought his eyes were soft and kind?

"Lady Olivia, as explained by Mr. Greenfield, a button from Mr. Grantham's coat —"

"A button that *may* have come from Mr. Grantham's coat," Edward interjected.

Olivia flashed her brother a small smile.

"Yes," Mr. Idleman agreed, although his brows pinched together, revealing his irritation. "The question remains, how did this button come to be found caught on your sleeve?"

Olivia looked at him and kept her voice steady when she replied, "I have no notion. I did not touch Mr. Grantham, and I cannot remember having anything caught on my cuff when I returned home."

Mr. Idleman stared at her.

She stared back.

"And the blood on your shoes and hem?" he asked at last.

"That information is in my statement." She smoothed her skirt over her lap. "I did not notice the stain on the floor before I opened the wardrobe."

On reflection, she regretted her cold response, knowing the gentlemen in the room were expecting her to act more like Farmer in the face of such terrible events. She would have done better to have fainted than respond rationally.

She'd have to remember that in the future. If she were accused, well, that would be time enough to meet expectations and become hysterical. The all-male jury would expect it of her and sympathize with her because of what they would consider to be a normal womanly reaction. Her heart lifted briefly. In fact, a male jury might be to her advantage. They'd find it difficult to believe that any woman, particularly a lady, would commit such a violent crime.

It was a bitter, cynical thought, but not without some promise of hope.

"Lady Olivia has supplied a statement that covers matters to the best of her knowledge," Edward said before Mr. Idleman could speak. "I don't believe she has anything more she can contribute at this juncture."

"The button — how do you explain the button?" Mr. Idleman said, a fleck of spittle forming in the corner of his mouth. His hands moved impatiently on the table, pushing the documents forward and back.

Olivia reached across Lord Milbourn to touch her brother's sleeve before he could speak. "I believe that question lies within the boundary of Mr. Greenfield's responsibility. I never saw the button and have no knowledge of when or where my maid apparently found it. For all I know, Farmer found it somewhere and tucked it in her pocket until Mr. Greenfield terrified her into producing it." She tilted her head to one side and studied him. "I would ask, however, how you know *when* Mr. Grantham lost his button? If it is his, of course."

"A drop of dried blood marred its surface, my lady," Mr. Idleman replied.

"I am only speculating, of course, but might he have had a nosebleed? Did you examine his handkerchief?"

The coroner and Mr. Greenfield exchanged glances.

Mr. Greenfield shrugged and said, "It was stained. As to when that happened, we do not know."

"Then we appear to know very little about that button, or the circumstances surrounding its presence in my wardrobe," Olivia pointed out gently.

Mr. Idleman cleared his throat and poked at the papers in front of him again with his index finger before looking at Olivia. "I would like to return to the question of your maid, Miss Alice Farmer, and your statement concerning her discovery." His gaze wavered, and he cleared his throat again. "Am I to understand that you believe your maid had something to do with Mr. Grantham's death?" Mr. Idleman asked, his brows rising almost to his hairline.

"I have no notion of where you obtained that ridiculous idea. I am not saying anything of the sort. If you are referring to my previous comment, I was merely trying to explain that I have no knowledge of that button." Her hands clasped more tightly together. "And that should cover the matter sufficiently."

Her reply might not have been quite as forceful as Cynthia's might under the circumstance, but she could see by the nonplussed expression on Mr. Idleman's face that she had left him no choice but to proceed along other lines of inquiry. He shuffled through the papers in front of him and then picked up her statement, only to replace it on the table.

Olivia stood. She didn't look at either of her brothers, although she was aware of a flurry of activity on either side of her. "If that is all, I shall be leaving." She stared at Mr. Idleman.

His mouth opened, then closed again. He glanced from her to Edward and Peregrine. "The inquest is not over, Lady Olivia."

"I have written a full statement and told you everything I know," she replied gently. "Have you any other questions with which I could assist?"

Mr. Idleman looked around the room, his face flushing a dull red. "Questions? No, Lady Olivia. And I wish to thank you for your cooperation. There are no other questions at this time."

Mr. Greenfield jerked and glanced at her, clearly startled at this decision. But he didn't comment. His patience, and the confidence in his gaze, suggested that he expected there to be plenty of time in the future to fix the noose around her neck.

Assuming he could make his case sufficiently strong to convince a male jury.

For the first time in her life, she was relieved to be a lady.

She smiled and nodded graciously in his direction. She was not going to accept their conclusion, no matter what it was. She was going to fight to prove her innocence and discover precisely who had murdered Mr. Grantham.

And why.

Chapter Twelve

As Alexander expected, the coroner's verdict was unlawful killing by person or persons unknown. His failure to name a suspect meant he could escape from the political fire that might be lit were he to name the sister of an earl as the possible murderer. The decision also encouraged Mr. Greenfield and Constable Cooke to continue their investigation and uncover enough evidence to eliminate all reasonable doubt.

Unfortunately, in addition to the button, Greenfield had revealed other troubling facts, as well, after Lady Olivia departed. The inquiry agent had searched Grantham's rooms and discovered a journal.

"Well, what do you think?" Belcher asked as they wandered outside into the cold, fresh air.

"An interesting case," Alexander answered absently, searching the throng of departing men. Spotting Edward Archer, he hailed him.

"Lord Milbourn. Belcher." Archer waited for them to catch up to him. He seemed to be in a somber, thoughtful mood as he turned and began walking toward the Archer terrace. Archer's fascination with British jurisprudence meant he understood the implications of the inquest and subsequent inquiries better than any of them. And his subdued mood indicated he knew what the evidence they'd heard might mean for his sister.

No wonder a small knot of worry had formed over the bridge of Archer's nose.

"Well, that was certainly interesting," Belcher said. His blue eyes flashed with curiosity as he glanced from Alexander to Archer. "That Greenfield chap seems to know his business, doesn't he?"

The wrinkled knot between Archer's brows grew more pronounced, but he didn't answer. His pace increased.

Alexander grunted. Greenfield might be intelligent, but was he smart enough to continue his inquiries, or had he already made up his mind?

"What about that journal, eh?" Belcher chuckled. "I expect old Grantham had plenty to say about all of us. I don't fancy that Greenfield chap reading about my youthful peccadillos, eh?" He laughed and nudged Alexander with his elbow. "Don't suppose you will be any happier, either, Milbourn."

"I don't suppose Greenfield will be any happier reading it," Alexander said dryly. "Assuming Grantham even mentioned us, except in passing."

"Of course, you are correct, Milbourn," Belcher said, looking from Alexander to Archer.

Alexander shrugged, aware of the tension building in Belcher. The man had always hated silence and would rattle on forever, just to hear the sound of a voice. Which wasn't necessarily bad, except that he was also one of those cheerful, optimistic sorts one invariably ended up wanting to strangle.

Well, perhaps Belcher did have his uses. He might be as irritating as a flea under the collar, but he'd work himself into a lather to cheer one up, and right now, Archer seemed to need that.

Noting that Archer had strode on ahead, Alexander lengthened his stride to catch up to him, knowing Belcher would follow suit.

Alexander caught Belcher's gaze and gave a sharp nod in Archer's direction.

"Say, Archer, old chap, join me at the club? I could use a spot of brandy, eh? Join me?" Belcher hurried forward and slapped Archer on the shoulder.

As Archer glanced at him, his scowl deepened. He shook his head and hurried forward, his eyes fixed on his destination one block away.

Belcher looked at Alexander, raised his hands, palms upwards, and shrugged. He'd done his best. Clearly, Archer was not amenable to distractions.

When Archer opened the black wrought iron gate in front of his house, Alexander paused. He needed time alone to consider what he had learned at the inquest, and he suspected Archer felt the same way.

Alexander particularly wanted to consider the fact that Grantham had been unwise enough to keep a journal and had left it where Constable Cooke could find it.

What did it contain? Was there anything in it that would stir up a new storm of gossip, should the authorities unwisely reveal the contents? His thoughts left him with a cold sensation caressing his neck like the lips of an ancient ghost.

Belcher might be amused to think about the adventures of his youth, but Alexander had a darker past he had no wish to bring forth into the light.

He rubbed the back of his neck. He ought to return to his own house and think. Speak to Greenfield and Cooke. Instead, he followed Belcher and Archer up the shallow steps and into the large house.

Latimore accepted their gloves, hats, and coats, his face carefully expressionless as he solemnly intoned the words, "Lady Olivia is in the Ivory Drawing Room, sir."

Without a word, Archer mounted the staircase. Belcher and Alexander glanced at each other and followed.

"Edward!" Lady Olivia rose from her chair by the fire and turned toward the door, her right hand pressed against the base of her neck. Her skin was pale, and she appeared exhausted with worry, her eyes circled with heavy shadows. "What happened?"

Archer shrugged and walked to the chair opposite her. When he saw Belcher and Alexander, he waved to a nearby couch. "Please, be seated."

Lady Olivia glanced at them, nodded, and also gestured at the couch. Then she sank down onto the edge of her own chair as if her limbs could no longer support her. She clasped her trembling hands in her lap. "What is it? What was the verdict?"

"It was a coroner's inquest, Lady Olivia," Archer said. "The verdict was much as you would expect: unlawful killing by person or persons unknown."

133

She pressed her fingers to her lips for a second and took a deep breath. "They did not mention anyone, then? A suspect?"

"That is not the purpose of such an inquest," Archer said gruffly. He shifted in his chair and leaned forward to rub his hands together. "Only the manner of death is important at this juncture, and Mr. Greenfield will continue his inquiry."

"What else?" She gazed at each of them in turn. "They must have said more — you were a long time in returning."

"Greenfield mentioned a journal." Archer raised a hand to keep her from speaking. "They did not divulge any contents. Presumably, they have not had time to inquire into whatever Grantham wrote about on its pages."

"God alone knows what old Grantham would decide to scribble." Belcher gave a low chuckle. "I hope he did not include that time I —" he halted abruptly with a glance at Lady Olivia. "Well, I'm sure he could have included any one of a number of embarrassing incidents from our youths."

"You don't think they will publish it, do you?" Lady Olivia appeared aghast at the thought. Her skin paled even more, and her hand rose once again to press protectively against her slender throat.

"I would hope Greenfield would not be so irresponsible," Archer said. But his slow voice indicated he didn't have much confidence in the inquiry agent's discretion. He rubbed the side of his chin as he stared moodily at the fire.

Alexander studied him. He had the impression that Archer knew something not revealed during the inquest, and the information worried him. However, he also appeared reluctant to share his thoughts.

"I don't expect any of our families would appreciate the notoriety." Belcher nodded. He leaned forward to rest his elbows on his knees, clasp his hands, and stare at the golden flames. Suddenly, he straightened, smiled, and looked at Alexander. "Speaking of families; how is your daughter, Milbourn? Should have asked sooner, but this business...." He shrugged, his brows raised, and his blue eyes fixed on Alexander's face.

Alexander stilled. Out of the corner of his eye, he saw Lady Olivia stiffen.

She sucked in a quick, small breath. The rush of air was so slight it was barely audible, but it sounded like a low scream of pain to him. She sat so rigidly, with such pale skin, that she looked like a statue carved out of marble and labeled, *Lady in Shock.*

With more to follow.

"Maria is well," he said.

"Haven't seen her in months. Off to school, is she?" Belcher asked with a polite smile.

"Maria has been in Barcelona. With her grandmother." Alexander gazed at Lady Olivia, but she looked away, staring down at the fire, her face a polite mask.

Perhaps it was for the best that she knew the truth at last. She was engaged, after all, even if her choice of husband was ludicrous. So it could hardly matter to her that he'd been married and had a child. But at that moment, he could have run a sword through Belcher's cheerfully imbecilic heart.

"Delightful," Belcher said. "Travel is so educational. Do the girl a world of good, I'd say."

"No doubt," Alexander replied in a dry voice.

He had no doubt that his fiery daughter found that traveling with a dour, elderly Spanish woman little more than a terrible inconvenience and a bore, but her grandmother wished to see her. What Alexander's mother wished for, she inevitably got. One way or the other.

Belcher suddenly chuckled. "Travel, eh — that reminds me of that little trip the four of us — you, me, Wraysbury, and Grantham — took to Paris." He laughed again, his eyes flashing with amusement. "Don't you remember?" He shook his head. "If old Grantham saw fit to describe that in his little notebook, well, I don't suppose Wraysbury's new wife would enjoy hearing about that one little bit."

Belcher glanced up to find Archer studying him. Anger tightened Archer's mouth into a thin line, and he gripped the arms of his chair as if to prevent himself from leaping up and beating Belcher senseless.

Belcher looked around hastily as if suddenly remembering Lady Olivia's presence. He blanched and blurted out, "Enough of that, eh? The past is past. Well, I suppose that is that, then." Belcher straightened and rubbed his palms against his thighs. "Sure you won't join me at my club, Archer?"

"No. Not today." Archer seemed to shake himself and become aware of his duties as host. He glanced at his sister, but she remained as still as a statue, staring at the fire. "If you would care for a restorative? Claret, perhaps? Or sherry?"

Belcher stood. "Nothing for me. I'm off to the club, then. Milbourn? Join me?"

"I must leave as well." He stood, still studying Lady Olivia.

She seemed oblivious to their conversation. Her delicate hands clasped together so tightly in her lap that the knuckles stood out like white pebbles against the beach of her blue dress.

"Lady Olivia!" Archer rose as well and held out his hand. "Our guests are departing."

"Not guests, surely," Belcher chuckled. "Friends, my dear chap. Next thing to family, I daresay."

Lady Olivia rose slowly and looked at them. "Thank you for coming. It was very thoughtful of you." Her low voice sounded mechanical.

"Of course, of course," Belcher replied with a bow. "At your service, dear lady. Least we could do."

"Good day." Alexander bowed. There was really nothing else to say.

He studied Lady Olivia's face, but she refused to look at him, although she did give a stiff nod acknowledging his *adieu*. Despite her pallor and air of coldness, she remained a beautiful, unattainable figure, tantalizing and yet forever out of reach.

Well, there was something more he could do for her. He could find out who was behind Grantham's death and keep Lady Olivia safe. Even if it was just to watch her marry her wildly inappropriate, useless betrothed.

Chapter Thirteen

*H*e is married and has a child.

Olivia's thoughts whirled like dead, brown leaves in a storm. Or he was married — no matter which. What a fool she'd been, pining for him all these years. His amused indifference should have warned her, but she'd been heedless and determined to have her own way.

Although she loved fencing and wanted to share the excitement of the sport with other ladies, she realized now that a small part of her clung to another hope. Her academy represented a last, desperate effort to draw Lord Milbourn's attention, make him admire her — want her — before it was too late. Panic shivered through her, turning her hands to ice. In a few months, she'd be sewn firmly and inescapably in place as Lord Saunders's bride.

Too late. It seemed it had always been too late for her.

He had a daughter…Maria. Was she dark and sardonic like her father? Or did she take after the unknown mother? She'd probably been beautiful, perhaps Spanish like his own mother had been, with lovely dark eyes and rich black hair. Knowing her handsome father, Olivia couldn't help but believe the little girl would be a beauty.

She sighed with frustration and longing. She'd always wanted a little girl, a child to dress in ribbons and bows, someone who would shriek with joy and clap her hands when the beagles clattered into the room, upsetting the tea things and making a wild, wonderful mess of the sitting room. They could gossip, go visiting other ladies, and stop for sweets at Gunter's.

Suddenly, she felt abandoned and lost on a dark path she didn't want to tread.

Dimly, she was aware that Lord Milbourn and Mr. Belcher were taking leave of them, but it hardly seemed to matter. She nodded, unable to make her stiff lips form any words except rote platitudes.

Then they were gone.

"Lady Olivia!" Edward said in an abrupt, exasperated voice.

She had the impression that he'd already repeated her name several times, and she flushed. "What is it, Edward?"

"What are your plans regarding Alice Farmer?"

"Farmer?" She regarded him with surprise. "I don't plan to do anything with Farmer. Why?"

"She ought to be dismissed. You can hardly consider her loyal at this point."

"She was honest and did what was right. By your measure, we should dismiss Latimore, as well. He might at least have warned me." She pulled her chair closer to the fire and sat again, a shiver going through her. "Would you ring for tea?" She rubbed her arms. "Please?"

Edward scowled at her and grunted, before striding over to the bell pull. "Latimore has been with us for thirty years."

"I hardly think that excuses him," she said gently. She should have gone to her bedchamber for a shawl. The cheerful fire didn't seem as warm as it had earlier, even when she held her hands out toward it. "I am sure he did what he thought was right, under the circumstances."

"Then you may apply that same logic to Farmer." She sighed. "What is done, is done. Farmer found the button and gave it to Mr. Greenfield. We can do nothing about that now, and dismissing Farmer will not change matters." She smiled ruefully. "In fact, it will only make things worse as I shall be without a personal maid to help me dress. And so will Margaret and Hildie. We all use her services."

"Then get another maid."

Another maid, Mary, arrived at that moment, breathless and flushed. When she paused in the doorway, Edward said, "Tea. And make sure it is hot."

"Yes, sir." Mary sketched a quick curtsey and dashed off again.

Edward eyed Olivia, and although she'd hoped he had forgotten the topic of their conversation, it appeared he had not. "As I said, you may hire another maid. They cannot be that scarce. Not like trying to find a decent cook, after all."

"Apparently, Gray was at least partially correct: ignorance *is* bliss — I was a great deal happier before I learned about that wretched button." She rubbed her forehead again, thinking of Farmer's skill in creating hot possets that could vanquish even the worst headache. "And while I dislike disagreeing with you, I have to say that while good cooks may be hard to find, a competent personal maid is harder still. So please leave poor Farmer alone. You saw her — she was terrified at the inquest. She did not want to be there. Frankly, I would not be at all surprised if Greenfield forced both the button and a confession out of her."

"You are a trifle overly solicitous, my dear sister, but perhaps you are right." Edward sighed. "It shoves you into a devilishly tight corner, however. I don't like the situation."

"I cannot claim to be overcome with joy, either." She shook her head. "And I don't understand — why did you not mention Mr. Underwood? I told you that he was near the academy, and I thought I heard him mention a journal when he spoke to you. Was he not concerned about Mr. Grantham's diary?"

"Yes. However, I doubt it is relevant," he replied harshly.

"Very well," she said, hurt by the thought that her brother cared more for Mr. Underwood than for her. She looked up at Edward, smiled wryly, and changed the subject. "We Archers seem to be a rum lot, do we not? First Wraysbury was involved with that murder, and now this. I have never heard of a family dogged by such dreadful misfortunes before. Perhaps it is just as well that you studied law." Her smile broadened in an attempt to treat the matter lightly. "I should have listened to you sooner and not gone to the inquest."

"It would not have made any discernable difference." He clasped his hands behind his back as he paced back and forth in front of the door. "However, in the future, perhaps you should consider my recommendations before taking any action."

"I will." She bowed her head meekly to avoid letting him see her struggles to suppress her laughter.

He sounded so much like a lawyer, that it was difficult to maintain a suitably serious expression.

His next statement, however, instantly sobered her. "I wish you were safely married. Perhaps we should discuss moving up the wedding date with Lord Saunders."

"Married?" Her question rose shrilly. "How would marriage help me?"

Before Edward could answer, Mary returned to the room, huffing and flushed. She carried a huge wooden tray, laden with an array of cups, saucers, pots, plates, and silverware. The gold-rimmed china dishes clinked and clattered when she stumbled over the doorjamb, and Edward hastily took the tray from her and set it on the low table in front of Olivia.

"Miss Denholm," Mary gasped, standing sideways at the door. She glanced through it to the hallway. "And Mr. Underwood for Mr. Archer. I brung extra tea things, Lady Olivia."

"Thank you, Mary." Olivia stood as Cynthia Denholm strode briskly into the room.

"Getting to be a habit, Lady Olivia. Ramshackle way to run an academy, if you ask me," Cynthia said as she walked over to the low table, studied the tea tray, selected a slice of cake, and took a large bite. "Good cake. Who is your cook?"

"Our cook is none of your business," Olivia snapped without thinking.

Edward looked shocked. His gaze flickered from Olivia to Cynthia and back.

"I beg your pardon," Olivia said in a calmer voice.

"Not necessary — no offense taken, Lady Olivia. Good cooks are like pearls in oysters. Someone else always finds them." She threw her head back and laughed heartily at her joke before picking up another slice of pound cake.

"Would you care for some tea?" Olivia asked, gesturing to the seat across from her.

"Delightful to see you, Miss Denholm," Edward said. "However, I must ask you ladies to excuse me. Mr. Underwood is waiting. And we have an appointment — at the club — I really must go."

Cynthia's mouth was full, so she waved him off.

As Edward walked briskly through the door, Olivia pressed her hand to her mouth to keep from laughing. She couldn't help remembering one particular summer evening when Edward had courteously offered to show Cynthia the rose garden at their country estate. Olivia didn't know what they'd discussed or what her brother had said to Cynthia, but upon their return to the garden terrace, Cynthia had grabbed Edward's chin and forced a kiss upon his mouth.

"Wondered about that," Cynthia uttered cryptically before joining Olivia.

He'd never quite gotten over the shock, and Olivia knew for a fact that he had even begged Wraysbury's advice on whether he now had to make an offer for the dreadful woman. What Wraysbury had said remained a mystery, but Edward always grew grim whenever Cynthia's name cropped up in the conversation.

Olivia suspected that Cynthia saw the whole episode as a frightfully good joke, because her eyes sparkled with amusement every time Edward edged out of the room whenever she sailed through the door.

As she turned back to face Cynthia, two thoughts surprised her.

She truly *wanted* the fencing academy to be a success. She adored fencing, regardless of Lord Milbourn's opinion that she wasn't particularly gifted at the art, and even if she never saw him again, she desperately wanted to continue. Nothing could match the challenge and breathless exhilaration of a fight, and she couldn't give it up.

However, she would miss him. He'd provided at least some of the impetus to drive her to strive for more, to do better, to excel. Her stomach burned at the thought of the hole it would leave in her life if she lost his friendship and support.

Marriage to Lord Saunders would never fill that void. Their future together stretched out in front of her, filled with gray, dreary years.

But there were worse things, she supposed, even if she couldn't think of any.

She studied Cynthia. She wanted her other friends to share her pleasure in the art and science of fencing, and Cynthia had certainly felt something that first day. Her blue eyes had gleamed with the thrill of the experience.

To become an expert, teach someone else.

Olivia's mother had told her that so many times that she could still hear her mother's voice echoing in her mind. She'd taught Olivia to sew and then stepped aside to watch Olivia teach Margaret. Then Margaret taught Hildie. Poor Hildie had been relegated to teaching one of the younger kitchen maids to sew, but she'd done it.

If Olivia wanted to become proficient, teaching others was the best way to do so.

Perhaps Cynthia was doing her more of a favor than she knew.

Cynthia poked through the pots, rattling dishes, and throwing ingredients together before pouring herself a cup of milky tea. She slurped it down and looked at Olivia. "Excellent tea! Are you ready, then? The other ladies are waiting for us at the academy."

Olivia's head jerked up. Her mouth hanging open, she stared at her. "Ladies? What ladies?"

"The other students, I presume." Cynthia shrugged.

"How many are there?" Olivia asked in a strangled voice.

"Three when I left. Could be more now, of course." She eyed Olivia and strode toward the door with a brisk air. "Well, are you ready?"

"I — well, yes."

The explanation for the sudden influx of students had to be the effect of the inquest. The ladies were eager to hear the details and gossip about it, while experiencing the vicarious excitement of having fencing lessons at the very location where two corpses had been discovered.

Perhaps they even hoped for a private tour to see the stained floor, conducted by the presumed murderess, herself.

How ghastly. But their morbid curiosity is my advantage. A frisson of excitement shook her.

Regardless of their motives, she now had pupils, and she intended to make the most of the opportunity. Once the ladies tasted the excitement of the sport, they would become serious students of the art — Cynthia had already felt the thrill coursing through her veins. And Olivia would soon have friends who understood and shared her enthusiasm.

Olivia had just reached the door when she nearly ran into Latimore.

"Lord Saunders, Lady Olivia," he intoned sonorously, his impressive nose tilted toward the gilded crown molding.

Lord Saunders stepped out from behind the butler. He glanced from Olivia to Cynthia and frowned.

"Lord Saunders, how pleasant to see you," Olivia said. "You know Miss Denholm, I believe."

The two nodded and examined at each other like a pair of pugilists taking the measure of their opponent.

Oh, no, not another scene. The two didn't get along, and Olivia glanced from one to the other, unprepared to play the role of diplomat.

"I'm sorry, Lord Saunders," Olivia said. "We were just on our way to the academy."

"The academy? Now?" Lord Saunders's pale brown eyebrows rose toward his receding hairline. "The inquest is barely over. Surely, common decency should prevent you from indulging in such scandalous behavior at such a time."

As if hearing their voices, Margaret appeared at Lord Saunders's shoulder. She touched his arm and nodded. "Indeed, my dear sister. Common decency. Mr. Grantham was our dear friend. I don't see how you can even consider going to the academy at a time like this."

Lord Saunders smiled at Margaret.

She squeezed his forearm as she returned his smile.

Olivia felt ill with irritation.

"I have never heard such nonsense in my life," Cynthia declared, resting her hands on her broad hips. "You are not going to listen to such a pudding-headed sapskull, are you?" She eyed Olivia. "I wouldn't. I wouldn't recommend you to, either."

Two red splotches burned over Lord Saunders's plump cheekbones. He straightened and said, "I do not see that Lady Olivia is in need of your counsel, young lady, and I will thank you to keep your comments to yourself."

Margaret beamed at him. "You are so *forceful*, Lord Saunders," she murmured.

Lord Saunders lifted his chin and stared at Olivia.

"Well, Lady Olivia?" Cynthia fixed her gaze on Olivia, as well.

Before Olivia could answer, Lord Saunders added, "If you continue with this outrageous behavior, I am afraid—"

Cynthia snorted. "I can well believe *that!*"

"I am afraid," Lord Saunders repeated in a louder voice, "that I shall have to reconsider matters."

"Matters?" Olivia could barely speak. Ice encased her limbs and even her lips resisted her efforts to open them.

He cannot mean that — this cannot happen — not now, not when I need someone — anyone — to believe in me — trust me!

Lord Saunders gave one, tight nod. "With regards to our future union." His mouth tightened into a frown. "You do not seem to view me, or my opinions, with the proper respect."

"You are so right, Lord Saunders," Margaret agreed. "I have noticed it myself and have been quite appalled by my sister's disregard for any normal feelings or *common decency*," she repeated Lord Saunders's phrase with evident satisfaction.

He patted Margaret's fingers, which still clung to his forearm.

Olivia finally opened her mouth to speak, but her whirling thoughts refused to settle on a reply. In the distance, she heard the cheerful howl of her dogs, followed by the clatter of their toenails on the floor.

The beagles were coming. Her thoughts fled.

"Well, Lady Olivia," Cynthia said. "Answer the ninnyhammer. What is it to be? I cannot wait all day for my second lesson, and the ladies are waiting."

Olivia's gaze jerked from Cynthia to Lord Saunders to Margaret before landing on Latimore.

The butler appeared to be aware of the oncoming situation. His head was lifted and tilted toward the stairwell, clearly listening to the impending arrival of the next disaster.

"The dogs, Latimore. They have gotten loose again," Olivia said at last.

"Very good, Lady Olivia." Latimore left. Hopefully, he would apprehend the animals before they managed to make a terrible situation worse.

She rubbed her temple. What she really needed was one of Farmer's hot possets and a few minutes of silence.

If only Lord Saunders could be blamed for Mr. Grantham's murder.

Horrified at the thought, she straightened and smiled apologetically at him. "I am sorry, Lord Saunders. I have no desire to offend you or anyone, but I am going to the academy. You must, of course, do what you think is best."

Margaret, who had been staring down at the floor, seemed to choke. She quickly pressed her fingers to her mouth to suppress the peculiar sound. When she glanced up, Olivia caught her gaze and suffered a dizzying sensation of shock. Margaret's blue eyes were brilliant with gleeful triumph, and she was clearly biting the inside of her mouth to keep from smiling. Her right hand clasped Lord Saunders's sleeve tightly, and she'd wrapped her left arm around her own waist.

Her feet shifted in sharp movements as if she were dancing a very small jig within the restrictive circle of her gown's hem. As Olivia watched, Margaret made a series of peculiar noises and swallows.

She was *glad* to see Olivia's engagement crumble and was trying not to giggle.

How could she? Olivia stared at her, bewildered by the flushed pleasure in her sister's face.

"Good decision. No one could blame you, Lady Olivia. What I can't understand is how you came to accept such a ninny to begin with," Cynthia said. "Now I suggest we leave while you still have students left to teach."

"Of course." Olivia let her friend drag her down the stairs and out of the door, all the while wondering what had happened and what important fact she had missed.

En Garde, My Love

Chapter Fourteen

A block away from the fencing academy, Alexander saw Greenfield rounding the corner.

"Is that not Greenfield?" Belcher asked, gesturing toward the soberly dressed inquiry agent. Despite his professed intention to go to his club and drink as much as possible, Belcher remained at Alexander's side, almost as if he didn't want to be alone.

Well, he'd always been a social beast and preferred crowds to solitary enjoyments. In fact, Alexander had never seen him so much as pick up a book or even a newspaper. No such private interests plagued Belcher.

Alexander nodded and swallowed an impatient sigh.

"Perhaps he has discovered something new. Let us join him." Belcher picked up the pace and dashed across the street without the least concern for the passing carriages.

One team of horses, jerked back by the driver of a small cabriolet, neighed and danced over the curb to nearly trample the pedestrians on the walkway. The driver swore vociferously and shook a meaty hand in Belcher's direction.

Belcher laughed and shrugged.

After ascertaining that no one had been injured, Alexander hurried after Belcher. He wanted time to think, but more than that, he needed to know what progress Greenfield was making. If any.

Seeing him leaving the vicinity of the academy seemed hopeful, however. If he had already decided that he had enough evidence to convict Lady Olivia, he wouldn't have bothered to continue the search. Some doubt had to remain in his mind.

"Greenfield!" Belcher hailed the officer.

Greenfield paused at the corner and turned, an expression of polite inquiry on his face. "Mr. Belcher." When he caught sight of Alexander, he added, "Lord Milbourn."

"Still investigating?" Belcher asked, slapping Greenfield on the shoulder as he chuckled heartily.

Greenfield studied him briefly. "There are still questions to be answered, sir."

"Questions? You seemed fairly sure at the inquest," Belcher said. His fair eyebrows rose. "The button and all that nonsense."

"Not sure enough to name the responsible party," Greenfield reminded him gently. "Questions do remain."

Belcher glanced at Alexander and shrugged expressively, his brows rising higher still as if he were unable to conceive of any nails that had not been pounded firmly into the lid of Lady Olivia's coffin.

"Motive?" Alexander suggested.

Greenfield's gaze cut to him. "Motive, indeed."

"It seemed obvious enough to me," Belcher said.

"Obvious?" Greenfield asked, leaving the brief question hanging like a carrot in front of a donkey.

Belcher raised his hands, palms up, and took the bait. "Well, surely — an argument — clearly an accident committed in the heat of the moment. Lady — that is, any lady might panic if she were alone with a man who became too insistent."

"And the housekeeper?" Alexander asked, impatient with Belcher's easy explanation.

"Coincidence? Burglar? Must the two deaths be related?" Belcher shrugged.

"That is another question, indeed, sir," Greenfield said. He glanced around the busy street and edged closer to the curb.

A gap in the traffic presented itself, and Greenfield walked briskly across the street, followed closely by Belcher and Alexander.

"Where are you heading?" Belcher asked, undaunted by the officer's determined air and brisk pace.

The second of silence preceding Greenfield's reply spoke volumes about his annoyance at Belcher's persistence, but he answered calmly enough, "I wish to speak to Mr. Archer."

"Archer?" Belcher frowned.

"Mr. Edward Archer," Greenfield clarified.

"Surely, he is not implicated! Why, he never set foot near his sister's academy, did he? And surely he would not allow suspicion to fall upon Lady Olivia, if he were involved," Belcher said.

Grantham's journal. Belcher's words reminded Alexander of that awkward piece of evidence. Just what tales had he told within its pages?

Greenfield shrugged and hurried faster.

"Well, I, for one, believe you are following the wrong trail, Mr. Greenfield," Belcher said. He glanced at Alexander and winked. "Perhaps we can assist you?"

"Assistance is always appreciated, sir," Greenfield replied.

Alexander had to admire the man's self-control. There was only the slightest edge to his voice, revealing his irritation. Alexander almost pulled Belcher back to suggest he go to his club as planned, but he resisted the impulse. If he continued to annoy Greenfield, the inquiry agent might let something slip.

An amazingly obliging Belcher threw more questions at Greenfield, most of them so ridiculous that Alexander had to work hard to suppress his laughter. Not even an exasperated sigh escaped from Greenfield. However, as they approached the Archer's townhouse, his brief answers disintegrated into ambiguous grunts. Not that Belcher noticed. He just kept babbling on like a merry little brook.

"Here we are, sir," Greenfield said, his hand on the wrought-iron gate in front of the elegant terrace. "If you will excuse me, my lord?"

Both Belcher and Greenfield looked at Alexander.

He ignored the faint plea in Greenfield's eyes. "We will come in with you, Greenfield."

"That is not necessary. I'm sure you gentlemen have more important matters to attend to."

"Nothing more important than a large glass of brandy at the club." Belcher laughed and slapped Greenfield on the shoulder again.

Greenfield winced, sighed, and opened the gate.

A few minutes later, Latimore escorted the three of them into the library at the rear of the house. Edward Archer was seated, quill in hand, at a large mahogany desk near the windows at the rear of the room. He glanced up when Latimore announced them, signed the document in front of him, and placed the quill in a brass holder on his right.

"You two did not get very far," he said as he rose and leaned across his desk to shake their hands. While his expression was polite enough as he gestured for them to sit in the chairs in front of the desk, his eyes were slightly narrowed and tight at the corners with annoyance.

"Ran into this fine fellow." Belcher slapped Greenfield on the shoulder yet again before flopping down in one of the chairs. He stretched out his long legs, crossed his ankles, and grinned.

"Lord Milbourn?" Archer frowned at him as if he'd expected Alexander to show a trifle more consideration about returning so soon with Belcher.

"We were concerned, Archer," Alexander said mildly. He took the seat on the end, leaving Greenfield to either stand or sit in the chair in the middle.

Greenfield moved behind the chair and rested his hands on its back. "I apologize for the interruption, sir, but I have a few questions." He paused for a second before adding, "Perhaps you would prefer to speak in private?"

Archer caught Alexander's gaze and let out a long breath. He looked down at the top of his desk with a frown and pushed the top sheet of paper an inch to the right with his forefinger. Then he picked the papers up, tapped their bottom edges against the blotter to align the sheets, and set the pile on the left corner of his desk.

"We are old friends. I don't know what you could possibly ask that they do not already know." He sat heavily and folded his hands on the brown blotter in front of him. "Proceed."

"Very well, sir." Greenfield didn't look pleased with Archer's response, but he drew out a small notebook and pencil. He flipped the book open to a blank page and looked at Archer. "We have Mr. Grantham's journal, sir, and several other papers."

"Yes. You mentioned those at the inquest. What of them?" Archer's clasped hands tightened.

"His finances were of some interest, sir," Greenfield replied with a hint of chiding underlying his quiet tones. He glanced at first at Alexander and then at Belcher. "Perhaps one of you gentlemen knows the source of his income?"

"Why the devil should we know that?" Archer asked. "He had some source, obviously. Family money or some sort of an estate. He went to Oxford, for God's sake." He ran a hand through his dark hair, making some of the thick curls stand up like storm-darkened waves. "He always seemed well-off. Comfortable." He glanced at Alexander with raised brows. "He paid his wagers, did he not? Milbourn won enough of them — he certainly ought to be able to confirm that."

Alexander nodded and leaned back, bringing his right foot up to rest the ankle on his opposite knee. "He certainly never complained when he paid what he owed. He was never a poor loser, no many how many times he lost." A lopsided grin twisted his mouth as he tapped his fingers on his right ankle.

Greenfield cleared his throat. "He did not inherit a large estate, sir. As far as can be determined."

"Investments. Other holdings." Archer shrugged and lightly rapped his knuckles against the leather blotter. "One doesn't question one's friends about their finances, sir." He rapped twice, harder. "He was more Wraysbury's friend than mine." He glanced at Greenfield, his eyes glittering with sardonic amusement over the thought of the inquiry agent attempting to question an earl.

Greenfield would be fortunate if he was even permitted in the servants' entrance to the earl's mansion, much less allowed into his presence. If anyone questioned him, it would be the House of Lords, as part of the murder inquiry. Assuming it got that far.

"Though I doubt Wraysbury knows any more about Grantham's estate than I do," Archer added, before clasping his hands together on top of the desk. The gesture politely suggested that their interview was over.

"Why the interest in Grantham's finances?" Belcher asked, oblivious to the air of finality settling around Archer's rigid shoulders.

"He opened an account recently and initiated some investments," Greenfield replied slowly. Reluctance to reveal the details of the case was evident in the thinning of his mouth and the way his gaze drifted from one piece of furniture to another, avoiding catching the gaze of the other men in the room.

"What of it?" Belcher laughed and slapped his knee. "Must have won a few bets for a change. Good for him." His laughter turned into low chuckles. "And excellent for his heirs, of course."

Alexander listened and stared at the beveled edge of Archer's desk, perfectly aware of where Greenfield was so delicately and expertly leading them. He took a deep breath and looked at the inquiry agent. "You seem to be suggesting something more than luck at wagering, Mr. Greenfield."

"What?" Belcher straightened and with raised brows and wide eyes, he looked at Alexander and then Greenfield. "Are you suggesting he was blackmailing Lady Olivia?"

Greenfield tilted his head to the left and gazed at Belcher with an expression of mild curiosity. "What makes you suggest Lady Olivia?"

"Well, she — that is — you realize, well, I honestly don't know. I was just — never mind me." Belcher threw up his hands and shook his head. "I don't know what I am saying."

"Have you found evidence of blackmail, Mr. Greenfield?" Alexander asked when Belcher's babbling trailed off.

"There were some notes," Greenfield said slowly, as if cautiously measuring each word. "In the back of his journal." A brief smile flitted across his face. "Somewhat cryptic as they were written in the form of initials, dates, and amounts. And there were other letters...."

Belcher snorted. "Wagers."

"I have to say, Mr. Greenfield, that if Grantham were engaged in blackmail, he would find my brother, the earl, a difficult nut to crack." Archer smiled grimly. "As are all the Archers. You cannot have a loose screw like our cousin John Archer in the family without adopting a somewhat callous attitude toward public opinion." His grin twisted.

"And the fact that my sister, Lady Olivia, is engaged in founding a fencing academy for ladies, should indicate to you what *she* thinks of Polite Society's opinion." He flashed a quick, considering glance at Belcher, before he focused on Greenfield again. "And she is not here at the moment, even if you wished to speak to her. Therefore, I am afraid you will have to look elsewhere, if blackmail is your concern."

"Indeed, sir." Greenfield nodded in agreement. His gaze shifted to Alexander. He frowned briefly and stared down at his hands, folded together in his lap. "You know a Mr. Underwood, sir. Do you not?"

Archer's mouth tightened, and his gaze hardened. "I do. What of it?"

"Was he having any difficulties of which you were aware?" Greenfield put the question delicately.

"Nothing that I care to discuss with you."

Greenfield's brows rose. "Indeed, sir. Perhaps we might discuss the matter in private. At your convenience, of course. In fact, I had hoped to speak to each of you privately. I am sure you understand."

"We know each other too well, already, to worry about such things," Belcher said with a grin. "Light your fuses and fire the cannons, Greenfield."

Archer and Alexander exchanged glances.

Archer said, "I agree with Mr. Greenfield. Privacy is best for such matters." He stood, frowning. "You may use this room for your interviews. To whom would you prefer to direct your questions first?"

"As you say, sir, Mr. Grantham was more a friend to the earl than you, and Lady Olivia is absent. So if you don't mind, perhaps I may have a few minutes of Lord Milbourn's time." Greenfield raised his brows as he looked at Alexander.

It was clear that he wished to give Archer time to reconsider his position concerning Underwood and whatever he knew of him. Perhaps the inquiry agent thought that when Archer's initial anger cooled, he would realize that implicating Underwood might remove some of the suspicion from Lady Olivia.

If that were his reasoning, it showed how little he knew of Archer's character.

"I have no objection." Alexander nodded at Archer.

Belcher's brow furrowed with irritation as he stood and followed Archer to the door. "This is ridiculous."

Alexander waited for the library door to close behind the two men before he fixed his gaze on the inquiry agent. "Well, Mr. Greenfield, what did Grantham have to say in this fascinating journal of his?"

"He had a great deal to say about all four of you." Greenfield chuckled. "Quite the quartet of adventurers in your day, it seems."

Alexander shrugged. "And eventually, we all grew up." He considered Belcher and added with a grin, "Though some of us matured more quickly than others."

"So it seems." Greenfield paused to examine his fingernails again.

Perhaps he hoped the silence would encourage Alexander to speak, but he simply relaxed and sat back in his chair and waited, his calm gaze resting on the inquiry agent.

Greenfield sighed. "Prying is so disagreeable." He took a deep breath and shook his head before looking at Alexander. "Nonetheless, I must ask about some entries Mr. Grantham wrote in his journal concerning yourself. And your wife."

"I thought that might be your concern. No need to spare my feelings. It all happened a very long time ago." Alexander smiled, despite the bleak, cold feeling settling within him. It had indeed been a number of years, but some pain never seemed to diminish.

"She...died?"

"What a delicate way of asking if I murdered her." Alexander stared again at the clean, straight edge of Archer's massive desk. The line reminded him of the sharp edges of the stairs that night. The lamplight had caught them, turning them into bright yellow lines before the bottommost steps descended down into the darkness of the ground floor. "No. I did not."

The inquiry agent nodded. "An accident. She fell."

"Yes. We were arguing on the first floor landing. She backed up to grab the small statue sitting on the newel-post" — a grim smile fluttered over his face—"to throw at me. She liked to throw things — figurines mostly, because they shattered so satisfactorily — when she failed to win an argument any other way. She missed her footing and fell." He stared at the floor, remembering the sickening, dull thuds as she tumbled down the staircase.

"And she was pregnant at the time?"

Alexander felt an itching sensation on the side of his face from Greenfield's stare. He glanced up and shrugged. "Yes, so her physician said. Four or five months."

"You did not know at the time?"

"She had not seen fit to tell me before...it happened." Four or five months. A cold hollow remained inside him at the loss of the baby, whether it was his or not. A tiny little boy — a son he was unlikely to have, now. The specter of that painful question remained: was the boy his child or not? It might have been his if it was closer to five months than four. But four....

She had refused to share his bed the last few months of their increasingly acrimonious marriage. And she was not a woman to forgo her pleasures. She had welcomed someone with her lovely pale arms wide open, brilliant black eyes, and hungry, crimson mouth, but he didn't know whom.

He'd preferred not to know. Marriage had been a mistake — and blaming another man for his misjudgment was futile, especially when he had no intention of repeating his errors.

"Grantham seemed inclined to speculate," Greenfield said, before adding hastily, "A few initials only — no names."

"Initials." Alexander grunted. The gnawing, bitter anger, guilt, and frustration at his past failures with his erratic, tempestuous wife made him bite back the question forming on his lips.

Who, who, who? The question repeated like the mournful, low call of an owl. *When did her love for me turn to hate? Who stole her smiles and lithe body?* His foot, still propped up on his left knee, jiggled. *Better off not to know, n*ot to speculate.

It could have been anyone, even a servant. A footboy or groom. *Anyone.*

Knowing the initials would only drive him to discover whose name would match the letters.

"Grantham never mentioned it to you?" Greenfield asked, pursuing the answers doggedly.

Alexander laughed harshly, his foot jerking faster. He gripped his ankle and stopped the movement. "No, he did not. He did not try to blackmail me with any knowledge he may have had concerning her, if that is your concern."

Then it struck him. If Grantham wrote about Isabella's affair, then at least she had not seduced him. Greenfield's questions would have taken a dramatically different turn if that had been the case, and Grantham had noted it in his journal.

The tight bands of tension around Alexander's chest eased. Grantham had not betrayed their friendship — he'd never had an affair with his wife. One of the few men who had not.

The thought made Grantham's death seem even sadder. Unnecessary and tragic.

He'd been such a gentle man, unobtrusive and always the last to join in any activity, particularly those promising any physical danger. Although no one would ever call him a coward, he did not court risk, either. And knowing him, it was difficult to conceive of Grantham indulging in blackmail, unless he was sure he was safe in doing so. Or if he desperately needed the money.

"Greenfield, are you sure about your supposition that Grantham was blackmailing someone?"

"It is difficult to be sure of anything, my lord. However, there were some letters...." A self-deprecating smile curved Greenfield's mouth. "And there were those deposits...."

"When did they start?"

"About six months ago. At least, that is when he began investing." Greenfield stared at his hands clasped in his lap. "His accounts were in arrears before that — had been for the last year."

Six months.

What had happened six months ago that had brought Grantham's financial matters to a head? If he'd had a lack of funds for a year or more, he could certainly have continued a while longer. However, there was nothing that Alexander could recall.

"How much money was involved?" he asked.

"Each deposit was one hundred pounds, and there were ten deposits. One per week for ten weeks," Greenfield replied.

"And then they stopped?" Alexander frowned. One thousand pounds. A nice round sum, but hardly a fortune.

But a nice, tidy sum that you might be able to squeeze out of someone.

"There was a gap of three weeks, and then another series of deposits. Same amounts, at the same interval. The deposits continued until a month before Grantham died," Greenfield said.

"It does not appear to be the result of successful wagering." Alexander rubbed the back of his neck. "The amounts and times would have been more varied."

"Unless he were the kind of man who saved his winnings until he had one hundred pounds before depositing. Bookkeeping would be easier," Greenfield suggested, studying Alexander to see his reaction.

"Grantham was not that methodical." Alexander placed his right foot on the floor. "Are there any other questions?"

Greenfield stood politely as Alexander got to his feet. "No, my lord. I appreciate your patience."

"Archer or Belcher?" he asked as he strode to the door.

"Mr. Belcher, I believe," Greenfield replied. He smiled. "Fortunate I ran into the two of you, was it not?"

"Yes," Alexander agreed in a dry voice. "Fortunate. Precisely the term I would have employed for our meeting."

Chapter Fifteen

The fencing lesson went surprisingly well, and Olivia felt invigorated as she locked the foils and masks in her office. The exercise had almost made her forget the recent tragedies, although the occasional hesitant question, high giggle, and nervous, darting glances from the young ladies who'd decided to attend confirmed that they were there mostly for the sheer thrill of seeing the building where two corpses had been recently found. And of course, the excitement of learning fencing from a lady who might be a murderer.

However, Olivia thought that they also seemed to experience some of the thrill she'd always felt when crossing swords with an opponent. The excitement flaring in their eyes wasn't only because of the recent, sad events.

Olivia was grateful to Cynthia, though, for her snorts of impatience whenever one of the ladies showed too much interest in the more gothic qualities of the unfortunate deaths. Those inelegant sounds, and Cynthia's exuberant use of her foil, kept everyone focused on the lessons. Olivia could only hope this was not the first and last time the Misses Peterson and Miss Wilson would attend.

When Olivia returned home, she was surprised to find Edward occupying her sitting room. A bottle of sherry and two glasses sat on the small table at his elbow, and Lord Milbourn lounged in the chair opposite him, his long legs stretched out toward the fire burning merrily in the fireplace.

"Edward, Lord Milbourn," she greeted them, wondering why they were occupying the Ivory Drawing Room instead of the library, which was Edward's normal retreat. As she caught Lord Milbourn's dark gaze, she grew warm, conscious of her flushed, damp cheeks from her recent exercise. She raised a hand to her hair, sure that it was in wild disarray.

Why hadn't she gone to her room to tidy herself, first?

"You look very well, Lady Olivia," Edward commented.

"I just returned from the academy. Class went exceedingly well today. To what do I owe this honor? I rarely have you gentlemen visit me in my sitting room," she said.

Edward leapt to his feet and dragged another chair over to sit next to him, across from Lord Milbourn.

A half smile twisted Lord Milbourn's mouth as he drew his legs back to give her room to walk past him and sit. "We were routed from the library by Mr. Greenfield," Lord Milbourn said. His black eyes glinted with amusement. "He is conducting inquiries."

Olivia looked from Lord Milbourn's sardonic face to her brother.

Edward shook his head. Worried lines furrowed his brow and his mouth formed a tight line.

What does he have to worry about?

"He cannot possibly suspect *you*, Edward," Olivia blurted out.

"I suspect he might be more interested in me." Lord Milbourn's mouth twisted into a cynical smile. "After all, Archer did not murder his wife."

Murder his wife?

Olivia straightened and clasped her hands together in a tight knot. Her gaze was drawn to Milbourn's dark eyes. A flicker of pain tore through the depths and bitterness thinned his mouth. Looking deeper, she glimpsed the hopelessness he hid so well behind a cold indifference and a sardonic sense of humor that served better than any shield to keep others at a distance. She partially lifted one hand to touch him before she stopped herself. A gesture of pity would only make him angry.

"Well, my brother has never been married," she said. "So he has not had a wife to murder."

Edward, in the middle of swallowing a mouthful of sherry, sputtered and choked.

Lord Milbourn chuckled.

"And perhaps you would do better to be less melodramatic, Lord Milbourn," she said bracingly. "You were apparently never convicted of any such crime, so I am sure Mr. Greenfield will not make any ridiculous assumptions."

"No. I was not convicted. Not by the law, at any rate," Lord Milbourn said, his intense gaze fixed on her face.

"You refine too much upon the past," she said, clasping her hands together.

"Unfortunately, the past can be a very persistent ghost," Lord Milbourn said.

She stared into his eyes. "Only if you let it haunt you." She shifted and smoothed her skirt over her lap with restless hands. "I, for one, don't place too much importance on it." She smiled. "Except to ensure I don't repeat mistakes, of course."

"Precisely my concern," Lord Milbourn stared at the fire, his face an unreadable slab of granite. "I see we are in accord, *mi niña bonita*."

Edward cleared his throat. "Unfortunately, Mr. Greenfield appears determined to sift through all our pasts since he found Grantham's journal. I cannot blame him — it is his duty — but it is awkward, nonetheless." The V between his brows deepened. "I fear the reason for Grantham's death may very well have its seeds in the past. I did not wish to credit all that Mr. Und — a friend — recently confided to me, but perhaps he was not merely upset and imagining things as I supposed." He studied Lord Milbourn's harsh profile. "You knew Grantham far longer and better than I. Is there anyone you suspect? Any reason?"

Gazing at her brother, Lady Olivia realized that he was reconsidering his conversation with Mr. Underwood and her statement that he had been near the academy around the time of the murder. Edward had nearly slipped and named him, and his words seemed to imply that Mr. Grantham had been blackmailing Mr. Underwood. Although she had suspected something of the sort, having her suppositions even partially confirmed saddened her. She didn't want to think that such things could happen among her acquaintances. Mr. Grantham had been so kind, so nice to them. The revelation about his character made her uneasy about trusting anyone.

Worse, she realized that if Mr. Grantham had been blackmailing Mr. Underwood, he could have had other victims, as well. No one was perfect, and they had all done silly things that might embarrass them. So any of Grantham's victims could easily have murdered him.

Lord Milbourn barked a short laugh. "Grantham was a mild man and quiet. However, all men have the occasional argument. His death may have resulted from the heat of the moment. An ill-judged action. Or it could have been more deliberate, if you take the death of the charwoman into account. If the two are related. If so, you may be correct, Archer. There may be something in his journal that could point the way." He rubbed the center of his forehead before pushing his fingers through his thick, black hair. "I would like to see that journal."

"Then why not ask Mr. Greenfield?" Olivia stood. "I am tired of speculating without facts. Let us find out what he knows."

Her boldness surprised even her. Perhaps her recent, close association with Miss Denholm was having an unexpected influence on her. Unfortunately, she could not determine if others perceived it as salubrious, or as an unforgivable lapse of good breeding.

Edward appeared positively appalled by her suggestion. He exchanged glances with Lord Milbourn, who merely smiled and shrugged.

"I do not think—" Edward stumbled to his feet.

"Indeed." Lord Milbourn stood languidly. "Why not?" He gestured toward the door. "Shall we see if he has finished annoying Belcher?"

"He may take it amiss," Edward said, following him. "And I would not blame him."

Olivia trailed after the two men. "What if he does?"

She brushed past Lord Milbourn as he held the door for her, feeling flushed and self-conscious. She caught the warm scent of bay, leather, and the tingling aroma of something she'd always associated just with him. Something masculine and heady that made her want to lean closer to him, close her eyes, and breathe deeply.

The back of her neck tickled as Lord Milbourn followed her to the staircase. She could feel him behind her, his warmth seemed to bathe her back, even though she knew it was mostly her imagination.

"Do you want me to ask Mr. Greenfield?" she asked over her shoulder as they descended to the ground floor. "He already believes I am guilty, so my request cannot make my situation any worse."

"There are always ways to make matters worse," Edward answered grimly. "I will ask on behalf of all of us."

Lord Milbourn cleared his throat, and Olivia caught a glimpse of a frown as she glanced at him over her shoulder. Apparently, he would have preferred to be the one to put forth the request, but at this juncture, they didn't need any additional volunteers to throw themselves on their swords, and it would have been rude to argue with his host.

And even Olivia could see the advantages of allowing Edward to handle matters. He was not involved and had been out walking with Hildie when the murder occurred. Dozens of people must have seen them strolling sedately through the park.

As she stepped off the last stair, she turned to study Lord Milbourn's face.

He appeared thoughtful, and he held his broad shoulders stiffly as he joined her. She had the distinct impression that he was not pleased to allow Edward to take charge. She smothered a smile as warm amusement swept through her. Lord Milbourn was not a man to let others take the charge. He was the sort of man who would lead from the front, and the devil take the hindmost. The type who ended up standing with a bemused expression on his face as a general pinned a medal to his chest for heroics.

He would not see his actions as courageous, just as something that had to be done. The thought made her long to step closer to him and slip her hand within his warm fingers.

After edging around them, Edward took the lead. They walked down the wide hallway to the library. Just as they reached the double doors, they opened, and Belcher strode out.

"I don't know what more I can tell you," Belcher said over his shoulder. He didn't see the three of them immediately and turned back to face Greenfield, who had apparently stayed behind. "However, if you will let me have the journal for a few days, I will see if I can help you with those cryptic initials." He held out a hand.

Edward and Lord Milbourn exchanged glances over Olivia's head. She grimaced.

Before they could say anything, she stepped forward and brushed around Belcher. "Perhaps my brother and I could be of service to you, Mr. Greenfield." She reached back and pulled Edward forward. "As you are aware, Edward was escorting my sister, Lady Hildegard, to the park, and he has studied the law." She halted, aware that she was starting to babble. "Not that that matters. However, my point is that Edward was just saying to me that he would be willing to examine Mr. Grantham's journal and relate to you any information he can discern from the contents."

Greenfield stood in front of the large, mahogany desk and stared down at its shiny surface, a gentle smile on his face. He ran his fingertips over the smooth wood for several inches, apparently lost in thought.

"Mr. Greenfield?" Olivia repeated.

"I beg your pardon, my lady," Greenfield's head came up. He looked at her, a pleasant expression on his face. "You were saying?"

"The journal." She flicked her hand in his direction. "Lord Milbourn indicated that Mr. Grantham had used some abbreviations in his diary that puzzled you. My brother, Mr. Edward Archer, has offered to study the journal and provide you with any insights he gains."

The smile on Greenfield's face grew sadder, and the corners of his mouth drooped, giving him the slightly worried, long face of a bloodhound that fears he has lost the trail and might disappoint his master. All he needed was a long tail to wag slowly back and forth in an it's-bad-but-not-entirely-hopeless gesture.

"I appreciate the offer, Mr. Archer." He nodded to Edward, who stood just behind her on the right. "And Mr. Belcher's, as well. However, I think it best that I continue to puzzle over it myself for now." He caught her gaze and smiled, his blue eyes bright and penetrating. "Don't you, Lady Olivia?"

No, I don't think that at all! I think you ought to give it to me so we can discover what Mr. Grantham wrote about us all.

She returned his smile and nodded. "Of course. No doubt you know your business."

"I appreciate your confidence." Mr. Greenfield bowed. "Now, if you will excuse me, I will leave you in peace."

For now.

She knew he would not leave them alone for long. Like the bloodhound he resembled, he would continue to sniff around, searching for the right trail. And she didn't feel particularly peaceful about it, although there was little she could do.

If she were Cynthia, she might grab Mr. Greenfield by his dark gray lapels, give him a good shake, and then wrest the journal from his pocket. But she was not quite that bold. Yet. Given sufficient time and provocation, however, Olivia thought she might surpass even the indomitable Cynthia Denholm.

"I will walk with you for a bit," Belcher said as they trailed back through the hallway to the front door. He accepted his top hat from Latimore and doffed it at a rakish angle on his blond curls, grinning with good humor. "If you don't mind, Greenfield?"

"Not at all," Greenfield replied as he followed Mr. Belcher to the front door.

Olivia studied the narrow back of the inquiry agent. His coat hung awkwardly, sagging on the left side, suggesting he carried Grantham's journal with him. Her gaze fixed on that lumpy bulge. A flicker of anger burned her at the agent's careless reply. What gave him the right to tease out all their secrets and disappointments? Didn't he ever lose his temper? Do something he regretted later?

No. Not him. He was too controlled. And yet he always seemed so mild, so unassuming, despite the intelligence in his eyes. He seemed to be constantly weighing them and their words. If they made any mistakes or contradicted themselves, he'd recognize it and remember.

A shiver ran down her back that had nothing to do with the open front door. Even innocent people forgot or grew confused. It was so easy to blurt out the wrong thing because of nerves. She gripped the soft blue merino wool she'd draped over her shoulders as a shield against the February drafts that seemed to spill through unseen cracks and drift through the townhouse at random.

Fear slid icy fingers down her neck. Despite his meek demeanor, she was afraid of Mr. Greenfield and what he might be thinking. He revealed so little. He could be on the verge of arresting her.

She'd be tried and hung. The note and the button would surely damn her.

Her gaze followed him as Lord Milbourn quietly murmured goodbye to her brother.

What was in Mr. Grantham's journal? Had he said anything about Wraysbury? About Mr. Underwood? Or about her? She could not imagine why he would have written anything about her, but one never knew what thoughts ran through another's mind.

Her own diary contained entries about Cynthia Denholm that she would hate to have revealed. But at times, she'd been so frustrated with her forthright and undeniably tactless childhood friend. Cynthia was not always an easy person to be around.

And Cynthia would be shocked, perhaps even hurt by Olivia's words, if she ever read them.

No wonder Mr. Grantham had used abbreviations. One never knew if one's journal would fall into another person's hands, or what damage it might do.

I should burn my old journals and start a new one, just using abbreviations. And what would Farmer think if she should walk in while Olivia was burning her diaries? Or if she found the ashes in the fireplace? She would undoubtedly see such an action as a guilty one, and she might feel compelled to report it to Mr. Greenfield.

You should have fired her. Her brother's voice floated through her mind.

Olivia pulled her shawl closer around her shoulders and hugged herself. *Concentrate.* Her diaries were not her most pressing concern, Mr. Grantham's journal was. She needed to read through it and discover if anyone in the Archer family, including herself, had anything to fear from it.

Had Mr. Grantham seen anything shocking in her insistence on learning to fence along with her brothers? At that time, Lord Milbourn had been Mr. Alexander Bron, her brothers' dashing fencing master, and she would have done anything to provoke him to look at her with something other than laughter in his dark eyes. But slowly, she'd grown to love the fencing, itself. Had Mr. Grantham made assumptions about the two of them that were simply not true?

How could he? Lord Milbourn had always behaved impeccably and with complete propriety.

But Mr. Grantham would not know that. He hadn't been there to see her frustration with Mr. Bron's amused, distant air. He was the epitome of the cold indifference aspired to by students of the Spanish Style of fencing. Haughty and implacable. A dangerous man to face when armed with a sword.

But if not that, then what could Mr. Grantham possibly have written about her or Lord Milbourn?

Her pulse quickened as her fingers tightened against her waist under the fringe of her shawl. She had at least a partial answer already. Lord Milbourn's wife had died violently in a way that cast suspicion upon him. That much was clear from his comments in the sitting room. What had Mr. Grantham written about that tragedy? Had he accused him of murder?

If he had, Mr. Greenfield might believe the two men had argued, and that Lord Milbourn had killed Mr. Grantham.

But if he had, he would have admitted it. He would never have allowed suspicion to fall on her or other members of the Archer family. Her heart told her that much was true.

So if not Lord Milbourn, then who? Mr. Underwood? It always came back to Mr. Underwood, no matter who else she tried to place in the role of murderer.

As for the foolish and puppyish Mr. Belcher, well, he was a bit of a coxcomb and undoubtedly admired quite a few ladies, but that was hardly scandalous. Many men openly flaunted their mistresses. A lady simply smiled graciously and pretended not to notice while coldly snubbing the woman. Anything Mr. Grantham wrote along those lines would be unimportant.

Of course, it could well be that the journal shed no light upon Mr. Grantham's death at all.

If only I could obtain that journal. Just to be sure. She straightened her shoulders. Now was not the time for sighs, it was the time for action.

"Please wait, Lord Milbourn. I wish to go for a walk," she said as he brushed past her. She tore off her shawl and held it out to Latimore, gesturing for her pelisse and bonnet.

"Lady Olivia, perhaps Lord Milbourn has other matters to attend to." Edward frowned at her.

Latimore, holding her deep blue pelisse and matching bonnet in his hands, looked from him to her. She grabbed her coat and turned her back on her brother while holding out the garment, forcing Edward to help her don it out of sheer politeness.

"I will not be long," she said.

Lord Milbourn was watching the progress of Mr. Belcher and Mr. Greenfield down the walkway.

"Lord Milbourn?" she asked.

He turned to her with an amused expression on his face. "Yes?"

"It is unimportant, Milbourn," Edward said. "My coat, Latimore. If you wish to stumble along in the dark, I shall be more than happy to accompany you, Lady Olivia."

Olivia felt her smile slip as she glanced from Lord Milbourn to her brother.

"Good night, *mi niña bonita*. Take care." He tapped the crown of his hat to seat it more firmly, smiled at her, and walked away, following Mr. Belcher and Mr. Greenfield.

"Well, Lady Olivia?" Edward moved to stand on the stoop and offer his elbow to her.

She took a deep breath of frustration. This was not going precisely as she imagined, but she couldn't forget that pocket sagging at Mr. Greenfield's side, with its bulky burden. She needed to read the journal — she simply had to.

How hard could it be to pick a pocket? Children on the streets of London seemed to do it quite regularly with near impunity, and it was dreadfully dark, despite the lamplighters' efforts to light the streetlamps. The shadows would hide her actions if she could get close enough to the inquiry agent.

Edward seemed to want to walk at a sedate pace, but Olivia tugged him along faster. Ahead of them, she could see Lord Milbourn's tall, broad-shouldered form, and a block further ahead, the hats of Mr. Greenfield and Mr. Belcher bobbed past other pedestrians. As she pulled her brother to trot more quickly through the alternating pools of shadow and golden lamplight, she saw Lord Milbourn's long legs eat up the intervening distance between him and the other men.

She jumped up a few inches to see around another pair of men. Lord Milbourn paused to slap Greenfield on the back and joined him and Mr. Belcher.

"Come on, Edward. Can you not walk at least a bit faster?"

"I will not run, Lady Olivia," Edward said in a low, angry voice. "What is the matter with you?"

"I want to catch up with the others. I — I forgot to tell Mr. Greenfield something."

"You can tell him tomorrow. I refuse to chase them down the street. It is unbecoming in a lady, as you well know."

"I rarely indulge in *becoming* exercises, as *you* well know." She dragged him with her, running a few steps, walking a few, and then running again.

The three men turned the corner ahead of them. Fearing to lose them, she let go of Edward's arm and dashed forward. As she rounded the corner, she was brought up short by a small crowd. A horse was snorting and rearing back with white-rimmed eyes, rattling a fragile, yellow-wheeled gig. One man was trying to grab the reins near the bit, while others, including Lord Milbourn and Mr. Greenfield, were bending over something in the street. Mr. Belcher stood a short distance away, watching them.

"Dead," Lord Milbourn said. The single word sounded harsh and stark in the shifting shadows. He lifted a small form from the road and set it carefully on the walkway. "Does anyone know this child? Who he was?"

Several people in the crowd shook their heads and took a few steps back as if afraid of being held responsible.

A well-dressed man descended from the gig, his face white in the golden light from the streetlamp on the corner. "I never saw him — could not stop. He ran out right in front of my gig. I could not stop."

"Did any of you witness the accident?" Mr. Greenfield straightened and looked around the crowd as he pulled out his small notebook.

A burly man stepped forward and yanked a tattered cloth cap off his head. "I seen it, sir. It were an accident — I seen it. No way to avoid it, poor lad."

"What is your name?" Mr. Greenfield asked.

"Tom Willow, sir." The big man shifted from one foot to the other.

"Can any of you others confirm this?" Mr. Greenfield revolved slowly, writing down murmured statements and names.

Several of the passersby at the edges of the crowd started drifting away into the darkness, having seen enough of the sad accident and unwilling to be dragged forward as possible witnesses. No one knew the child, and from the look of his tattered, ill-fitting clothing and dirty face, he appeared to be one of the impoverished, anonymous urchins trying to survive as best they could on whatever they could glean from the streets.

"Poor little mite, it'll be a pauper's grave for him, I fear," Mr. Greenfield commented as he closed his notebook and slipped it into a pocket under his lapel.

The man in the gig frowned and dug around under his overcoat, drawing out a small leather coin purse. He plucked out a few coins and handed them to Mr. Greenfield. "At least give him a decent burial. And a name. Mine is Todd — give him that, if nothing else."

"That is good of you, Mr. Todd," Mr. Greenfield slipped the money into his pocket. "I shall certainly do as you ask. He shall get a proper grave under a stone with a name."

The crowd had mostly dispersed, though the men who had provided Mr. Greenfield with names and statements remained. Olivia edged closer to the inquiry agent. A flash of red caught her attention.

She glanced around to see Cynthia Denholm and the Misses Peterson standing nearby. The red cloak draping Cynthia's tall figure stood out vibrantly in the golden glow of the streetlamp. As Olivia watched, Cynthia strode forward, her cloak flapping around her in a swirl of crimson.

What was she doing here?

"Good thing I happened to be passing. You are obviously in need of assistance and a bit of common sense." Cynthia's voice boomed, startling everyone into silence. "Men...." She shook her head. "Don't know a child's head from its feet." She thrust past Greenfield to kneel next to the lad, oblivious to the mud and grimy patches of melting snow. She ripped off a glove and held it over the child's nose and mouth for a minute. "Dead." Sighing, she struggled to her feet and brushed the mud off her knees. "Not that you did him any good, standing around him like a lot of henless chicks."

"I am sorry." Mr. Greenfield ask, his voice rising in polite enquiry, "Miss?"

"Denholm. Cynthia Denholm." Hands on her broad hips, Cynthia studied him. "Are you that Greenfield chap? The one annoying Lady Olivia about that other murder?"

The corners of Greenfield's mouth twitched in a hastily hidden smile. "Yes. I am afraid so, Miss Denholm." A somber expression slipped over his face. "And I am sorry, but I must attend to the matter of this poor child's accident."

"Death. He is clearly dead. No need for mealy-mouthed sentiment." She sighed and glanced around. When her forceful gaze landed on the spectators, the men shuffled their feet, flushed, and more often than not, stumbled away on some other urgent business. "Well, carry on, then, though I don't see what you can do for him now, Mr. Greenfield." As she strode past him, she slapped him on the back before rejoining the two ladies standing with linked arms at the corner.

Olivia studied them fleetingly. How had they happened to be passing? True, the Peterson family lived nearby, and as they were friends of Cynthia's, it was not beyond the realm of possibility that they were simply taking a walk before dining. The fashion-conscious Petersons would never have supper before nine, so they could well be passing the time before returning to their townhouse in ample time to change.

Perhaps there was nothing very unusual about their presence on this street, after all.

Once again, the large man, clutching and twisting his cap between large, reddened hands, spoke up. "I'll fetch the undertaker, sir. He be my brother-in-law."

"Very well." Mr. Greenfield glanced around and almost bumped into Olivia. His eyes widened in surprise, and he nodded abruptly.

His left hand patted his coat pocket, and he stilled. Shock rippled over his face, and he patted more vigorously. Then he slipped his hand into his pocket and pulled out...nothing. Jerking his head around, he stared at Lord Milbourn, Mr. Belcher, Edward, and finally, Olivia.

She looked at his coat. It no longer sagged to the left.

The journal was gone. A cloud of butterflies fluttered inside her chest. She felt lightheaded and then queasy as her pulse quickened. Her fingers tingled with cold.

Someone had stolen Grantham's journal!

Chapter Sixteen

Much to his chagrin, Grantham's journal continued to torment and elude Alexander. Greenfield proved so obstinate in his refusal to let anyone even glimpse it that Alexander was beginning to think he didn't have Grantham's diary after all.

The thought raised interesting possibilities.

He spent Sunday considering the case, and the following Monday, he attended the coroner's inquest into the death of Mrs. Adams. When Edward Archer walked in alone and sat next to him, Alexander was relieved. Lady Olivia had obviously decided not to attend and had provided a brief statement, which Idleman read aloud to the jurymen.

"Lord Milbourn, we have read your statement. Is there anything you wish to add?" Idleman frowned grimly at him as if he could force him to remain silent through sheer force of will.

"Yes." He walked over to the pitiful body, already ensconced in a simple wooden box in the corner of the room.

The cold February air had not kept all signs of decay at bay, and the corpse's round cheeks appeared bloated and multi-hued. The putrid smell overlaid even the cleaner smell of the casket's fresh wood and was so dreadful that they'd left one of the small windows nearby open, despite the blustery winds that swept through it.

Mr. Idleman and his jurors ranged themselves around him, although none of them seemed inclined to stand too close to the simple box.

"Well, my lord?" Idleman prompted him. He clasped his thin hands behind his back and fixed his gaze firmly on Alexander.

"You will recall that I requested various articles of Mrs. Adams's clothing to be present." Alexander gestured to his left.

A battered, black bonnet, shawl, and short pelisse were draped over the top of a square table shoved against the wall. Alexander picked up the bonnet and tilted it so that the gentlemen ringing him could see the brownish-red stains covering the interior.

"You see where the blood has pooled and dried?" he asked. "It is on the right side of her bonnet." He placed the bonnet on the table and went to the wooden box. "If you examine the face of the deceased, you will also notice a livid area on the right side, running over the chin, cheek, and temple. This is blood that has pooled under the skin immediately after death."

"Are you a physician, my lord?" one of the more elegantly dressed jurors asked. He stared at Alexander with an arrogant air that suggested he didn't consider Alexander's observations to be worthy of their consideration.

"No. I have seen death before, however." He glanced around the circle of men. "Many of us have. There can be no question that the fluids in the body will naturally settle at the lowest point."

"Well, what of it?" the elegant man asked, shifting his feet impatiently and gazing around as if unwilling to look at the pitiful body of the dead woman.

"You have heard Constable Cooke's report. There was no sign of Mrs. Adams when he first searched the house on Wednesday, the thirteenth of February. And when we discovered the body, it was lying on its left side, not the right, and she had been dead for at least a day. This means the body was hidden somewhere and then moved to the kitchen."

"Very well. I believe we can accept your assessment," Idleman stated curtly. "Have you any additional points you wish to make?"

"I would also encourage you to examine the wound on her left temple. There is a pattern" — he pulled the drawing he'd made out of his pocket and handed it to the man standing on his right—"still visible, imprinted in the flesh. I suggest you find the weapon that made that wound, if you wish to uncover her killer."

The men dutifully filed past the corpse, taking turns to bend over and examine her bloated face. The processes of decomposition had done much to destroy the delicate pattern, and several men shook their heads doubtfully. But enough saw the purplish-brown traces to grow thoughtful.

"I would only add," Alexander said as he studied the coroner, "that her key to the premises where she was found is also missing. It would appear that she might have met her end *because* of that key. Whether the murderer intended to kill her with that blow or only wanted to render her unconscious long enough to take the key, the end result was the same. That is all." He nodded sharply to the coroner and walked back to his seat.

The rest of the inquest passed rather prosaically.

The elegantly dressed man, Mr. Carter, brought up the apparent connection between the deaths of Mr. Grantham and Mrs. Adams. "There can be no doubt that the two poor souls were both foully murdered by the same despicable individual." He looked at each of his fellow jurors in turn, before fixing his gaze on the coroner. "It is inconceivable that there should be two such desperate persons in London."

The coroner nodded once in agreement, before catching himself and frowning at Carter. "Speculation, sir. Our purpose is only to determine the manner of death. The proper authorities will investigate the matter to identify the individual, or *individuals*, responsible for this outrage."

A few minutes later, Idleman announced a verdict of unlawful killing by person or persons unknown and terminated the inquest. The decision was no surprise to anyone, though several jurymen, including Carter, clustered together near the doorway. Alexander heard them whisper Lady Olivia's name as he passed them on his way through the door.

At least he had time, now. No one had been named, or taken into custody, at either inquest as he feared might happen. Idleman seemed curiously reluctant in that regard, though Alexander could well understand it if Idleman thought the evidence pointed to Lady Olivia. The coroner would not want to risk an accusation against an earl's sister. He wisely left it up to Constable Cooke and Mr. Greenfield to uncover sufficient evidence to hand the entire affair over to the House of Lords; let them deal with Lady Olivia.

With luck, it would never reach that august body.

Chapter Seventeen

Considering how best to prove her innocence, Lady Olivia went about her duties Monday morning absentmindedly. Her inattentiveness led to incorrectly addressed correspondence, and a strange menu with multiple desserts, but no meat course. Her errors were gently brought to her notice, and by mid-morning, she felt that a cup of tea was not only deserved, but required.

Mary dutifully brought her a tray, including a few Bath buns wrapped in a napkin. The fresh bread smelled heavenly of yeast and were still steaming when Olivia unwrapped them and slathered on some rich, creamy butter.

"Mary," Olivia called as the maid approached the door on her way out. "Ask Latimore to join me. I wish to speak with him."

"Yes, Lady Olivia." Mary bobbed a curtsey and scurried through the door.

A few minutes later, Olivia heard Latimore's firm tread clattering over the marble floor in the hall. "Did you wish to see me, Lady Olivia?" Latimore asked. He remained standing in the doorway, one white-gloved hand on the doorknob.

"Come in, Latimore," Olivia said. She shifted in her chair, feeling like a child about to chastise her father. It felt wrong and unseemly.

Latimore moved to stand in front of her, his hands clasped in front of him, and a calm, patient look on his face.

"About that button," she said hesitantly, unsure how to ask him why he hadn't warned her, why he'd left her to suffer such a terrible surprise at the inquest. She didn't want to sound like a whimpering little child, even if she felt like one.

He nodded majestically. "I thought it might be a matter of concern to you, Lady Olivia. We did not mean to upset you. However, Mr. Peregrine thought it best not to worry you."

"Not to worry me! I would have appreciated a warning, at least."

"Yes, Lady Olivia. Perhaps it is best if I explain the circumstances."

"I should think you would."

"Mr. Greenfield insisted on examining your wardrobe—"

Sucking in a sharp breath, Olivia stiffened. "My wardrobe? Why was I not informed?"

Latimore bowed deferentially, his gaze fixed on the far wall. "I beg your pardon, Lady Olivia. You were at the academy at the time. Mr. Peregrine granted his permission."

"Peregrine?" She frowned, feeling betrayed, before she waved for him to continue.

"Miss Farmer was cleaning your pelisse at the time. She attempted to stop him from taking the garment from her. Unfortunately, she had discovered the button while handling your clothing, and it fell from her hand. She had no choice but to allow him to take the item."

"No choice?" Olivia asked bitterly.

"No, Lady Olivia. Mr. Greenfield picked it up before she could regain possession of it. She went immediately to the housekeeper, Mrs. Keene, as was appropriate, and Mrs. Keene brought the matter to me. Miss Farmer was fearful that she would be dismissed, and Mrs. Keene was in favor of that course of action. Mr. Peregrine overheard our discussion and decided otherwise since he had given Mr. Greenfield permission to search in the first place."

"I see my dear brother has a great deal to answer for," Olivia murmured.

"Mr. Peregrine then told Miss Farmer to remain silent if she wished to remain in service here. He felt it would be best not to worry you, unnecessarily."

She eyed him coldly. "Indeed."

"Mr. Peregrine insisted." He raised a gloved hand and covered his mouth as he coughed twice. "Pardon me, Lady Olivia. I hope you do not take this amiss, however, I must say that honesty is preferred in these circumstances. Hiding information or clues from the authorities can only do harm. I agreed with your brother. I felt that your honest and obviously shocked reaction at the inquest would stand you in good stead. The entire staff supports you, Lady Olivia, and believes in your innocence, if I may say so. I am sure Mr. Greenfield will do his best to discover the miscreant, but he can only do so if he is in possession of all the facts."

Somehow, Latimore had reversed their positions. Once more he gently assumed the role of a parent, and for some reason, she wanted to cry. At least he thought she was innocent; they all did.

But that didn't change the fact that they had plotted behind her back and hid crucial things from her. That was the one action she couldn't quite forgive. She hated being left out, or having others decide what she should or should not know, as if they were superior to her and she were a fragile child needing protection from the truth. Frustration churned inside her. How dare they assume they knew what was best for her?

"You should have told me, nonetheless," she said. "It concerned me directly, and I also appreciate honesty." She bit off her words before she descended to the level of a petulant infant and exclaimed, *it isn't fair! You left me out!*

The expression on Latimore's face softened, and he allowed himself a small smile. "I am sorry, Lady Olivia. In our judgment, we were taking the best course—"

"I should have been consulted."

"I see." He straightened. His face turned to stone. "Shall I inform Miss Farmer?"

"Inform Farmer?" Olivia stared at him. "Inform her of what?"

"That we have been dismissed," Latimore said. His brown eyes, encircled by dark purple pouches, appeared sad, and his mouth drooped. His short white hair barely covered his pink scalp and fluffed up like the freshly dried down on a newly hatched chick. The vertical lines running from the sides of his long nose to frame his mouth deepened as he studied her, and his jowls sagged even lower, pulling the corners of his mouth down.

He looked defeated.

She was suddenly aware of how old he was. He'd been with them for as long as she could remember. He'd always seemed to be the same, middle-aged man: never changing and eternal.

Though her feet shifted, she didn't stand and hug him the way she wanted to. He would have been appalled if she'd even attempted such an action, so she simply said, "No — no, that is not what I meant at all. I simply meant that I should have been informed, and I expect to be included in any discussions concerning me in the future."

He blinked several times and raised a fist to his mouth as he cleared his throat. "Thank you, Lady Olivia." He bowed. He coughed again and fumbled around in his pocket, before finally pulling out a piece of paper that he handed to her. "I had meant to give this to you earlier. It is the list of visitors we received the week of the tragedy. Mr. Edward also has a copy, as does Mr. Greenfield."

"I don't suppose there are any names that would surprise me." Olivia glanced over the sheet. Latimore's neat handwriting listed the names of their guests in two long columns.

"No, Lady Olivia. I did not record any unusual visitors in the log book."

"No strangers?"

"No."

The paper rustled between her nervous fingers. *One of these — one of our friends or acquaintances — tucked that button into my cuff to shift the blame to me. Someone I know might be a murderer.* A chill ran down the back of her neck, and she shivered. She found it difficult to even read the list, not wanting to imagine any of the friends listed therein as a killer, willing to betray and implicate her.

Someone is willing to see me hang.

Then the irony of her thoughts struck her. A slow, self-deprecating smile stretched her mouth. She'd just chastised Latimore for not informing her of the button, and here he was, trying to give her a list of names, one of which might be responsible for Mr. Grantham's death, and she didn't want to read it.

In the distance, Lady Olivia heard the deep thrum of the front door knocker. She glanced at Latimore.

"Is there anything else, Lady Olivia?" he asked politely, as if he had all the time in the world.

And he did, she reflected. Whoever was waiting at the front door would have to wait until he opened it.

"No. That is all." She dismissed him and then spread the list out on her lap to read it.

A quick glance through the names only disheartened her more. The majority of callers were ladies of her acquaintance and their mothers. *Miss Madison, Lady Emerson and daughter, Mr. Henry Franks, Miss Swainson, Mr. Thomas Willow,* and so on. On the back were *Mr. Underwood, Mr. Grantham, Lord Milbourn, Mr. Belcher,* and several more men who were friends of her brothers. They almost seemed to be an afterthought, as if the meticulous butler were merely trying to be thorough. The list seemed endless, and each name seemed even less likely to commit murder than the preceding one.

She went through it several times before throwing it in frustration onto the small, oval table next to her.

Olivia was about to return to her room to exchange her pale rose morning gown for a walking dress when Latimore reappeared in the doorway.

"Miss Denholm, Lady Olivia," he announced with a bow.

As usual, Cynthia failed to wait like a proper young lady in the hallway and followed closely after Latimore. He'd barely finished speaking when she edged past his shoulder and said, "Good morning, Lady Olivia."

"Surely we do not have another lesson scheduled for today," Olivia said, glancing at the window to reassure herself that it was too early in the day for a lesson, even if she had forgotten it. "I had thought we were going to wait until Wednesday afternoon for the next one."

"Yes, yes." Cynthia strode into the room and waved at Latimore. "Go on, back to your post, my good man. We have no need of you."

Latimore stared at Olivia.

She sighed. "You may go, Latimore."

"Very good, Lady Olivia." He bowed and closed the door behind him.

"Would you care to sit down, Miss Denholm?" Olivia asked politely, gesturing to the gold and ivory brocade cushioned chair opposite her.

"Yes, well, a cup of tea would be welcome." Cynthia flung herself into the chair and eyed Olivia expectantly. Her fingers tapped the armrests.

While Olivia rang for more tea, Cynthia slapped the armrests, leaned forward, and helped herself to the last Bath bun, happily using Olivia's plate and knife. As she took a huge bite, Olivia reflected that her friend's governess must have despaired of ever teaching the energetic girl any sort of good manners. She'd never let politeness stand in the way of positive action.

But in a way, Olivia found her refreshing, and she was always warmhearted. She always knew where she stood with Cynthia Denholm and didn't have to worry about making a mistake or inadvertently insulting her. Cynthia would undoubtedly let her know of any misstep and then promptly forgive her.

The maid arrived a few minutes later, and Olivia ordered an assortment of cakes, as well as tea.

Cynthia was already peering hungrily at the empty plates. As Olivia watched, Cynthia licked her index finger and picked up several remaining crumbs nestling within the napkin folded around the buns.

"The tea will be here shortly," Olivia said as she sat, arranging her pink muslin skirts around her. "It is good to see you."

"Yes, yes. Delightful. Lovely day. You are looking well, as am I, so on and so forth." Cynthia brushed away her words impatiently. She pulled a rather large reticule onto her lap. The bag had elaborate embroidery in bright red silk and a matching crimson fringe dangling from the bottom. She gripped the strings holding the reticule shut and pulled it open. "Found this — thought you might want it." She pulled out a book and thrust the object out toward Olivia.

The brown leather cover looked worn, and a mysterious darker stain had spread over the bottom half. She eyed it with distaste and kept her hands clasped together firmly in her lap.

"What is it?" Olivia asked. Unease prickled the skin between her shoulder blades.

Cynthia shook the book and then tossed it into Olivia's lap, just as Mary walked through the door with the tea tray. Reluctant to touch the thing, Olivia pushed it to the side, letting it slip between her hip and the arm of her chair. She busied herself with serving the tea and tried to forget it was there, but cold dampness seemed to seep through her gown where the book touched her.

After a shrug, Cynthia piled her plate with several slices of pound cake and a few of the delicate frosted tea cakes, for which Mrs. Peale, their cook, was justly famous.

Soon enough, however, Cynthia was slurping her third cup of tea and she spied the ragged corner of the leather book. "Go ahead, Lady Olivia. That is Grantham's journal, you know."

"What?" Olivia dropped her plate. It slipped off her lap and tumbled to the floor with a thump before she could catch it. Fortunately, the delicate, gold-rimmed china did not shatter since it fell but a short distance onto a thick carpet. Equally lucky, only a few crumbs remained on the plate. She rapidly brushed them back onto the plate and placed it onto the tea tray with shaking hands.

"Mr. Grantham's journal," Cynthia repeated, picking up the last small cake and taking a large bite out of it.

Olivia sat back and picked up the leather-bound book. The stain on the cover still felt unpleasantly cold — almost wet. "How did you obtain it?"

"It was lying in the gutter where that child was killed." Cynthia shrugged. "Terrible thing to happen." Her eyes glinted with a martial light. "That child should not have been in the street at all. Schooling, a full stomach, and bed — that's what he needed."

"Yes," Olivia agreed hastily, before Cynthia could launch into a more strident lecture about the evils of poverty and her determination to create an orphanage for the unfortunates in London.

It was a laudable goal, and Olivia had promised to help and had even given Cynthia her entire allowance on several occasions to fund the school, but she'd heard the speech so many times that her head rang with it. She wanted Cynthia to succeed, but in one small matter, the two ladies differed greatly. Olivia preferred simply to *do* something without a great deal of discussion and planning, while Cynthia seemed to discuss, bully, and consult endlessly, forever running around in vigorous, excited circles without accomplishing much of note.

Of course, if Olivia had done the same with her academy, her brother might have rented the townhouse to someone else, and her procrastination might have saved Mr. Grantham's life.

She glanced at Cynthia and noted that her gaze was growing unfocused. Her plump, red mouth was opening and shutting in preparation to launch into her favorite lecture.

Hastily, Olivia cut her off by saying, "Why did you not return it to Mr. Greenfield?" She held up the book by the dry corner.

"Didn't know what it was until I got home and opened it." Cynthia shrugged and looked wistfully at the empty plates on the table. Once more, she licked the tip of her index finger meditatively, but then appeared to think better of picking up the remaining crumbs because she finally clasped her hands together in her lap. A droopy, disappointed expression remained on her face, however.

"You read it?" Olivia asked.

"Naturally."

"Then why bring it to me? Why not return it to Mr. Greenfield? You must know it may contain information important to his investigation," Olivia said, watching her friend curiously.

Although she had previously wanted the journal, she now found herself reluctant to touch it, much less read it. She wasn't sure she wanted to know what Mr. Grantham had written about all of them, especially Mr. Underwood. The book seemed dangerous and tainted with more than melted snow.

Cynthia's gaze focused on Olivia's face, her blue eyes filled with sympathy. She sighed lustily and shook her head. "Thought you should read it. You wear your heart upon your sleeve, Lady Olivia. Always did. Too soft." She shook her head again, her red curls bouncing around her round face.

"I was not in love with Mr. Grantham!" Olivia exclaimed. "Why would you think such a thing?"

"Grantham?" Cynthia laughed and waved one hand back and forth in front of her face. "Not Grantham, no. That fencing chap — calls himself Lord Milbourn now."

"He does not *call himself* Lord Milbourn. He *is* Lord Milbourn," Olivia said frostily as she straightened.

Cynthia gestured at the book. "Read that, Lady Olivia. It mentions others of your acquaintance. Sad, really." Her hefty shoulders lifted up and down as she sighed. "Shouldn't like to see that information made public. Bad. Very bad."

"Why don't you just tell me what it is you believe you've discovered if you think it is that important?" Olivia's heart battered against the walls of her chest. She wanted desperately to read the journal, and yet she was afraid of the contents. What had he said about her brothers, or about Lord Milbourn? She didn't want to know their boyhood misdeeds, didn't want to go through that dismay such knowledge would bring, even if she could forget later.

She wanted to believe the best about them, and about herself. Whatever mistakes Mr. Grantham had recorded were better left in the dark.

"No need to kill the messenger and all that." Cynthia grimaced, the pinched corners of her eyes betraying her discomfort. For once, she seemed reluctant to blurt out whatever she was thinking. "Thought you should know. Not a nice surprise. Your Mr. Grantham—"

"He is not *my* Mr. Grantham," Olivia interjected. Her fingertips ran over the top of the journal. The leather felt old and flaky, already starting to decay where it was not still damp. "You must have — he wrote something about Mr. Underwood, did he not?"

"Underwood?" Cynthia frowned at her. "There was a letter. Concerned his wife."

"He was here the day it happened. He was distraught," Olivia whispered, staring down at the book.

"As well he might be if he knew what Grantham had. At least he is above suspicion, or that alone would have condemned him."

"Above suspicion?" Olivia asked, her gaze searching Cynthia's face hopefully.

Cynthia nodded. The red curls framing her face shook loose, and she brushed one long strand out of her eye and tucked it behind her right ear. "Thought you knew — his wife had a baby. He only left briefly to fetch a physician—"

"I saw him on the street," Olivia interrupted.

"Yes, but he was not gone long enough to do ought else but find a physician. So he was there that day and the next — still there for aught I know. They lost two babes before, but this one is alive. So far. A boy."

Edward had known. That was why he had not mentioned his conversation with Mr. Underwood to Mr. Greenfield.

But Mr. Underwood hadn't been home the entire time. Olivia's gaze searched Cynthia's face. "Mr. Underwood did leave his house. I saw him, spoke to him. He was walking past the academy."

Cynthia nodded, clearly unimpressed by the revelation. "Went to fetch the doctor. He was only gone a short time — barely long enough to find a physician and return home."

That explained the panic in his eyes and strain on his pale face. Mr. Underwood had been in a desperate hurry to fetch medical assistance for his wife.

While part of her was relieved and pleased to hear about the new arrival in Mr. Underwood's house, she also felt a great, gray emptiness seeping into her. If Mr. Underwood was not guilty, then.... Her grip on the journal tightened. She couldn't imagine who else might have wanted to see Mr. Grantham dead. That lack placed her even more firmly at the top of Greenfield's list.

Perhaps the journal might still hold some other name, another answer. She studied Cynthia's expectant face before asking, "Did the journal mention someone else? Someone who might have done such a terrible thing to Mr. Grantham?"

"Yes. Grantham had an affair with Isabella Bron — bragged about it in that journal." Cynthia flicked her hand in the general direction of the diary again.

"Isabella Bron? Who is Isabella Bron?"

"Apparently, she was Lord Milbourn's wife — before he inherited his title. Sensuous and quite insatiable by all accounts. Spanish, you know. Passionate. According to Grantham, that is." Cynthia shrugged. "Never knew her, myself."

Lord Milbourn's wife had an affair with Mr. Grantham?

Olivia felt numb, her mind empty of all thoughts except Cynthia's stark statement. The words circled round and round, making it difficult to concentrate.

"Wh-what?" she stuttered. She couldn't think. Why couldn't she *think*?

"I suppose that's why he killed him."

Olivia stared at Cynthia. "Killed him?"

"Why Lord Milbourn killed Grantham," Cynthia repeated patiently. She stared at the empty plates again, licked the tip of one finger, and picked up a few globs of icing and some crumbs. She cleaned off two plates before she said, "Thought you should know. Knew you wouldn't believe me, so I brought you the journal." A look of sympathetic concern wrinkled her forehead. "Stay away from him, is my advice. Dangerous."

"I don't—" Olivia stuttered to a halt.

"That will be best. And as for the journal, it'll look better if you return it to Greenfield." She grinned. "Might make him trust you a bit more and look to the real culprit, Lord Milbourn."

"I don't know what to say," Olivia said at last. *Lord Milbourn?* He couldn't possibly be guilty. She could hardly breathe, and her heart felt as if a giant hand were squeezing it until her entire chest ached.

No, he couldn't have killed Mr. Grantham, he just couldn't. She refused to believe Cynthia's conclusion. If Lord Milbourn had done such a thing, he would have admitted it. He was an honorable man. He would have accepted blame before allowing even the slightest suspicion falling upon her.

She remembered his hand clasping hers at the inquest and his words, "Steady, *mi niña bonita.*" He couldn't have shown her such sympathy if he were to blame.

186

And if he had wanted to kill Grantham, he would have challenged him to a duel — there were foils in the room. He wouldn't have hit him over the head with a marble cherub. It made no sense.

Unless he'd lashed out in hot anger after discovering Mr. Grantham had cuckolded him. But why now? Why would Mr. Grantham admit such a thing to him after so many years?

No. The sharp denial steadied her. That supposition didn't explain Mrs. Adams's death, and Olivia refused to believe there were two murderers. The deaths had to be connected, and they had to have been planned. Coldly planned.

Lord Milbourn could be cold. Distant. And he knows how to develop a strategy. Find the weaknesses in an opponent. That's why he was a fencing master.

Doubts nagged her, biting and itching like a swarm of fleas infesting the nape of her neck. Her pulse thundered in her ears. For a second time, a sure sense of *wrongness* steadied her. It could not be him — it didn't *feel* like him. She refused to accept the theory.

"What other reason could there be for Grantham's death?" Cynthia asked, tilting her head to one side. Her shrewd gaze challenged Olivia.

"I don't know," Olivia said, opening the journal and flicking through the pages. Skimming the entries, her brow wrinkled. There were no names — just enigmatic abbreviations. "Surely this affair was not recent — I understood Lord Milbourn's wife died a number of years ago."

Cynthia nodded in agreement. "Ten years." Again she gestured at the diary. "Read it."

"How can I read it? There are no names mentioned — at least none I recognize."

Cynthia laughed and flung her hands up as she shrugged. "It is not hard to interpret — you will puzzle it out as well as I did. It is not difficult."

"It is ridiculously obtuse — can you not simply translate it for me?"

"You give up too easily, and I have already told you the gist of it. Milbourn's tragedy is described, as well as several youthful escapades that your brother participated in. You will certainly recognize those and from there, the rest of the entries become clear."

Olivia shut the book with a frustrated flick of her hand. Why couldn't Cynthia just provide her with a key? Why did she have to be so difficult? "But—"

"Grantham thought Milbourn might have pushed his wife down the stairs." Cynthia studied her. "That is the important point. Killed her. Probably knew about her affairs. A young hothead. Impulsive. Dangerous, as I said."

"He was never accused, never arrested," Olivia said, leaning forward. Her hands twisted in her lap.

"He is a slave to his impulses." Cynthia reached over the table to clasp Olivia's forearm and give it a squeeze. "Best to be prepared. Dreadful thing, but it's got to be faced. Stay away from him — best to be safe."

Olivia shook her off and sat back. "I need to think — to consider this information."

"Naturally." Cynthia stood and sighed, her gaze drifting one last time over the decimated tea tray. "Read the journal before you return it to Mr. Greenfield. Best to face the facts. Sorry." She leaned over and gave Olivia's shoulder an awkward pat. "Must be off." She hesitated a second before adding, "And burn that letter concerning Mrs. Underwood. It's an ugly thing — arranging to get rid of an unborn baby. Must have been a year or two before she married. Can't blame her. Terrible position. No wonder she's had two miscarriages after that experience. Sheer butchery." She heaved a sympathetic sigh and shook her head as she stood. "Almost burned it, myself. Don't know why I didn't. A man wouldn't understand. Terrible to be alone and with child. Good thing you have Lord Saunders. He will support you — make you forget. You'll see."

"Lord Saunders?" Olivia rose to her feet and stared at Cynthia, feeling deserted.

"You're next to betrothed, are you not? Best thing for you. Forget Milbourn — the devil take him. Now, I must be off. Good day to you, Lady Olivia, and don't forget the journal. Read it. Best to face the truth now than cry about it later," she said before striding through the door and disappearing from view, leaving Olivia with Mr. Grantham's journal resting, heavy and cold, in her hands.

The clammy feel of the stained leather cover was not the only reason Olivia stared down at it with distaste. She wanted to remember Mr. Grantham as a kind, gentle man who was always happy to provide a listening ear when one felt overwhelmed and needed a strong measure of sympathy. The fact that he might have then gone home and written about all their little foibles and tales of woe made her queasy with a sense of betrayal.

But if there was something in the diary that could provide a clue as to who had murdered him, she needed to discover it. Flipping through the pages again, her frustration mounted. She hated puzzles, particularly when others, like Cynthia, found them so easy to interpret. Olivia stopped to read a few passages here and there as her anger with her inability to understand Mr. Grantham's cryptic references burned. But after a few minutes, she found several events that were familiar to her from her brothers' accounts. She could not claim complete victory, however, because Mr. Grantham had referred to the participants by names like M. Dull, M. Somber, and M. Simple. And her brothers had never shared all the details with their sisters, so Mr. Grantham's appellations made it very difficult to decide precisely to whom Mr. Grantham referred.

After an hour, her head throbbed, and the only definite progress she'd made was to decide that "M." designated "Mr." while "Mdme" meant either "Miss" or "Mrs." depending upon the lady he noted. And she often doubted her conclusions about that, as well.

Throwing the book to the floor, Olivia stood and paced in front of the fire until she could control her irritation. Mr. Grantham's arrogant, mocking tone only increased her angry frustration. After five minutes of walking, she picked up the leather volume again, sat, and rubbed her brow before plunging once again into the diary.

After rereading one section three times, she felt almost sure that Mdme Ice was actually Mrs. Bron, Lord Milbourn's wife. That should have meant that she should have been able to identify M. Dull, M. Somber, or M. Simple as Milbourn, but Grantham's entries were so coy that she could not make that association, although she felt sure that he was one of them. None of the names seemed appropriate.

Nonetheless, one thing was clear despite Grantham's efforts at obfuscation; he'd had a brief affair with Mdme Ice. In his own words, "I have broken through the ice, at last, to find nothing but a great deal of hissing steam and hot, salty water beneath the beautiful surface." Mr. Grantham had betrayed Lord Milbourn in the worst way possible and still pretended to be his friend for ten years.

She slammed the journal shut. Perhaps she would find the resolve to read more later and work out his ridiculous nicknames. Or she might simply hand it over to Mr. Greenfield and be done with the filthy thing, because for the moment, it seemed certain to only bring them all more pain without the hope of an answer.

Chapter Eighteen

B y mid-morning on Tuesday, Alexander finally resigned himself to ignorance concerning the contents of Grantham's journal. Greenfield steadfastly refused to allow him to even see the bloody book. He'd been so obstinate that Alexander had almost come to suspect that the inquiry agent had created the diary in his imagination to trick those involved into confessing, and that it didn't actually exist.

Considering the case for the one hundredth time, Alexander experienced a now-familiar prickling of the skin between his shoulder blades. He had facts aplenty and could almost see how the puzzle fit together. Almost, but not quite. He'd hoped that Grantham's journal would supply the final nudge to align all the pieces.

His frustration led to restlessness, and Alexander left his townhouse abruptly. He walked aimlessly and soon found himself on Oxford Street, just a few blocks from the Fencing Academy for Ladies. He paused at Holles and then turned down the street toward Cavendish Square. Hands in pockets, he stared up at the dreary building, his thoughts straying to Lady Olivia.

Greenfield had to be insane to believe she had anything to do with Grantham's death. Or that of the charwoman.

Thinking of her made him walk in the direction of the Archer house. He wanted to see Lady Olivia and know that she was safe. And free.

The walk was not long. While he was waiting in the hallway of the Archer house, he studied the huge portraits. Slowly, he grew aware of the deep quiet penetrating the rooms and hallways around him, like a cold, dense fog masking all signs of life.

Something is wrong.

His senses sharpened. In the distance, he thought he could hear the soft sibilance of distant whispers, so low they barely intruded upon the silence. The faint noise could almost have been the rushing of blood through his veins. Or an illusion — a desire to hear any minute sign of normal life.

"Lord Milbourn, if you will please follow me?" Latimore intoned from the bottom step of the staircase.

Alexander nodded sharply and followed the butler up to the gallery on the first floor. Latimore ushered him through the colonnaded space into the Ivory Drawing Room and performed the introductions before bowing his way out again.

Edward, Peregrine, and Lady Olivia faced him. They stood in a semicircle in front of the fireplace, and their strained, pale faces bore such similar, grim expressions that Alexander halted. He'd interrupted a serious discussion of some sort. Something terrible had happened.

Had Greenfield made a move against her?

"I have come at a bad time," he said, moving closer to Lady Olivia. He searched her alabaster face, noting the worried lines around her shadowed eyes and the downward turn of her mouth.

Edward exchanged glances with his brother and stepped forward to shake Alexander's hand. "Not at all."

Peregrine shook his hand in turn and looked at Edward with raised eyebrows.

Edward nodded absently.

"B-beg your p-pardon, Milbourn. On my way out, you see," Peregrine said, clearly relieved at the prospect of escaping whatever situation they'd been discussing.

Oddly enough, his rapid retreat alleviated some of Alexander's anxiety. Peregrine would never abandon his sister if she were truly in trouble. Whatever else he lacked, he didn't lack for courage.

"How are you, Lord Milbourn?" Lady Olivia asked, initiating the polite preliminaries of a social call. "Would you care to be seated?"

"Yes. And I am quite well." He glanced from Lady Olivia to Archer. "Has Mr. Greenfield been harassing you?"

Lady Olivia exchanged looks with her brother before she gestured for him to sit and sank into a nearby chair. She clasped her hands in her lap and smiled. "No. He has not been here recently. Has he been troubling you?"

"No."

"Would you care to be seated?" Lady Olivia asked again, half-rising.

Archer sat abruptly on the damask couch facing the fireplace and leaned back, leaving Alexander to sit in the chair opposite Lady Olivia.

"Have you learned anything more about the case?" Archer asked.

"Nothing. Though I assume Greenfield knows what he is doing," Alexander said as he took a seat. "I had hoped to get a look at Grantham's journal, but he has avoided granting me that privilege." He studied Archer. "There must be a clue somewhere — a motive — and that is the most likely place. Perhaps he would allow you to read it."

Another sidelong glance flashed between Archer and Lady Olivia.

"What is it?" Alexander asked sharply.

"Mr. Greenfield refused to allow you to see the diary because he does not have it," Lady Olivia said slowly. She looked at her brother. "I have it."

"You? How did you obtain Grantham's journal?"

"Miss Denholm found it in the street. The night that child died," she said.

"And she gave it to you?" He leaned forward, sitting on the edge of his chair. "Why?"

"Lord Milbourn, there were some references to you that some might believe point to a motive," Archer said before his sister could explain.

"So you and Lady Olivia—"

Lady Olivia straightened and opened her mouth.

However, before she could speak, her brother shook his head. "Not at all. You misunderstand us, Lord Milbourn. We do not believe you are involved. But a man like Greenfield — or others who do not know you as well — might not understand."

"Understand what, exactly?" Alexander studied Archer, before transferring his gaze to Lady Olivia.

She flushed and glanced down at her hands, twisting them together in her lap. She looked up, caught his gaze, and her blush deepened. "Perhaps it would be better if you were to read it for yourself."

"I hope you will allow me to do so," he replied dryly. "However, in the meantime, you could grant me the favor of telling me what has caused you such distress."

Archer cleared his throat. "Very well. It is indelicate, Milbourn, and I am sorry. Perhaps Lady Olivia should leave?"

"Let her stay," Alexander answered abruptly.

"Very well. It seems that Mr. Grantham had an," he cleared his throat and cast an uncomfortable glance at Lady Olivia, "affair with your wife."

So that was what they were discussing with such intensity: his wife's charming lack of loyalty.

"Indeed," Alexander said coolly. He leaned back and hooked an arm over the back of his chair and crossed his right ankle over his knee. "Old news, I'm afraid. Grantham didn't mention why he thought this would trouble me now, did he?"

"No," Archer answered. "And as you say, the events happened a long time ago."

"Do not take it to heart, Lady Olivia," Alexander said when she refused to meet his gaze. He smiled bitterly. "I am sure such sordid things will not trouble your marriage. Lord Saunders is not the sort to stray."

"Why should that trouble me?" she asked in a sharp voice. She straightened and stared at him, her mouth tight and her eyes flashing with irritation. "I have not the slightest interest in Lord Saunders's affairs, although I suppose loyalty to my sister, Lady Margaret, should make me somewhat concerned for the sake of her happiness."

Alexander studied her bright, angry eyes and flushed face before he chuckled. "Cried off, did he?"

"He did *not* cry off," Lady Olivia replied, turning away to stare at the floor. She still refused to meet his gaze.

Archer cleared his throat, frowned in consideration, and finally said, "Merely a misunderstanding. But as an old friend of the family, you will soon hear anyway. Lord Saunders has signed a marriage contract."

"I see. And his bride?" A slow, lopsided grin twisted Alexander's mouth as he looked at Lady Olivia.

"Lady Margaret," Archer said. His brows drew together as a brief wave of irritation passed over his features. He flicked a hand as if he could brush away his annoyance. "We were all surprised." He shrugged and fixed his gaze on the floor with the uncomfortable air of avoiding his sister's eyes. He seemed unaware that she was staring at the floor with equal intensity. "Well, all of us, except for Lady Margaret, of course. And Wraysbury, who officially accepted Saunders's offer. The two are well suited, and both seem eager for the match."

"Then please, offer my sincere congratulations to both parties."

"The nuptials are planned for next month." Archer's face twisted. "It seemed preferable to Lady Margaret's notion to proceed posthaste to Gretna Green to avoid the annoyances of banns and licenses."

No wonder Lady Olivia had appeared stunned when Alexander arrived. Her younger sister had snatched Lord Saunders right out of her grasp. He studied her face. Her irritation had faded, leaving a relieved twinkle in her gray eyes and a soft smile curving her lips, when she finally raised her gaze and shyly looked at him.

He'd never seen her look more alive. Or beautiful.

"Mr. Edward, sir," Latimore's voice came from the doorway. "You have a visitor."

"Who is it?" Archer asked, an annoyed look tightening his face at the interruption.

"Mr. Underwood, sir. I have shown him into the library."

"Oh, yes. It is that matter of his son, I suppose. Tell him that I will join him in a minute."

"Very good, sir." Latimore bowed and disappeared, his quiet tread gradually growing more distant as he descended the stairs.

"Beg your pardon, Milbourn. A small matter I must attend to. Perhaps you will allow Lady Olivia to offer you some tea?" Archer moved toward the door and paused to glance over his shoulder. Without waiting for a response, he nodded. "I will send Mary up with a tray." Then he was gone, the leather soles of his shoes clattering firmly across the marble floor of the gallery.

Alexander could have sworn that Lady Olivia groaned.

"What is it, *mi niña bonita*? Are you disappointed?"

"I am afraid I am not overly fond of tea, and I have had far too much of it of late." Her low laugh drew an answering smile from him.

"And what of Lord Saunders?" he asked, rising and moving to stand in front of the fireplace.

"He was sweet, but the beagles would never have approved of him." Her eyes shone with a mischievous gleam as she stood and looked up at him. "And I am sure Lord Saunders will adore Lady Margaret's rabbits just as much as she does. My brother is correct; they are very well suited." She moved nearer and rested a hand against his chest as if to feel his thundering heart.

Slowly, she leaned against him. The fragrance of lavender filled the air around her soft brown hair. The warmth of her palm against his chest radiated through him. This close, her skin looked as smooth and fine as cool marble with a faint pink flush coloring her cheeks and lips.

She tilted her head up and paused. When he failed to move, she pressed a soft kiss against his mouth.

He drew in a sharp breath and looped his arms around her to draw her closer, deepening their kiss.

His feelings, denied for so long, threatened to overwhelm him. This was what he had longed for, what he had wanted for years. And it was what had caused him so much pain.

Once again he felt a rush of that tortuous brew twisting through his gut, an emotion that had never quite faded since that terrible night, ten years ago. His wife had fallen to her death, and as he had stared down at her tumbled body, his first emotion had been relief. The guilt, and then grief, had only come later, when he'd checked for a pulse in her rapidly cooling wrist and remembered their daughter.

How could he explain it to Maria? How could she trust him to protect her if he could let this happen to her beautiful mother?

He pushed Lady Olivia away gently. She deserved something better, nobler than he. And she would find a man to love, given time.

Isabella's ghost stood between them, the same old malicious smile curving her red lips. She would always be there, intent on destroying anything of value in his life.

He should never have married her. But they had both been young and foolish and had allowed their physical needs to overcome their better judgment. She'd been beautiful and rapacious in her need for male admiration. He knew that, but thought his adoration would be enough. And he'd shook with anger the first time she threw her head back and laughed at his demands for loyalty and fidelity.

Only a fool ignores a chance for pleasure when it is offered, she'd mocked him. Life was hard — why not grab what opportunities arise?

And he was inattentive, she'd said. Then she'd begun her complaints. Over the months, she railed at him so often that he could still hear the angry sneer in her voice as she complained, "All you care about is fencing. Why deny me my happiness? Is it so bad to want a little pleasure? You care nothing for me — you are cold — as cold as that sword you love so well. Take your blade to bed, if you want love. See if *it* will return your love."

Her words had tainted his life and haunted him, nearly killing his pleasure in the one thing she'd left him, the art of fencing.

"Lord Milbourn," Lady Olivia whispered, her gaze roving over his face as her hands smoothed his lapels.

His memories fled like shadows at dawn. He caught her hands and gently pushed her away. "My apologies." He forced a cold smile. "I don't believe I will wait for tea, after all."

"Don't go. Please, stay and talk." She caught at his sleeve. "The journal — I don't believe you had anything to do with Mr. Grantham's death."

"Surely, you are not naïve enough to believe I am incapable of killing a man?" he asked with a sardonic twist to his mouth. "I assure you I am quite capable of doing so."

"I have no doubt you are," Lady Olivia replied. Her grip on his arm tightened. "In a duel or a fair fight. You would not have killed Mrs. Adams for her key to the townhouse and then murdered Mr. Grantham."

"Not even if he had an affair with my wife?" He pried her fingers off his arm. It was for her own good.

"You would have done it *then*. Not ten years later." She walked over to her chair and bent down to rifle through the sewing box on the floor next to it. When she straightened, she held an old, brown leather book in her hands. "You wanted to examine Mr. Grantham's journal." She held it out to him. "Take it."

"Why not give it to Mr. Greenfield?"

"You give it to him," she flung the words at him.

Her tight mouth and the look of confusion and hurt in her eyes forced him to harden his resolve. She wanted something more from him, something he couldn't give her.

Better disappointment now than a deeper pain later.

But the scent of her hair and taste of her lips lingered like the taste of the sweetest Madeira wine.

He stiffened. She would forget him soon enough. He reached out and took Grantham's journal. After slipping it into his pocket, he bowed and bid her good day.

She gazed at him, her eyes glittering with unshed tears, as he walked away.

Chapter Nineteen

Olivia watched Lord Milbourn leave with feelings of confusion and abandonment. What was wrong with him? Or with her? First, Lord Saunders had decided to offer for Margaret, instead, which was actually a relief, and now, Lord Milbourn had rejected her, as well. She'd always assumed she'd marry and have children — lots of children — who would each have his or her very own beagle to sleep at the foot of the bed and follow them around with wagging tails, long, flapping ears, and adoring eyes. For the first time, the lonely misery of spinsterhood loomed in front of her as a very real possibility.

Perhaps she should never have kissed him. She'd been too forward and made him angry. Maybe that was the flaw in her that frightened men away; she was too bold and presumptuous. Even her academy provided ample proof of that. Why would she have pursued such a grossly inappropriate activity unless she lacked a sense of propriety and understanding of polite behavior?

Now, when she hoped her actions would bring her closer to Lord Milbourn, she'd only driven him away.

The only man she'd ever loved — would ever love — was gone.

The numbness of despair made her limbs feel leaden and heavy. She stared at her work basket. A few pale green silk threads spilled limply over the edge, taunting her with her inability to complete anything successfully. She'd promised Margaret a pair of elaborately embroidered sleeves over a month ago, and they were still unfinished. But now, sewing seemed tedious and too much effort.

She was still staring down at the basket when Mary brought up the tea tray, just in time for a series of social calls from ladies of her acquaintance. Most were avidly curious about the inquests and tragedies, probing delicately for titillating details and perhaps hoping to elicit a thrilling confession from Olivia.

She answered their questions mechanically.

The day dragged on. Despite her visitors, part of Olivia kept reviewing what she had read in Grantham's diary, restlessly searching for a clue. The discipline was better than thinking about the uncertain London weather, the inquests, or the kiss and Lord Milbourn's reaction to it.

After the last lady left, however, she couldn't think of anything except Lord Milbourn.

Her heart had soared when he first put his arms around her and crushed her against him. She thought she'd found love at last and an answering need within him. Now, she wondered if his embrace had only been a reflex, like a boy who throws up his hands to catch a ball thrown at him without warning. What she had thought was passion might only have been surprise.

How embarrassing. And how dismal.

Such a reaction suggested that, despite his bitterness about his wife's behavior, he still loved her. She was the only woman he'd ever given his heart to, and no other would ever match her.

One couldn't fight a ghost, and time only made them stronger as their faults melted away, leaving only the memory of their perfection.

I can't compete with her, or the perfection of their past together.

Mrs. Bron's specter would always stand between them. Olivia slowly went upstairs to change for dinner, her feet dragging with the effort.

That evening, when Hildegard, Edward, and Peregrine decided to go to the theater again after supper, Olivia begged off, pleading a headache.

"You have had a lot of headaches recently," Hildegard remarked as they stood to leave the men to their after-dinner port. "Perhaps you should send for a physician."

"I don't require a physician. I simply need a little peace and quiet. An evening at home will do me a great deal of good," Olivia said.

"You will just brood. You know you will. You should come with us," Hildegard pleaded. She grabbed the newel-post, placed one foot on the first stair, and began to swing gently back and forth around the post. As she swung closer to Olivia, she flung a calculating look over her shoulder. "Mr. Belcher is joining us at the theater. Perhaps you should come. Don't you think he's angelic looking?"

"Will you stop swaying like that? You are not a child anymore. You are a young lady and should act like one."

"What about the theater? Are you not interested?" Hildegard grinned. "In going with us, that is."

"I am not interested in going, nor am I interested in Mr. Belcher."

"Well, you ought to marry someone, you know, as you are the eldest. You should marry before Margaret."

"Lady Margaret," Olivia corrected her and then winced. She sounded exactly like an old maid — an old *bluestocking* maid. And while Mr. Belcher was certainly handsome, she couldn't make herself feel anything for him, even if that decision doomed her to remain alone for the rest of her life.

She frowned. He'd always been pleasant, almost too pleasant at times and rather irritating when she considered him as a potential mate. Obviously, blond curls and a square chin failed to attract her as much as they should have, so it was her own fault if she slipped into spinsterhood without a protest.

But then Lord Milbourn's sardonic features shoved Mr. Belcher's pretty face out of her mind. The mere thought of him made her contrary heart beat faster. Why couldn't she forget him and turn her attention to the charming Mr. Belcher?

Hildegard snorted. "You know mother would have been quite disgusted with you, if she were still alive. She always believed in order, and it is certainly the height of disorder for Lady Margaret to marry first. You should take your responsibilities more seriously and set a good example for those of us who are younger than you. And still impressionable," she added in a mockingly sweet voice.

"Margaret—"

"*Lady* Margaret," Hildegard said, interrupting her.

"Lady Margaret has certainly impressed her bad habits upon you," Olivia said. Hildegard sounded almost exactly like Margaret had before her shocking betrothal to Lord Saunders.

Hildegard eyed Olivia over her shoulder, but didn't stop swaying. "You have been in the most terrible mood lately, and you used to be such fun." She wrinkled her nose. "I thought you would be relieved that *Lady* Margaret is marrying Lord Saunders. Surely, you knew that she's been in love with him *forever*."

"What?" Olivia stared at her sister.

Hildegard swung around the post in another arc. "Did you not notice what a foul mood she has been since everyone started talking about your betrothal to Lord Saunders?" She rolled her eyes. "It was obvious to everyone that she was horribly jealous."

Suddenly, Olivia understood why her sister had grown so difficult and contrary. Olivia shook her head ruefully. If only Margaret had said something — Olivia would gladly have relinquished her claim on Lord Saunders if she'd known Margaret loved him.

"Clearly, she failed to make it obvious to Wraysbury or he would never have considered matching me to Lord Saunders," Olivia said, trying to paint over her own blindness in the matter.

"Well, you and Wraysbury were the only ones who did *not* know," Hildegard said. She paused in her swaying to examine Olivia's face again and sniffing. "You should be pleased. No one thinks you are guilty, you know."

"I am not worried about that."

"Then is it truly Lord Saunders? You did not love *him,* too, did you? I was sure you did not. I fail to understand the attraction he holds for both of you. I told Margaret—"

"*Lady* Margaret," Olivia said triumphantly, cutting her off.

Hildegard wrinkled her nose and swung faster from side to side, left foot flying as she balanced on her right and clung to the post. "Don't be so stuffy. No one is here but the two of us."

"Nevertheless, it is Lady Margaret, just as you are Lady Hildegard. It shows respect for your family and yourself. Mother never referred to father as anything but Lord Wraysbury."

"Oh, I'm sure she referred to him as something else. At certain times." Hildegard giggled. "In private."

Olivia felt her face flame. "You are incorrigible."

"Oh, pooh. Titles are all very well if we have guests, but if you ask me, it is just ridiculously stuffy to worry about such things when we are alone."

"Have you been visiting Her Grace, the Duchess of Peckham, again?" Olivia asked.

Hildegard was fast becoming far too lackadaisical in the matter of polite manners, and she grew worse each time she visited their cousins. The duchess had been born in the former colonies, now the United States of America, and she took the matter of titles very lightly. Perhaps a little too lightly to make her a good influence on the younger members of the Archer family.

"What if I have?" Hildegard countered as she hopped off the bottom step. "The boys will be done with their brandy and gossip soon. Are you sure you don't wish to join us?"

"No." Olivia laughed. "Honestly. I am looking forward to a quiet evening. Enjoy yourself, and don't annoy Edward too much."

Hildegard giggled. "How am I supposed to enjoy myself if I cannot annoy Edward? It is one of the primary joys of my poor, benighted life. And he hates it so when I disappear from our box at the theater, even though he knows I'm only visiting friends. He seems to believe I'm on the verge of running off with an actor, or the groom, or some such person."

"Don't even suggest such a thing." Olivia held her hand over her mouth to hide her smile. "I think he fears Wraysbury will hold him personally responsible if any of us behaves outrageously. Or more outrageously than I have behaved already in founding my Fencing Academy for Ladies."

"Then it is a good thing Margaret is getting married. One female crossed off his list of responsibilities, and only two more left to burden him." She slanted a sly glance at Olivia. "Unless he can cross you off, as well. I saw Lord Milbourn here today. And you spoke to him in private." She snorted. "La de dah, de dah!"

"Stop that noise! And it was for less than five minutes — just long enough to say our farewells. Now if you're going to the theater, I suggest you get ready, or they may leave without you, and you will miss annoying the beautiful Mr. Belcher."

"They would not dare!" Hildegard yelped as she turned to dash up the stairs. "I would never forgive them."

Olivia waited until her sister disappeared around the curve in the staircase leading up to the third floor before she followed at a more decorous pace.

Much to her relief, she spent a quiet evening at home and was able to mend the torn flounces around the hems of two dresses, although the green silk for Margaret's sleeves still taunted her. Ignoring the embroidery work, she started reading *The Pirate*, instead. She'd wanted to read it ever since it had been published the previous year by Sir Walter Scott, but her brothers had insisted on their rights to read it first.

Shortly before midnight, she blew out her lamp and settled into her bed, pulling the heavy covers up to her chin. Her worries failed to keep her awake as she half-feared, and she soon sank into a deep slumber.

Ordinary life thankfully continued the following morning. Olivia caught up on her correspondence, discussed household management with Mrs. Keene, and prepared the menus for the rest of the week. Edward and Peregrine wanted to invite some friends to supper Thursday evening, so she expanded the menu to include cray fish soup removed with a roasted turkey, *poulet a la duchesse*, oysters, a loin of pork, matelot of eels, and fish removed with a fillet of veal for the first course, followed by a pheasant, asparagus, macaroni, cederata cream, ratafia pudding, jelly, omelet soufflé, cardoons with sauce, and wild duck for the second course. The list should provide a welcome variety for even the most delicate appetite, and since Mrs. Peale did an excellent job with most of the dishes, she couldn't lodge too many complaints.

Olivia had just sifted the drying sand off the menu when Latimore appeared at the door to the sitting room.

"Lady Olivia, Miss Denholm has sent a note." He bowed as he held out a silver salver with a creamy card on top.

"Is she here?" Olivia picked up the calling card and glanced past his shoulder.

No one had shadowed him through the gallery. She studied the card. Cynthia Denholm's name was printed on the front, and a few scrawled lines covered the back. Olivia frowned. The writing didn't have the bold flourishes and curls she normally associated with Cynthia, but it was obviously hastily written. And she'd used pencil, so perhaps that accounted for it.

The terse message certainly sounded precisely like Cynthia.

Where are you? Time for a lesson.

— Cynthia Denholm

A lesson? It was at least two hours before they were supposed to have the next session at the academy.

Olivia sighed and rose, looking through the doorway again. "Is she waiting in the hall?"

"No, Lady Olivia." Latimore shook his head. "She sent a boy with the card."

"She must be at the academy, then." Olivia shook her head. "I suppose I must go. If my brothers ask, please inform them that I have gone there. I should return in a few hours, four at the latest." She handed him the menus for the week. "Please, see that Mrs. Peale receives these."

"Very good, Lady Olivia." He took the menus and bowed his way out.

She listened to his steady tread echo across the marble as he descended the staircase again. Although she was pleased that Cynthia had caught some of Olivia's pleasure in the art of fencing, she was beginning to recognize some of the disadvantages, as well. Particularly as it was taking an increasingly large chunk of her time.

Well, the sooner she went to the academy, the sooner she could return to her social responsibilities here.

Upstairs in her room, she had Farmer gather up her soft curls and pin them into a tight knot at the nape of her neck to keep the wayward locks out of her way. When fencing Cynthia, good, unobstructed vision was crucial.

"Where are my new kid half-boots?" she asked the maid as she smoothed the lapels of her dark green Spencer and stared out the window of her bedchamber. Soft sunshine glittered over the hodgepodge of mews' roofs and chimneys. For once, it promised to be a fair day, with only a few fluffy, white clouds scudding across the pale blue skies.

The short jacket would be warm enough with the addition of her thick cashmere shawl. And that light clothing would be more comfortable than her fur-lined pelisse when she was flushed and perhaps overheated on her return.

"Here they are, Lady Olivia." Farmer held out the white boots, which Olivia had had ordered especially for fencing.

The white leather was soft and supple in her hand, and the thin soles should provide for excellent footing on the wooden floors. Olivia smiled as she draped them by their laces over her arm.

"Is there anything else, Lady Olivia?" Farmer asked, watching her with anxious eyes. She twisted her thin hands together in front of her, obviously still fearful that Olivia would decide to let her go without a recommendation.

Olivia impulsively reached out and squeezed her maid's wrist. "No, and please, stop worrying so. I am not going to terminate your employment simply because you told Mr. Greenfield the truth."

"Oh, Lady Olivia, I am so sorry." She grabbed Olivia's hand and clasped it tightly between her cold, damp palms. "I never meant to — honestly — I never would have done so. But he came up here when I was brushing the mud off your good pelisse, and he saw it fall from my hand onto the floor. I couldn't do anything — honestly." Her voice broke under a deluge of tears. She gulped and sniffed between gasping out in desperate phrases, "I never meant — I would never do such a thing — truly — you have been so kind to me — you must believe me!"

"I do, and you must believe me, Farmer." Olivia hugged her before wriggling her hand out of the maid's grasp. "I am not angry and will not let you go. Who else would make such wonderful face creams and possets? We would all be lost without you. Now please, stop this nonsense. Your future here is quite safe."

She studied Farmer as the maid dug through the pockets of her apron and pulled out a large handkerchief. She blew her nose and murmured a confused series of damp expressions of gratitude from behind the folds of the linen square.

"You know I am innocent, do you not?" Olivia asked.

Every twitch, every sob stopped with such sharp suddenness that Olivia blinked several times. Even Farmer's breathing desisted. In that appalled silence, Olivia knew with absolute certainty that her maid believed she had killed Mr. Grantham.

Olivia went rigid with the deep sense of betrayal. But she had told Farmer she wouldn't let her go, and she meant to keep her word.

The only question that remained was why the maid wished to continue working for a murderess.

"Oh no, Lady Olivia. I would never believe such a thing," Farmer said awkwardly, her eyes flicking left and right before focusing on the floor.

There was little to be gained from trying to convince her of Olivia' innocence. Protesting only made one seem guiltier, not less. The thought had barely ceased echoing through her mind before she felt the tickle of an idea, something about the murders, that refused to coalesce. She shrugged it off. The notion would return, fully formed, when it was ready to do so. She could not force it.

"Never mind. I mended the flounces on two of my dresses, however, there is still the lace on my white satin gown that needs repairing. Please attend to it." Olivia patted Farmer on the shoulder, grabbed her cashmere shawl, and made good her escape.

She managed to avoid the necessity of an escort by the simple expedient of brushing past Latimore in a flurry of words that granted him no opportunity to send for a maid, or one of her brothers.

Walking rapidly, she had one foot in mid-air, about to step off the curb at the first intersection, when the thought that had escaped her earlier shook her like a strong wind. She took a step back and frowned. The unpleasant notion grew stronger and terribly unpleasant.

All of her previous suspicions had centered around men, or rather one man, Mr. Underwood.

What if a woman had murdered Mr. Grantham, the way Mr. Greenfield thought she had? She remembered Cynthia shoving her during their first match. That hadn't been the first time Cynthia had hit someone.

Her stomach churned. When they were younger, Cynthia had given one of their grooms a resounding slap across the face when she thought he grew too forward in his attentions.

What if she had gone to the academy searching for Olivia, and Mrs. Adams had let her in? She could have met Mr. Grantham — though why he was there was still a mystery — and he might have grown a bit too familiar. Cynthia could easily have misunderstood his kindness for flirtation, the same way she'd mistaken the groom's actions.

Olivia could see the two of them standing in her office, a frown of disgust on Cynthia's broad face. Without thinking, Cynthia could have reached out, picked up the marble cherub, and hit him over the head. Then far below, the front door creaked as Olivia and Peregrine had arrived.

Panicked at what she'd done, Cynthia might have shoved Mr. Grantham into the wardrobe. She was certainly strong enough to manhandle his body. Then, as Olivia and Peregrine walked to the main staircase, Cynthia could have dashed down the servants' stair at the back of the house.

It wouldn't take her long to realize she had blood on her clothing and needed to avoid being seen. If she ran into Mrs. Adams in the kitchen, the older woman would surely have exclaimed about the stains. Fearful of being caught, Cynthia might have hit her, too, with one of the old utensils left behind by the previous tenants.

Cynthia had already have been overwrought and upset over what she had done, and she never knew her own strength. Consequently, the blow might have been more than necessary to render Mrs. Adams unconscious. And again, terrified of meeting Olivia or Peregrine, Cynthia could have dragged the charwoman away and hid her body in one of the small buildings behind the townhouse.

Once rational thought returned and Cynthia realized what she'd done, she could have returned Mrs. Adams's body to the kitchen so that it would be discovered and given a decent burial.

That would account for her lack of interest in Grantham's journal. It had nothing to do with his death. And knowing Cynthia, her crimes had to be weighing heavily on her conscience. Perhaps that was why she wanted to see Olivia; she wanted to confess.

Wait! She stumbled over a curb and regained her balance at the last moment.

"Isn't that your friend, Miss Denholm?" The echo of Peregrine's words rang through her mind. She and Peregrine had both seen Cynthia, striding away down the street.

So there was proof that she'd been in the vicinity of the academy when the murders occurred. The only thing that changed in her theory was that Cynthia had left before Olivia and Peregrine arrived, not after. It was an insignificant detail, and the rest fit so neatly she didn't know why she hadn't seen the answer sooner.

Olivia tried to find flaws, anything to prove that she was wrong. She liked Cynthia and didn't want to think of her committing two senseless murders. There were certainly some holes, perhaps enough to give her hope that her theory was incorrect.

After all, there was the matter of Mrs. Adams's missing key. Cynthia would have no reason to take it. That suggested that someone might have killed the charwoman in order to obtain the key, otherwise, they would have found it by now.

So Olivia could be wrong. Thankfully, someone else had to have murdered Mr. Grantham and Mrs. Adams. And she was no further along in her private inquiry, except for the feeling that she'd noticed some clue at some point and knew more than she thought she did. She only needed to let that notion float forward into the light, like a feather floating from the shadows to a beam of sunlight streaming through the window.

When the tall, gray building housing her academy rose into view, she paused, demoralized anew. She couldn't help feeling that she'd touched off this terrible series of events when she recklessly decided to start her fencing school. She'd flouted the rules of Polite Society in doing so and had gone her own way like a refractory horse, wild and stubbornly refusing to take the bit into her mouth. All because she wanted to share the exhilaration she felt when her blade found its mark and the sizzle of excitement burning inside her.

Maybe if she hadn't invited Cynthia Denholm to join her, Mr. Grantham and Mrs. Adams might still be alive. Even if Cynthia *weren't* the murderer, their deaths might never have occurred had Olivia not done such a nonsensical thing.

Give in and give it up — I'll have to, now. It's too scandalous. I should have recognized that before this.

What was once only outrageous, was now dark and bloody with tragedy. It was time to end it before anyone else suffered. Be the sweet, biddable lady she should have been all along.

By the time she stepped up to the academy's door, she felt coldly chastened and heavy with bleak hopelessness. Her dreams were well and truly shattered. There seemed nothing left for her to do but smile politely and conform to expectations. Marry the next fool who asked her. Forget the feel of fire in her veins, the challenges, and the exhilaration of crossing swords with an opponent.

Settle down. Be sensible. The words crushed her with their unbearable weight.

Hand on the doorknob, she pushed the door open, vaguely surprised that it was unlocked. With a shrug, she remembered the authorities coming and going at random, as if staring at the filthy floorboards would answer all their questions. Reminding them to lock the door had little effect.

But though leaving the door unlocked was not the best situation, there was so little in the building to steal that it seemed silly to worry about it. Mr. Greenfield would be done soon enough, one way or the other.

Then she could hire appropriate servants, preferably a husband and wife, to take care of the property and keep it secured.

Or rather she would have found servants, if she were to continue the academy. That possibility seemed ridiculously remote.

So much I should have done, so many small details overlooked.

She should already have made those arrangements, but she'd put them off, thinking Mrs. Adams would suffice. Olivia sighed, drowning in guilt and shame. If she'd hired a couple as she'd initially planned, perhaps Mrs. Adams would still be alive. But the agency had sent Mrs. Adams, and Olivia had been too lazy and careless to interview more servants.

That fact simply proved she was unfit to run an academy in the first place. Unfortunately, it was too late for such regrets. But she could correct the untenanted state of the townhouse, so the place would be cared for until her brother rented it to someone else.

She'd simply have to make another appointment with the employment agency and find a suitable man and woman. Today would have been ideal, of course. Perhaps she ought to have Latimore send one of the footmen over to stay at the academy tonight. That would provide temporary help until she could hire more appropriate staff.

Walking into the dusty hallway, Olivia glanced around. The hushed silence made the building seem abandoned. A chilly breeze lifted a small curl at the nape of her neck. In the dim light, she shivered and held her breath, trying not to think about ghosts.

She cocked her head to one side, but she couldn't even hear the whispers of shoes sliding across the floor, or the voices she should have heard if Cynthia and the Peterson sisters were already practicing.

"Miss Denholm?" she called, removing her bonnet. She dropped her white leather boots on the floor, and held her hat by the ribbons as she threw off her shawl and draped it over her arm. "Miss Peterson?"

Perhaps they were upstairs in her office. She'd left the masks and foils on her desk, not wanting to use the wardrobe again, although it had been cleaned.

Her thoughts returned to the problem of servants as she climbed the stairs. No doubt she'd have difficulties. Few would want to work here when they realized that two people had been killed in the townhouse. Many might refuse to stay overnight, for fear of being murdered in their beds. Or the horror of seeing a ghost leaning over them as they slept.

She shivered and rubbed her arms. That wasn't the worst of it. The murderer hadn't been found and still had the key. Even if Mr. Greenfield locked the door, the killer could come and go as he pleased. She'd be lucky if she could find anyone willing to stay here under those conditions, until she had the locks changed.

The floor above her head creaked. She halted and glanced upward at the shadowy landing, her nerves fluttering.

She was scaring herself. There were no specters — it was daytime, after all. She took a deep breath. "Miss Denholm? Are you there?"

No response. Where was she?

Olivia frowned and climbed the rest of the way up the stairs.

The door to her office was partially open, and a fan of grayish light glowed across the floor, showing puffballs of dust, and grains of sand in stark relief against the dark wooden planks. Despite the sunlight, the room felt gloomy and cold, with a hushed quiet that made Olivia think of the tense silence of someone hiding and holding her breath. She glanced around uneasily, almost willing to believe that hauntings were real and not simply the result of a sensitive person's own fears.

"Miss Denholm?" She pushed the door the rest of the way open and stepped into the room.

The grainy sunlight leaking through the dingy windows behind her desk glinted off the foils tangled in a heap on the scarred, wooden surface. The room appeared to be empty. It wasn't until she walked closer to the desk that she noticed a slumped heap of skirts in the shadowed corner behind the large piece of furniture.

"Miss Denholm?" Her voice rose shrilly with shock. She pressed a hand on the edge of the desk, her heart pounding.

Cynthia sat on the floor, her head lolling against the wall to her left. One hand rested in her lap and the other lay, palm up and fingers curled, on the floor beside her. She still wore her thick, black pelisse over a dark brown dress, and stout walking boots. Her bonnet hung askew over her right ear, and with her mouth hanging partially open and her eyes closed, she appeared to be peacefully asleep.

Edging quickly around the corner of the desk toward her friend, Olivia flinched when something jabbed into the center of her back. She dropped her bonnet in surprise.

Then, without thinking, her new empty left hand reached out and clenched the hilt of one of the foils resting on the desk. The heavy shawl draped over her arm slid over the desktop with the motion, hiding the surface.

"Don't turn around," a man ordered as she jerked forward again at another vicious jab into her back. Even though she couldn't see him, he sounded as if he were smiling maliciously — she could hear it in his voice. "Where is it?"

"Who are you?" she asked sharply, ignoring his question. "What have you done to Miss Denholm?"

"Where is it?" He thrust her forward sharply.

Her hip hit the corner of the desk, and she almost sprawled over the surface. Clenching her jaw, she pressed her lips together and pushed off the desk, spinning around to face the intruder. She took a step back, flicked the foil from her left to her right hand, and brought up the unprotected tip.

A man stood in front of her, his face covered by a dark cloth with two holes cut out, showing his glittering eyes. He wore a large, wide-brimmed black hat and a dark coat. In his hand, he held a walking stick with an elaborate gold knob.

She drew a sharp breath. She recognized that stick. "Mr. Belcher!"

Suddenly, Mr. Grantham's cryptic notes in his journal made sense. Crispin Belcher had been Isabella Bron's other lover. Mr. Grantham must have been blackmailing him.

With a flamboyant gesture, Mr. Belcher pulled off his hat and the attached mask, and threw it on the desk with a taunting bark of laughter. As he did so, a large brass key clattered to the floor.

She stared at it. It was the key she'd given to Mrs. Adams.

"So you guessed," he said. "Well, it matters naught."

"What did you do to Miss Denholm?" Olivia leaned against the edge of the desk, her legs hardly able to support her.

"That cow?" He chuckled and pulled his walking stick apart to reveal the sword inside. "Unfortunately, she is not dead, though she may wish she were when she awakens."

He backed up a few feet to assume a fighting stance, a look of disdain on his face. He touched her blade with his.

"Why? Why are you doing this?"

"That is not the question, Lady Olivia." He studied her. His contempt giving way to anger. His golden brows thrust together. "Where is the journal?"

"I don't have it." As quickly as she could, she took the measure of the room. Her office was not as large as the room they used for the fencing lessons. The furniture took up valuable space. However, obstacles could be useful.

She eased away from the desk, seeking more space to maneuver.

"Don't lie." He lunged forward, almost slipping under her guard.

She parried and tried to control her harsh breathing. Panic fluttered in her chest, squeezing out the air.

Think! What are his weaknesses?

Her brothers had discussed dueling techniques and the relative strengths and weaknesses of their friends — she'd heard them countless times. Edward had once remarked that Mr. Belcher was a decent swordsman. That tepid praise meant that, in fact, Mr. Belcher was good — most likely, very good.

"I am not in the habit of lying," she replied coldly, moving past the wardrobe. She didn't want to be trapped in the smaller space between the desk and that large piece of furniture. "I do not have it."

Smiling grimly, he teased and tested her blade, his blue eyes fixed upon her, searching for an opening. "That cow found it and gave it to you — what did you do with it? Hide it? I assume you read it."

"I gave it to Lord Milbourn," she said, retreating a step and watching his movements. Her ragged breathing and rapid pulse made her reactions shaky and graceless. She took a deep, steadying breath.

Cool indifference.

It sounded so easy, but it was difficult to achieve when she faced an opponent bent on killing her.

"Milbourn?" He lunged again, slipping in under her guard and nearly disarming her. "That blind fool. It will be as useless to him as it was to you."

She managed to swirl out of the way and slid her foil under his to force him back. When she stepped back, a burning pain over the ribs on her left side told her that he'd been more successful than she realized. He'd sliced through her Spencer and nicked her. Warmth trickled over her waist and hip.

"It will be of some use, however. And I am sure Mr. Greenfield found it very interesting," she said smoothly.

Mr. Belcher's grin widened and grew more spiteful. "Interesting or not, it won't do you much good now, my little dove."

A breathy moan from the corner behind her desk reminded her of Cynthia. Why hadn't he killed her? Suddenly, she remembered the first lesson she'd given her friend and how Cynthia had nearly killed her.

"You are going to blame this on Miss Denholm — are you not?" Her voice sounded harsh to her ears.

"Very good, Lady Olivia. I fear your lessons with Miss Denholm will shortly come to a sad end." He scornfully tested her blade again.

With great effort, she forced him to retreat a step. The fire in her side deepened.

"Why?" the question whispered over her lips.

"Why not? She's been a bloody nuisance, and I can think of no more deserving party. She will be surprised, of course, when she awakens to find you dead, the offending blade in her hand, and no recollection of what she has done. Accidents do happen. And perhaps she should not have confided in me that she loved Grantham and feared he was preparing to offer for you." He clicked his tongue and shook his head. The tip of his blade danced in front of her eyes. "Jealousy, you know. Dreadful thing."

"Sheer nonsense. No one will believe you. You forget Lord Saunders."

"You forget that Lord Saunders is marrying your sister. Not you. I am afraid they will be all too happy to believe me when I sadly explain Miss Denholm's terrifying jealousy."

"The journal—" She stopped abruptly.

"What about the journal? Even that featherbrained Greenfield will realize the journal means nothing when I explain about Denholm." In a quick gesture, he pressed his left hand over his heart in an exaggerated expression of grief. He smiled and continued reciting the tale he obviously intended to relate to Greenfield, "I just wish I had realized the danger to you sooner, before you were tragically murdered by a clearly unhinged Miss Denholm. Her unbalanced state also explains why a previously rational young woman would be so enthusiastic about learning to fence. It is unnatural, after all, and a plain indication of how disordered her mind was. It explains so much, you see."

Olivia barely heard him. She pressed her left arm against her side, grateful for the shawl still draped over her forearm. The folds and the darkness of her dress hid the blood she was sure was seeping through her clothing. Mr. Belcher already had too many advantages — he didn't need to know he'd wounded her.

She had to end this soon, before she weakened too much. She made a few feints, but Mr. Belcher parried her thrusts easily, his condescending smile never wavering.

He's the better swordsman.

"I still do not understand — why should it matter to you if Grantham knew of your affair? He was guilty, himself," she said, hoping to gain time. She needed a minute to catch her breath and find a vulnerability, an opening she could exploit.

"Grantham was nothing but an annoyance. But he could have made my new business endeavor with Milbourn a trifle awkward. Grantham discovered the truth — I don't know how — and he threatened to tell Milbourn. He knew I had loved Isabella, and the baby was *mine*, not Milbourn's." His blue eyes burned in his bleak face. "And Milbourn killed them both — pushed her down the stairs. I lost everything I loved while he lived to gain a title and a fortune. Well, now *he* will discover what it feels like to lose everything he loves."

With a flash of steel, he charged.

Chapter Twenty

"What do you mean, she is not here?" Alexander faced Latimore in the Archer's entryway. His driving need to find Lady Olivia strengthened as he eyed the elderly butler's impassive face.

It wasn't until that moment that he realized where he'd seen the circular pattern left in the broken skin of Mrs. Adams's temple. His sense of urgency deepened.

"She had a lesson, Lord Milbourn. With Miss Denholm," Latimore replied, his voice growing so slow and ponderous that he gave the impression of a turtle frozen in winter ice.

"Who went with her? Mr. Edward Archer?"

"No, Lord Milbourn. She professed to be in a hurry and would not wait for an escort."

"Alone? She went alone?"

"Indeed, Lord Milbourn." As Latimore stared at him, his mouth tightened with disapproval at Alexander's persistent questions.

Or perhaps he was still annoyed with Lady Olivia for leaving without a proper escort. Alexander's lips twitched with a flash of amusement, but it didn't last.

Olivia was alone at the academy. Or perhaps not alone enough.

He'd reviewed Grantham's journal several times last night, before sending the diary back to Mr. Greenfield. Although it took him a while to break the code Grantham used in place of names, he'd been able to do so largely by associating his memories of the events described with Grantham's references to Sharp, Simple, and Somber. Alexander was M. Dull, Belcher was M. Somber, and Wraysbury was

M. Simple. The appellations seemed to be largely the opposite of each man's underlying character — or so Alexander assumed. He'd been described as a great many things over the years, but dull had not been one of the more popular choices, and no one could consider Belcher somber or Wraysbury simple.

However, if Alexander had guessed correctly, Grantham's notes explained a great deal and confirmed some of his suspicions. The recent deaths did seem to have their genesis in the past — specifically, his and Isabella's fiery past.

Grantham's derisive entries still rankled, even though what he'd written about was over more than ten years ago. He'd known almost from the beginning that his wife had been insatiable, but he had not expected her to betray him with his closest friends. And he'd never really suspected how contemptuous Grantham had been of all of them, including Wraysbury. He hid it well behind a gentle, friendly exterior, so ready and willing to listen to any confidences.

Good old Grantham — friend of everyone, critical of none. Or so it had seemed.

Apparently, Grantham's kindness had earned him a place in Isabella's bed, even if it only lasted a few days. He'd written of her with a disdain that made even Alexander angry for her sake, and his words revealed something about Grantham that perhaps even he had been unaware. Grantham had been in love with Isabella, and his cruel words about her only revealed his own pain when she inevitably abandoned him for the attentions of another.

Not enough excitement for her, it seemed. But then, no one would ever have been exciting enough. And with sharp spite infusing his ink and dripping from his quill, Grantham had documented his brief affair with her and the lover who replaced him: Belcher. No one could fault Grantham for a lack of awareness. He had been more observant of Isabella's behavior than Alexander, himself, and he'd recorded everything he'd seen or guessed in his quite comprehensive diary.

How Grantham discovered that Isabella had taken Crispin Belcher as her last lover remained a mystery, but he seemed confident in his knowledge. And the words he'd read rubbed huge handfuls of salt into his wounds.

They still burned through him.

The entries echoed the same complaints Isabella had always hurled at his head, and he could hear her shrill voice screaming them at him.

You care more for your silly swords than for me!

The final remark about her affairs, recorded in Grantham's journal, was the speculation that her unborn child may have been fathered by Belcher. The pain of that thought twisted inside Alexander until he thrust it away.

The past was important only as far as it affected the present. Isabella had been dead for ten years — she no longer had the power to torture him. So how did that sordid tragedy cause Grantham's death, now?

There was at least one possibility. Grantham must have been blackmailing Belcher. If Alexander assumed that, it explained why Belcher was so anxious to sign the papers for their proposed business venture. He was afraid Alexander would back out if he ever discovered that Belcher had had an affair with Isabella.

Well, Belcher needn't have worried. Alexander would never let Isabella's old betrayals affect him. If he had, he'd have had to cut his acquaintance with most of the men he knew. Grantham had been aware of a few of her affairs — her last affairs — but even he hadn't been aware of them all.

The thought was bitter, but Alexander had come to terms with his wife's character years ago. She hadn't been evil, she'd simply been desperate for admiration and attention. She needed to be told she was beautiful and desirable, the way most people needed to eat. One man's sweet words would never be enough to fill the gaping chasm within her.

He looked up to see Latimore staring at him, the disapproving frown still creasing his face.

"Tell Mr. Edward Archer, or his brother, to meet me at the academy." Alexander turned on his heel and strode away, a sense of urgency filling him.

Where was Belcher now? What was he doing? The image of the gold knob on the end of his walking stick arose, vivid and stark. The ball of the knob had a series of raised rings girdling it, making a pattern exactly like the one he'd sketched after examining Mrs. Adams. Belcher had clubbed her with his walking stick and killed her, all for the sake of a key.

Perhaps he was not at the academy. Or if he was, he had no reason to harm Lady Olivia. Most likely, Alexander feared for her safety for naught.

Or maybe it was already too late.

His stride lengthened until he was almost running, dodging other pedestrians and carriages and ignoring the angry yells of coachmen who had to rein in their teams to avoid hitting him. He turned the corner at Mortimer and took a deep breath as the ramshackle building housing the academy rose into view.

From the outside, it looked peaceful and deserted, all the gray-tinged windows shut. He ran up the shallow front steps and grabbed the doorknob. The house was unlocked. The door creaked as it swung open under a light touch. Lifting his head, he almost called out when he heard the creak of floorboards.

The sound came from the first floor. Maybe she was simply in her office and would be justifiably annoyed when he interrupted her.

He welcomed her displeasure, if that was all that would greet him. He raced up the stairs. As he set foot on the landing, he heard the metallic clash of swords. Every fear he'd ever suffered coalesced at the harsh sound.

He ran into the office and slammed to a halt in front of the desk. Out of the corner of his eye, he caught a swirl of gray. He grabbed one of the rapiers scattered amongst the foils on the desktop and turned. A man stood between Alexander and Lady Olivia. He was hunched beneath a shawl, struggling to throw it off.

Lady Olivia had thrown her shawl over her opponent. Alexander let out a breath, but instead of following through, she had stepped back, her face pale. The tip of her foil wavered.

She couldn't do it — couldn't make herself take that final, awful lunge to kill the man facing her.

And he had already looped the shawl over his left arm. He raised his sword.

Alexander closed the distance between them and touched the man's back with his rapier. "Halt, Belcher. It is finished."

Lady Olivia retreated another yard, her gaze fixed on Alexander, and the tension in her face relaxing into relief.

Throwing the shawl aside, Belcher whirled to face Alexander. When he began to raise his sword, Alexander ruthlessly slashed at his arm, then upward to slide his blade around Belcher's, down, and force the weapon out of his hand. Alexander completed the move by pointing his foil at his opponent's heart.

Wild-eyed and flushed, Belcher stared at him. Desperation widened his eyes.

"It is finished," Alexander repeated, jerking his rapier to catch Belcher's attention.

"No, it is not!" Belcher ground out. "You don't know — don't understand."

"I do, Belcher. There is no point in continuing. Drop your weapon." He looked at Lady Olivia. "We must send for the constable. Or Greenfield."

Belcher flashed a glance over his shoulder at Lady Olivia and back at Alexander. The whites of his eyes revealed his panic. "No — you cannot. Wait—"

"No. There is no point in waiting," Alexander said gently. "You must realize that. Delay will not help you — it will only prolong a difficult situation."

When Lady Olivia took a step toward the door, Belcher jerked and shifted to block her path. "Please — you cannot — *please.*"

"I am sorry, but you must have known there would be consequences," Alexander said.

"No, no — just allow me to depart. You will never see me, again. I swear it — upon my honor — I swear it!"

Alexander shifted uncomfortably. Belcher was visibly crumbling as he realized that his future was dimming and shrinking to the size of a cold jail cell and noose. "We cannot allow that. Come, Belcher, you know we cannot let you leave."

"Then finish it!" Belcher screamed at him, hunching forward, with his angelic features contorted in desperation.

Alexander took one step back. "No."

"Do it — you must! Kill me!" Belcher thrust his chest out, flecks of spittle collecting in the corners of his mouth. "Will you force me to face the humiliation of a trial? Kill me — now!"

"No — this is unnecessary."

"Would you deny me an honorable death?"

"You denied yourself that courtesy," Alexander said in a hard voice.

"I will not hang — I am not a common criminal," Belcher said, near madness twisting his face, his eyes flicking around the room wildly.

Then, before Alexander could completely withdraw, Belcher threw himself forward. Alexander's reaction was automatic. His blade lowered without conscious thought, and Belcher thrust himself into Alexander's blade.

He grunted, a low, animal sound. His eyes grew wider. He stared into Alexander's face, smiled, and with one last effort, he hunched forward and reached out to grab Alexander's hand. He pushed the foil deeper and gave one final, long gasp.

Grim and sick at heart, Alexander yanked the sword free. The action was far too late. Belcher slumped to the floor as Lady Olivia watched in horror, her hand pressed to her mouth.

He studied her pale face and took a step forward. Her left side was dark with blood. Gripping her elbow, he flicked open the top button of her Spencer with his free hand.

"Mr. Belcher...." Her murmured words drifted off.

"Dead," he said gruffly. "By his own choice. Perhaps it is for the best."

"How could he?" She frowned and brushed his hand away. "What are you doing? Stop that!"

"You are injured — we need to stop the bleeding."

"Are you a doctor?" She dragged her elbow out of his grasp and pressed her arm against her left side before walking past him to the desk. Pallid and shaking, she perched unsteadily on the edge and faced him.

A twisted grin lifted one corner of his mouth. "Of course, not, but you must allow me—"

"On the contrary, I must *not* allow you such liberties, Lord Milbourn, and I am shocked you would suggest such a thing." Her face grew bleak as she cast an uneasy glance at Belcher. "Mr. Belcher — are you sure he is...."

"Yes." Alexander knelt to roll him over on his back. Belcher's left hand thudded against the base of the wardrobe. "It was his choice. I should have realized sooner—"

"We all should have realized sooner. I fear I suspected first Mr. Underwood, and then, even poor Miss Denholm." She winced and caught her breath. "Is she all right? He said he did not kill her, but she has been unconscious for a terribly long time."

He strode over to the woman slumped in the corner. He hadn't noticed her before — his attention had been focused solely on Lady Olivia — and he studied her briefly. Her chest rose and fell in a strong rhythm, and she snorted abruptly. Despite her strong signs of life, he bent to hold his hand under her nose. Warm air fluttered over his palm. When he pressed his fingers against her inner wrist, a steady pulse thrummed under his fingertips.

"She is breathing and will most likely recover. You must let me bind your injury before you bleed to death."

"I will not. You have admitted you are not a physician, and I repeat, I have no intention of allowing you such intimacies. Not as matters currently stand." She fastened her cool gaze on his face.

As matters currently stand?

He raised one brow.

A smile flickered over her mouth before she sighed. "We must send for Mr. Idleman and Mr. Greenfield. Again."

"Not until I stop that bleeding." He threw open the wardrobe and pulled one of the fencing costumes out of the bottom drawer.

"What do you propose to do with that?"

He pulled out a pocketknife and inserted the blade into the divided skirt to tear off long strips of white muslin. "Bandages," he replied shortly. His mouth twitched, and he glanced over at her with a lopsided grin. "If you feel the urge to faint, I would encourage you to do so. It will be far less troublesome for both of us."

"I am not in the least danger of fainting, and I wish to know if something Mr. Belcher said to me is true." Her expression grew tense with concern as she studied him.

Holding half a dozen long strips of material in his hand, he straightened. He could guess what Belcher had told her and anticipated her question. "Yes," he answered tiredly. "I suspect he did have an affair with my wife. Women always did seem to find him attractive. And she needed adoration — anyone's adoration. He must have feared that if Grantham told me, that I would not go into partnership with him." He shrugged. "He was a trifle short of funds, but he had one trading ship left that he hadn't sold. I would not have let past misdeeds influence me. He should have realized that."

She flicked her right hand with impatience. "That is all very well, however, that is not my question. Mr. Belcher said he wanted you to discover what it felt like to lose everything you loved." A momentary flush lit her wan cheeks, and her glance dropped briefly to the floor. Her voice lowered to a breathless whisper when she asked, "What did he mean?"

Blood thrummed in his ears. This was not the right time — she would be better off not knowing. Ignorant.

Innocent, the way she'd been at eighteen, when he'd first seen her.

He lifted her roughly to sit on the desk before unbuttoning her Spencer, despite her exasperated attempts to stop him. He shook off her cold fingers and peeled back her short jacket, revealing the sprigged muslin dress beneath. Blood was soaking through the thin fabric to stain the left side of her bodice and the upper portions of her skirt.

She grabbed his wrist. "Stop that and tell me, what did he mean?"

"Nothing that should concern you," he answered tersely. He flicked his wrist out of her grasp and studied the complex folds of her bodice.

"He wanted to kill me. To hurt you," she said, crossing her arms over her bosom.

His frown deepened. "I apologize, but I must remove that garment."

"Really?" she asked sweetly. "And what happens after you wrap those ridiculous bandages around me? Do you expect me to walk through the streets partially dressed? Speak with the coroner and Constable Cooke? I'm curious how you will explain to my brothers your behavior in taking truly unforgivable advantage of me, as well."

"I will assist you to dress. Afterwards."

"That doesn't seem quite proper to me." Her head tilted to one side, her eyes bright with amusement. "And I question your skill as a lady's maid."

"Trust me, Lady Olivia. I will ensure you will have no cause for concern — at least about your apparel. And your shawl can hide any errors."

"Perhaps." She thought for a moment. "Very well, I will consent to your demands to brutalize my person, but only if you explain what Mr. Belcher meant. After all, you see me in a very weak and vulnerable state. I should think you would have the grace to answer that one, small question."

He searched her pale face and gleaming eyes, filled with sympathy and a vulnerable emotion he'd hoped he would never see there. "You know what he meant. *You* — he wanted me to lose *you*, because he thought I loved you."

"And you do not?" A hint of disappointment filled her soft voice.

"I—"

"Don't lie to me," she interrupted harshly. "Not now. *Please.*"

"Yes, then. I loved — love — you. I've loved you since the first time you walked into the room and interrupted my lessons, demanding to be included. I loved your determination and laughter and the light in your eyes when you first crossed swords with me." He cradled her head in his hand, her soft hair curling over his fingers. "And I loved your stubborn refusal to remain locked outside."

When she smiled at him and touched his cheek with soft fingers, he pulled her closer and pressed a kiss against her warm mouth. Need filled him, and his grip tightened until he felt her palm pressed lightly against his chest.

She caught his gaze, and although her lips retained her tender smile, her eyes glittered with unshed tears. "However, there was a caveat in your voice — an unspoken *but*. You loved your wife, and still love her, more."

"No." He closed his eyes and pressed his forehead against hers briefly, wanting to hold her against him and feel the deep beat of her heart. "No. I don't know that I ever loved her — I was too young when we met to understand the difference between passion and love. She was so beautiful — I was enamored with her smile — and she knew how and when to bestow it to achieve the greatest effect. She was vivacious and demanding. Alive in a way few women are. And then...." He shrugged. "She needed more than I could give her. Complete adoration — all my attention." His mouth twisted. "And she hated fencing. Particularly when I engaged in it."

"Oh, my poor dear." Lady Olivia stroked his cheek and laughed, though her eyes shown with dismay. "Caught between love and the sharp point of a fencing foil."

He caught her hand and kissed the soft palm. He would do anything to wipe away the anxiety and pain in her eyes.

A low moan from the corner behind the desk made him lift his head. "However, this is not the time, nor the place, to discuss this."

"And Miss Denholm awakens." She crossed her arms once more over her bosom. "She can assist me while you go find the authorities, I hope, for the last time. They must be quite sick of urgent summons to visit this address."

He smiled at her, and took hold of one of her hands. "It might be selfish of me, but I hope you have not developed an aversion to the thought of reopening your academy." He glanced around, the smothering darkness lifting from his heart. "This building is sorely in need of restoration. But it has good bones and an adequate design for your original purpose. I would not see you give up your dreams."

"Then we must hope this third tragedy does not close it for good."

Chapter Twenty-One

After bandaging Olivia's ribs so tightly that she could scarcely breathe, Cynthia took Olivia's elbow and dragged her home, ignoring the outraged demands of both Mr. Idleman and Mr. Greenfield for a complete accounting of what had occurred. Cynthia released her into Latimore's care and, wincing whenever anyone spoke, she refused to wait for a physician and departed, gray-faced and obviously suffering from an aching head.

When Latimore saw Olivia, he immediately sent one of the footmen for the physician and sent her upstairs in the custody of a very stern-faced housekeeper.

"I'm sending for that lazy Farmer," Mrs. Keene said as she propelled Olivia into her bedchamber. "You shall go straight to bed. The doctor has been sent for — there is no need for you to leave this room until he has seen you and pronounced you fit." She frowned and touched the dark, crimson stains on Olivia's side with distaste. "Disgraceful — we shall all be murdered in our beds if this keeps up."

"I really don't think so," Olivia murmured as she relinquished her shawl to Mrs. Keene and sat on the ladder-backed chair in front of her writing desk. "You may go."

"Yes, Lady Olivia," Mrs. Keene said by habit as she brushed the shawl and examined the soft cashmere for stains. Her frown deepened when she poked a finger through the hole sliced through the soft folds. She hummed and cast a dark glance at Olivia. "I can try to mend this, but I can't promise it will be as lovely as it once was." The stern note in her voice seemed to accuse Olivia of a terrible negligence with her clothing.

Amy Corwin

"I am sure it will be fine." Olivia glanced at the door, wishing she would just do as requested and leave.

Her side ached miserably. All she wanted was to lie down and drift away to sleep. Every muscle in her body seemed to throb, and although she ought to weep with pain, she felt herself smile at the thought of Lord Milbourn's warm lips pressed against hers.

Farmer soon arrived with one of her possets. She bullied and clucked over Olivia, forcing her into a nightgown and then proceeding to browbeat the poor physician, as well, when he arrived to clean and bind her wound.

"It is only a small scratch," Olivia said as the thin, wiry physician put on a pair of reading glasses to peer at the array of bottles in his case.

He nodded and tsked, making small clicking sounds with his tongue as he worked. Despite her questions, he refused to comment one way or the other, as if discussing her injury would precipitate her into a fit of nervous prostration. The wound did require a few stitches, however, which she bore silently with a clenched jaw and eyes squeezed shut.

He actually had the gall to pat her on her head when he was done. "You will do now. Plenty of rest."

He snapped his case shut and took Farmer by the wrist to pull her toward the door. The two of them whispered back and forth for several seconds, Farmer periodically casting anxious glances at Olivia, before closing the door after the doctor.

"There now, Lady Olivia, you just lie back and rest. I will take care of everything." She glanced at the empty glass next to Olivia's bed and picked it up, frowning. "Another posset is what you need."

Since Olivia's head was already whirling dizzily and her cheeks felt numb, she tried to refuse. But like the doctor, Farmer ignored her protests and dashed out. Olivia leaned back against her pillows. The tight bandages made it hard to breathe, and her side itched and ached. But she refused to use the laudanum from the small blue bottle the physician had left next to the pitcher of water on her chest of drawers. Farmer's concoction was more than sufficient, and she already felt too hot and drowsy.

228

She closed her eyes and let sleep wash over her, dimly aware of the squeak of the door opening and then closing again.

Night came and went in a restless blur, and the next day her family united to prevent her from escaping from her bedchamber. At one point, Edward threatened to take her key and lock her in if she didn't stop trying to sneak downstairs. Farmer was more than happy to supply her with gossip, however, so her imprisonment wasn't too onerous, particularly after she persuaded Peregrine to bring her both *Sense and Sensibility* and *The Orphan of Tintern Abbey* to while away the time.

The second day, she joined the family in the breakfast room despite Farmer's threats and dire warnings. Latimore held firm in refusing visitors, so Olivia was left to her correspondence, sewing, and composing new menus for the coming week. A vague sense of disappointment caught at her like a kitten's claws snagging her skirt, when she realized Lord Milbourn had not visited.

"Did Lord Milbourn leave his card?" Olivia asked Latimore as he handed her the morning mail.

"Lord Milbourn has not visited us today, Lady Olivia." Latimore bowed and backed a step toward the door.

"Yesterday, perhaps? Surely he has been here to see Mr. Archer. After all, there must have been an inquest."

"Yes, Lady Olivia. Both Mr. Archers attended the inquest. They may have met with Lord Milbourn during the proceedings."

With a jerk she half stood. A sharp pain in her side made her slowly reseat herself. "They went and did not tell me? What—" Observing the disapproval on Latimore's face, she stopped. One didn't discuss such matters with the servants. She waved her hand in dismissal. "You may go. However, if you see either Mr. Archer, please inform him that I wish to speak with him."

"Very good, Lady Olivia," Latimore intoned as he bowed again and eased out of the room.

Why did everyone insist on treating her like a fragile invalid? While it was true that quick or sharp movements hurt, she was nearly recovered, and she hungered for news.

And she longed to see Lord Milbourn. Had he forgotten her? Was that kiss simply a fleeting desire? He had admitted he loved her, hadn't he? If he did, why hadn't he come to see how she fared? Even if he harbored no deeper feelings for her, it was simple courtesy to ask after her health.

The normally sunny Ivory Drawing Room seemed cold and gray this morning and even the sky outside the large bow windows appeared dingy, with dark gray clouds blocking the sun. Sharp gusts of wind rattled the panes, sending eddies of cold air to swirl around her shoulders. Another storm seemed to be brewing.

She sighed and sorted through the letters Latimore had brought to her, thinking she'd even welcome Cynthia's energetic company today. She felt forgotten and alone, like a little girl's doll relegated to the attic after being outgrown.

Her gaze flickered to the window again, and she listened to the clatter of carriage wheels, horses, and the loud calls of street hawkers. Life was passing her by while she sat here, growing old and tired.

In the distance, her beagles yodeled and barked. She straightened and smiled. They, at least, still loved her. And neither Edward nor Peregrine could stop her if she decided to take her dogs for a walk.

Mindful of her side, she rose carefully to her feet. She was halfway to the door when Latimore reappeared.

"Señora Doña Luisa Benéitez de Velarde, Lord Milbourn, and Miss Bron, Lady Olivia." Latimore bowed and held the door open while the three visitors brushed past him.

A silver-haired *grande dame,* dressed in heavy black silk and lace, entered first, her black eyes fixed upon Olivia. Her high cheekbones and stubborn chin gave her face strength and still retained vestiges of the beauty she must have enjoyed when she was young. She paused six feet away, her black lace gloved hands clasped at her waist.

With the ironic grin that never failed to catch at Olivia, Lord Milbourn followed, holding the hand of a small, dark-haired girl about eleven years of age.

"Lady Olivia," — Lord Milbourn bowed and gestured to the lady on his left—"may I present Señora Doña Luisa Benéitez de Velarde and Miss Maria Bron?"

"I am pleased to make your acquaintance," Lady Olivia curtseyed, and nodded to the older woman and child.

"Charming," Doña Luisa murmured, her sharp, black eyes taking in the details of Olivia's ice blue morning dress.

"Señora Doña Luisa Benéitez de Velarde is my mother, and Miss Bron, my daughter," Lord Milbourn said, completing the formal introductions. "They recently returned from our home in Barcelona."

"I hope your trip was uneventful," Lady Olivia said.

"Traveling is never as uneventful as one would wish," Doña Luisa said in a dry voice. Her tone and sardonic expression were so similar to Lord Milbourn's that Olivia had to bite the inside of her cheek to keep from laughing.

The girl's grip on her father's hand tightened when Olivia glanced at her, and she frowned, lifting her small, pointed chin. Lord Milbourn shook his hand loose and then placed his palm against her narrow back to push her forward a step. Her lower lip thrust out in a silent pout, but she did execute a polite curtsey.

"Would you care to be seated?" Olivia gestured to the comfortable group of ivory silk couches clustered in front of the elegant fireplace.

A fire was crackling merrily on the hearth, and on this blustery, gray day, it was the most cheerful spot in the room. Doña Luisa nodded and glided over to the closest couch, where she sat, straight-backed, on the edge of the seat. Miss Bron followed and sat next to her grandmother. One small hand drifted over to grip one of the luxurious folds of Doña Luisa's skirt, but the older lady gently disentangled the girl's hand and placed it on the girl's lap without glancing at her.

For some reason, Olivia found the small gesture heart wrenching. She flicked a small smile to the girl as she sat on the couch opposite. Lord Milbourn sat in a gilded chair next to his daughter. Before Olivia could say anything else, she heard the beagles yodel again and a shout.

Then the inevitable happened. The loud clatter of dogs racing over the marble floors and up the stairs, followed by the pounding of the footmen's feet as they gave chase, echoed through the room.

"Oh, dear," Olivia murmured. She gripped the right armrest and looked at Doña Luisa.

The older lady's dark eyes glittered with amusement, and Miss Bron sprang to her feet and faced the door. Her lithe body was rigid with tension.

Slipping and sliding, the dogs scrambled into the room, tails wagging and tongues lolling out of their mouths. The animals took one look at the little girl and galloped across the gold and ivory carpet to encircle her, shoving their damp noses under her hands and pushing each other aside in their efforts to be the sole dog privileged to be petted by the stranger.

"I am so sorry!" Olivia flushed and rose to her feet.

Lord Milbourn chuckled and sat back, hooking one arm over the carved arc of the seatback.

Doña Luisa shook her head and smoothed the black silk over her lap with apparent unconcern.

To Olivia's relief, Miss Bron giggled in delight and bent over, trying to hug and pet as many of the dogs as possible.

In the doorway, two footmen shifted from foot to foot, looking too embarrassed to enter the room.

"I suppose I should introduce the dogs." Olivia dragged each dog back by its leather collar as she said their names, "This is Caesar, with the black spot over his eye, and these are Bathsheba, Brutus, Justinia, Octavius, and Titus. As you can see, they are completely without manners." When she was done, she waved the footmen away.

They'd failed to keep the dogs kenneled, and there seemed little point in their staying. The two men left with alacrity.

After sniffing the carpeting, furniture, and the three guests, the dogs made themselves completely at home. The tan and white beagle, Titus, lay down at Doña Luisa's feet, and from the way the lady shifted, Olivia suspected the dog was on, rather than near, her toes. Caesar and Brutus sat next to Lord Milbourn, leaning against his legs and staring up at him with huge brown eyes while he stroked their heads and fondled their long ears.

"I like them," Miss Bron said, staring at Olivia in challenge. "Especially Bathsheba." She stroked the dog's floppy, soft ears, and Bathsheba leaned against her, almost pushing her off her feet.

"The child is mad about animals," Doña Luisa said. Her soft voice held almost no trace of an accent. "Her father is the same." Despite the exasperation in her words, she smiled indulgently at her son.

Watching the young girl, Olivia desperately wanted to put an arm around her narrow shoulders and give her a warm hug. She looked so uncertain, and every few minutes, she would blink rapidly as if wanting to cry but too proud to do so. Dark smudges under her large brown eyes suggested that she hadn't spent a quiet night, and it struck Olivia that Miss Bron was frightened. Her sidelong glances at her father made Olivia think she feared her father would send her away again, soon, or that he had threatened some terrible punishment if she dared behave improperly.

The thought broke her heart.

What, if anything, had her father told her about Olivia? Perhaps nothing at all, she realized with near despair. She felt a deep kinship with the child — they were both lonely and wanting the attention of the man sitting so carelessly near the fireplace.

On impulse, Olivia said, "Then she is yours — we have far too many dogs at the moment. However, if you take Bathsheba, you must take Octavius, as well, so they do not get lonely."

Miss Bron glanced at her father, who nodded with a smile. Olivia looked at him, surprised at his easy acquiescence.

"What do you say, child?" Doña Luisa prompted her.

Miss Bron studied Olivia with a frown creasing the smooth skin of her brow. "You cannot make me like you, you know. Even if you give me a dog."

"Miss Bron!" Doña Luisa said, a stern look hardening her face. Her mouth compressed into a thin line as she studied the girl.

Miss Bron's chin tilted up, and her eyes flashed with defiance as she looked from her grandmother to Olivia.

"Of course, I cannot," Olivia agreed complacently. "However, I am sure we can be friends. And I can provide you with a near endless supply of puppies, if you are interested in such things."

Eyes widening in surprise, Miss Bron stared at her for a full thirty seconds before she covered her mouth with one thin hand and giggled. She jerked her head up to push a long, dark lock of hair over her shoulder before she dropped a quick curtsey. But as if she needed the reassurance, her left hand never left Bathsheba's smooth head.

"Thank you, Lady Olivia," Miss Bron said.

"You are quite welcome." Olivia brushed off her skirt and returned to her seat, only to have Justinia lean against her and sit on her feet. She looked around and almost laughed. The dogs had disposed themselves cleverly amongst the three guests and Olivia, so each animal could receive as much attention it wanted.

Doña Luisa sighed and brushed a few tan and white hairs from her dress. "I regret that our visit must be short, Lady Olivia. I have promised Miss Bron a trip to Gunter's Tea Shop."

Miss Bron's hand paused in stroking Bathsheba's ears, and a wide smile glowed on her elfin face as she looked at her grandmother. "I am to have a cake — whichever cake I want!"

Olivia stood. "Certainly. I am pleased to have made your acquaintance, and I hope you will visit me again. Perhaps, if you are going to Gunter's, you should leave the dogs here." When she saw the look of panicked disappointment in Miss Bron's face, she hastened to add, "We will send them to you this afternoon, however. Never fear."

Miss Bron glanced at her father. He smiled and nodded, encouraging her to relax enough to smile at Olivia and say, "Thank you, Lady Olivia." She curtseyed and moved to lean against her grandmother's knee.

"My son may stay, however," Doña Luisa said. "I understand he has other business here."

"And he may bring the dogs home — *please*, Papa?" Miss Bron ran to her father and draped herself over his lap to gaze up pleadingly into his face. Bathsheba yipped and followed quickly to also press against Lord Milbourn. "Please, Papa?"

Lord Milbourn's eyes warmed with amusement as he looked into his daughter's eyes, and he pushed her long black hair off her shoulders. He sighed in mock exasperation and shook his head. "Very well, *mi niña bonita*. I shall bring the dogs with me when I return.

But I shall only do so if you promise not to annoy your grandmother, or grow ill from eating too many cakes."

"I shall not, since I can never eat too many." She stifled a giggle as she leaned against her father and looped an arm around his neck to press a kiss against his cheek.

"Your promise fails to reassure me," her father replied wryly.

His daughter giggled again and then pressed her hand over her mouth as she cast a measuring glance at Olivia.

Olivia smiled reassuringly and shook her head.

"Say a proper goodbye to Lady Olivia," Lord Milbourn said, "and then you may go."

Miss Bron was quick to comply with the required social conventions. She curtseyed and remarked grandly that she had enjoyed meeting Lady Olivia, all the while her eyes glowed and her feet danced to be on her way.

Olivia rang for Latimore, who came, accompanied by a footman and several leashes. The butler escorted the two ladies to the carriage, waiting for them in the street, while the footman led the dogs away.

When Olivia turned away from the door, she found Lord Milbourn had moved to stand next to her. Her breath caught in her throat. She took a step forward, leaving only six inches between them. Warmth radiated from him, filling the space between them, and her gaze fixed on the soft, white folds of his starched linen neckcloth.

Slowly, hesitatingly, she placed her palm against his chest. His heart beat strong beneath the smooth wool of his jacket. He smelled of bay and cloves, and she closed her eyes briefly to breathe in the heady scent.

When she lifted her head, he slipped a hand around her neck and pulled her closer to press a kiss against her lips.

"Honestly, you might give a fellow a b-bit of warning," Peregrine said in a disgusted voice.

Lord Milbourn released her abruptly, and Olivia stepped away, her cheeks flaming.

Her brother stood in the doorway, his fists on his hips. He looked from one to the other before he sighed and shook his head. "I suppose you expect me to c-call him out now, and d-defend your honor."

"I expect nothing of the sort," Olivia said. "Other than to have the decency to turn around and grant us some privacy."

Peregrine smiled, his eyes twinkling. "I would be happy to oblige, except you have another visitor — I s-saw her on the s-stairs coming up." He turned his head. "Miss Denholm."

Cynthia brushed past Peregrine briskly, drawing off her gloves. The fading remnants of a bruise colored her left temple and the area around her eye with a vivid combination of blue, green, and yellow splotches. Unfortunately, her dark green walking dress highlighted it beautifully, making it even more noticeable than it might normally have been.

Cynthia nodded to them. "You are looking well, Lady Olivia. Lord Milbourn." Striding over to the fireplace, she held her hands out and rubbed them vigorously. "Dreadful weather. Starting to sleet, so I suppose all the walkways will shortly be covered with ice."

Olivia exchanged glances with Lord Milbourn. One of his dark brows rose, and a half-smile twisted his mouth to one side.

"You ought not stay, t-then," Peregrine said, crossing his arms over his chest. "W-would you like a c-coach?"

Olivia frowned at him and shook her head. Much as she would like to have been alone with Lord Milbourn for a few moments longer, she was not so rude as to suggest Cynthia leave immediately after her arrival.

After all, it was her duty to endure fifteen minutes for a social call.

"A coach? Why would I want a coach?" Cynthia stared at Peregrine, her eyes wide with astonishment. "A little sleet does no harm." She studied Lord Milbourn and Olivia, a smile growing on her face. "Ah, I see. Private conference and whatnot. Don't need to hit me over the head." She grimaced. "Again. Well, I won't stay, then. Just came to ask after your health." She drew her green leather gloves back on and walked toward the door. "Is Mr. Archer about?"

Peregrine straightened and looked at Olivia, his mouth opening and shutting with surprise. "W-what?" He cleared his throat and hastily added, "At your service, of course."

"Not you — Mr. Edward Archer," Cynthia replied.

"Edward?" Peregrine's expression of confusion deepened. He stared at Olivia as if seeking enlightenment.

Olivia raised one hand, palm up, to signal she had no further knowledge than he had.

Poor Edward, I hope he is already at his club, or he could find himself buttonholed again by a very determined Miss Cynthia Denholm.

"I saw Mr. Edward Archer leaving just as we arrived," Lord Milbourn said. He cupped Olivia's elbow in one hand, and she could almost feel the subtle rumble of a smothered chuckle shake him.

"Well, that is that, then. I must say, Lady Olivia, that it is time he found himself a wife. Past time. These eternal bachelors — not a good thing. Leads to bad health and whatnot." Cynthia flashed a stern look at Peregrine.

Peregrine turned pale, and his fingers began to fidget with one of the brass buttons adorning his sky blue waistcoat. "Right. W-well. He is not here." He politely stuck out his elbow to escort Cynthia down the stairs, although the grimly desperate expression on his face looked like he'd much rather dash off without her than perform this particular duty. "Are you leaving, t-then?"

"No point in staying, is there? Good day to you, Lady Olivia. Lord Milbourn." She slipped her hand around his elbow and allowed him to drag her toward the staircase.

"Poor Mr. Archer," Lord Milbourn murmured in Olivia's ear.

"Which one?" Olivia laughed and looked up at him, so filled with love that she thought she would burst. "I fear if Mr. Peregrine Archer is not careful, he will have a betrothal to announce upon his return."

"Then he will not be the only one." He brushed her cheek tenderly with his fingers and caught her gaze, his eyes dark with an intensity that caused a cloud of butterflies to flutter in her stomach.

"No. My sister, Lady Margaret—"

He gave her a slight shake. "Not Lady Margaret. *Lady Olivia.* Did you not guess when I brought my mother and daughter here to meet you, that I hoped you would consider a more permanent place in my life?"

"Permanent? As a fencing partner?"

He chuckled and wrapped his arms around her. "We can fence as often as you wish when you are Lady Milbourn."

"Or Lady Olivia—"

He pressed a long kiss to her lips before she laughingly pushed him away.

"I have not agreed," she complained, leaning away to stare up at him. Joy constricted her throat, and all she could do was grin idiotically.

"Have I been presumptuous, then, in speaking to the earl?"

She had to swallow a bubble of excitement before she could say, "No. High-handed, perhaps, but not quite presumptuous."

"And what is your answer?" His voice was rough as his strong arms tightened around her.

"You have not spoken of love—" she complained.

"I have, as you well know." He gave her a small squeeze. "To repeat, I love you — I've loved you for these past ten years."

She laughed, unable to speak, and reached up to trace the high curve of his cheekbone with her fingertips and the faint line of his freshly shaved beard.

"And you?" he whispered.

"I have loved you since I was eighteen, as *you* are well aware." Bubbling joy broke through her words, making them froth in a merry little stream.

Before she could say more, he pressed another kiss to her eager lips. Finally, she relaxed against him, feeling his warmth and strength fill her.

She was beloved, and she belonged. And her dreams did not seem so out of reach at all.

THE END

Your Opinion Matters: Thank you for reading my book. Your opinion is important to other readers, as well as to me. Authors are always desperate to obtain reviews because 4 and 5 star reviews are required to advertise and promote our books. I know that the time and effort required to write a review can make the task daunting, but even a few words are helpful. So if you have time to write a review at http://www.amazon.com/ I would really appreciate it.

Thank you again for taking the time to read my book. I sincerely hope you enjoyed it.

Amy Corwin

Other Titles by Amy Corwin

The Archer Family Regency Romance Series
The **Archer Family series** are traditional Regency romances spiced with a mystery.

While these books do not need to be read in order, the list below presents them in the series order.

The Necklace (Prequel to the series)
The Unwanted Heiress
A Lady in Hiding
The Earl's Masquerade
A Stolen Rose
En Garde, My Love
Love Across the Pond
Lady Victoria's Mistake

Second Sons Inquiry Agency Regency Mystery Series
The **Second Sons Inquiry Agency series** are traditional historical mysteries set in the Regency period in England. The books all feature the Second Sons Inquiry Agency.

While these books do not need to be read in order, the list below presents them in a series order.

The Vital Principle
A Rose Before Dying
The Dead Man's View
The Illusion of Desire
Honeymoon with Death

A Second Chance Paranormal Romances

The **Second Chance Paranormal Romances** are paranormal tales spiced with mystery, danger and an "Urban Fantasy" feel. They do not have to be read in any particular order as each book stands alone.

Her Vampire Bodyguard
A Fall of Silver

Paranormal Suspense

Mysteries

A new series of contemporary, cozy mysteries is underway, set in fictitious towns near the Outer Banks of North Carolina.

Whacked!

About the Author

Amy Corwin is a charter member of the Romance Writers of America and recently joined Mystery Writers of America. She writes historical and cozy mysteries with a touch of romance, as well as paranormal romances. To be truthful, most of her books include a bit of murder and mayhem since she discovered that killing off at least one character is a highly effective way to make the remaining ones toe the plot line.

Join her and discover that every good mystery has a touch of romance.

Connect with Me Online at http://www.amycorwin.com